Pen Pals

Follow the author on twitter: @martingore
website: www.martingore.co.uk

Pen
Pals

Martin Gore

Acknowledgement:

I would like to thank the Strawbs for the use of the lyrics to their iconic seventies song "Part of the Union" and Splinter for the splendid "Costafine town". Both capture the images and social context of the time.
I would also like to thank editor Alice Baynton and designer Simon Hartshorne.

Dedication:

To my long suffering wife Sandra Gore
and my late sister in law Sue Vaudin Gore,
for their editorial advice and editing.

1.

2000 – A new millennium

Jean Murgatroyd sat in her high backed chair. It was early yet, just getting light. It was raining too. A good morning to be inside she thought, although she could see that the mornings were getting lighter. Spring was just around the corner.

She had always been an early riser. These people knew that. They had come to realise that she expected to be in her chair early; not cooped up in bed. The kindly nurse, whatever her name was, had dropped by and helped her out of bed. She would use the loo without her help thank you. Now she was looking out of the window down the valley towards the factory.

Although it was some distance away she could see people scurrying into work through the rain. The morning shift was starting. The gates set into the imposing stone archway were just visible, but the name engraved in the stonework was not. Her name. She would need to visit soon. She hadn't been in since her fall. This place was temporary they said. You'll soon be better and back in your own home they said.

A lorry was leaving the factory now through the new entrance. She could see the barrier lift. The old gates under the arch weren't used much now. Unsuitable for modern traffic. The gateman didn't need to leave his hut. He just pressed a button.

The Murgatroyd neon sign above the old mill building was still lit, although one side was flickering. 'They need to get that seen to,' she grumbled to herself. The new factory was further round near the mill pond. It was ugly she thought, all prefabricated metal cladding. The old mill was a thing of beauty, but was now more offices than factory. 'I'm not sure what old Josiah would make of it,' she muttered.

She wondered if her friend would visit this morning. Her friend whose name escaped her. Frustrating. She had always been so good with names. Bill had said that she never forgot a face. She looked at his picture in a silver frame, in his RAF uniform. A beaming smile beneath jet black receding hair. 'Handsome bastard' she murmured to herself. He was long gone now. How many years?

Still searching in her mind for her friend's name the old lady picked up the picture she had left when she last visited. It showed her friend with young Vicky on new year's eve. Mother and daughter in posh frocks holding champagne flutes. Brenda. That was it. Brenda.

She would get dressed soon. When the lady came. She

would visit the factory today. With Bill. They would eat fish and chips in the canteen. Derek would come too. Bill said that you always needed to tour the factory to keep people on their toes. Perhaps James would come too? She missed him, her only son. When had he last visited her? It could have been last week or the week before she thought. Or perhaps it was longer?

Her mother wouldn't approve she knew. Her mother never did approve of Bill. Or of the Murgatroyds. They were the bosses. They weren't for the likes of us. But she'd done okay hadn't she? She would have her mother round for tea soon. When she got back to the hall. Marjorie would make a lemon drizzle cake. Then she realised. Her mother and Marjorie were both long gone too, weren't they? She'd lost her train of thought.

The lady had laid out her clothes. Her electric blue Berketex twinset, complete with her Country Casuals cream blouse. She would wear her pearls of course. She always wore her pearls. The ones Bill gave her for the Queen's Award visit all those years ago. They were in their place on the dressing table she noted. In their faded blue box. Good.

*   *   *

It was just another Tuesday morning. Early March. Wet. Vicky was doing the school run. She'd dropped the kids off, trying to get out of the pouring rain as soon as possible. Then she saw the lunchbox. On the back seat. Bethany's. Again. Wearily she got out of the car and ran to the entrance. Inside she saw her daughter happily chatting to her little friends. Completely oblivious. She tapped her on the shoulder and Bethany turned. A motherly glare and a sudden glimpse of understanding. No words spoken, but there would be words spoken later as both knew. Vicky headed off. She got in the car and her phone rang. She sighed. It was going to be one of those days. She was going to be late for work. They'd got up at the usual time, but as always getting the children's minds focussed on getting ready had been impossible. Various little ailments, a lost sock, money for a future school trip, then some sisterly bickering over whose turn it was for the front seat.

'Shit,' she said aloud. She'd forgotten to take the lasagne out of the freezer too, and as she sat in the driver's seat she realised that her short coat had not covered her backside and her bottom was soaking wet. She looked at the phone. Her Mother.

'Hi Mum,' she said as she wrestled with the seatbelt and turned the radio down. 'Oh God.... really? You still there? Okay, I'll be there as soon as I can.'

She rang Mark, her all too understanding boss. He knew Jean Murgatroyd. Everyone in the town knew Jean, and Vicky's mother Brenda Arkwright too. Two powerful women. Millview nursing home wasn't far away. On the hill above the town. A fine view of the Pennine hills and a grandstand view of Murgatroyd's pen factory. Millview was posh. Suitable for geriatrics of distinction. It had a discreet whiff of high class urine mixed with disinfectant and full English breakfast, which hit Vicky as she entered through the solid oak front door.

'Your mother's in the library. Would you like some tea?' said Melanie Clark, an old school friend, and now a school mum too. 'Yes please Mel,' said Vicky. Mel smiled sympathetically. 'It had to happen one day, even to the indomitable Jean Murgatroyd,' said Mel with a shrug.

Mel eased herself out of her chair and headed for the kitchen. She'd already spoken to her husband, who worked at Murgatroyds. It was a one factory kind of town, so the death of Jean Murgatroyd was going to be big local news.

Vicky entered the library. The books were mainly novels, predominantly romantic fiction favoured by an older female clientele. Some larger print versions. It was warm and the rain drummed on the windows as she entered. An old country house library with oak panelling and high ceilings.

Brenda Arkwright sat on a settee, sipping tea. She was

dressed for work. A deep maroon jacket, dark blouse and sensible skirt. Her hair was cut short and highlighted brown with auburn tints in a modern style. Immaculate. Just the right mix of executive authority with a dash of femininity.

Vicky hugged her mother warmly as she stood to greet her. As they did so Vicky realised that she was taller than her mother now. When did that happen she wondered? It was apparent to her that even her mother, the mighty Brenda Arkwright, was getting older now.

'Oh Mum. I came as soon as I could. How are you feeling?' said Vicky.

'Well I suppose it's still a shock even though I'd been expecting it,' said Brenda. She smiled a smile of inevitability. 'After all it had to happen one day.'

They both sat down, facing each other. As Vicky did so she was conscious of her rain sodden backside once more, and that her hair, only styled the previous day, felt in need of urgent repair. Joy. This was definitely one of those days.

'When did she go then?' asked Vicky.

'About an hour ago I guess. I often pop in on the way in to the factory. I tend to forget if I get embroiled in work. I was showing her more of the millennium party pictures, and some from Christmas. You know the ones of the kids? Well I showed her the one of you and me at the party, and she smiled. She began to drift off as she does, then I realised that she had stopped breathing. I called the nurse, but obviously her heart had given out. She died very peacefully.'

'At least she wasn't alone at the end. I always think that's the saddest thing.'

Mel arrived with more tea, and some custard creams. Vicky poured some fresh tea. Fresh, if somehow a little stewed.

'I don't suppose you've spoken to the family at all yet?'

'Oh no. James and I aren't in touch these days. The nursing home is trying to contact him. He spends so much of his time in the States now. I suspect that they'll have to contact Carol. At least she still lives locally, and I've met her here from time to time. She brings the grandchildren in now and again.'

Brenda paused and sipped her tea. She seemed to be struggling with something in her mind.

'So when did James last visit?' Vicky asked.

'Oh I don't know. Months ago. Even years maybe.'

'That's really sad. She had no other family then?'

Vicky sipped some tea as she spoke. She'd had hotter, but it would do. Nursing home tea.

'No. James was an only child. Jean was eighty three. Eighty four next week actually.' Brenda recalled.

Vicky could tell that her mother's mind was elsewhere. Work perhaps? As managing director she had a lot on her plate of course. No. It wasn't that. It was something to do with the events of the morning. She sensed a tension in her mother.

'Quite a life I suppose,' pondered Vicky. 'She must have seen some changes in her time. Two world wars. Watching Murgatroyd's grow from virtually nothing.'

Brenda thought for a moment, and then replied.

'A local girl from a council house was our Jean, and not afraid to tell you that either. Especially when her husband Bill did his pompous Tory bit. It was a shame when she had the two strokes in quick succession. Up until two years ago she was as independent and indestructible as ever. She was a bit lonely after her housekeeper died though. They were so very close; Jean missed her a lot. That's why I popped in a bit more. She got a new housekeeper, but Marjorie had been more of a friend than an employee for years, so it wasn't the same. It wasn't easy persuading Jean to come here from Murgatroyd Hall, but she had been going downhill rapidly. She was getting more forgetful and confused, and rather isolated in that big old house. We all told her it was temporary of course. At least her room had a view of the mill though, so she could keep her eye on things at the factory.'

'Reunited with Bill and Marjorie then? Up with the angels? Quite a reunion.'

Vicky smiled. Brenda smiled too.

'I guess. In the old days Jean would just rant away and Marjorie would just smile serenely. I don't think I ever saw her angry. Jean Murgatroyd was Jean Murgatroyd and Marjorie just accepted it.'

There was silence, except for the ticking of the grandfather clock and the sound of the rain beating down on the window. Vicky saw that her mother was now deep in thought. There was something on her mind. Something larger than the death of an old friend. She thought about asking what is was, but then decided that it wasn't the time. She decided to approach it a different way.

'Mum I know this is a bit soon, but have you thought about what this might do to your retirement plans?'

Brenda paused before replying, marshalling her thoughts.

'Well this isn't a complete surprise of course. Jean hasn't been at all well for a few weeks now, so I've been thinking about it. I can't retire from Murgatroyds until I see how the ownership works out, and that won't happen until we see the will. I've been managing director for twenty years, and I've worked there all my working life. I can't just walk away. The family will have their thoughts and I'm just a hired hand at the end of the day. We'll just have to see.'

'Well you know the girls would love to see their grandma more often. But it's going to be tough for you to walk away. It was going to be anyway, but now.'

Brenda looked distant for a moment, as if she hadn't heard.

'She was involved in the business up to the time she had the strokes you know? I used to take her around the factory from time to time, and if we ever had a royal visitor she'd come. She loved that.'

'I suppose if I'd been a Murgatroyd with my name on the business I'd still have taken an interest. She must have been so very proud,' said Vicky.

'Yes and she was no silent partner back in the 70's. She saved the business. A very feisty lady was our Jean. We had our moments. That's an understatement. William Murgatroyd and Bill built the business, but Bill died in 1974. After that Jean Murgatroyd was the chairman and matriarch.'

'But wasn't James involved too? At one time?' Vicky speculated.

'Oh yes. But that's a longer story for another day,' Brenda said.

Brenda stood and walked to the window. Silence took over. Sensing again her mother's unease a feeling of foreboding dug in Vicky's stomach, like the day when she'd been stood outside the headmaster's office for not doing her homework. She decided to let the silence hang. Let her tell me in her own good time. Brenda was actually wondering what to do. She wasn't prepared for this even though she knew that Vicky had to know sometime. She wondered why she hadn't planned how to deal with this event? After all it was going to happen one day? Play for time she thought.

'Look Vicky, we need to have a longer chat about things. But not here. Not now. I need a bit of time to think,' she said.

Vicky stood and went to the window. She could see tears welling up on her mother's face. She hugged her, suddenly she seemed vulnerable and old.

They sat once more, and Brenda composed herself. At length she took out her handbag, and ferreted about inside.

'There is one thing I do have for you.' Brenda put her hand inside the bag and took out a boxed fountain pen. She handed it over to Vicky.

'From Jean. She wanted you to have this. A keepsake.' Brenda said.

Vicky opened the Murgatroyd monogrammed box, which contained an old but exquisite fountain pen. She took it out. It was clearly well used, and very heavy. In fact she remembered it on Jean's desk at Murgatroyd Hall. She had been collecting jumble for the local Brownie pack some years previously, and Jean had invited her in. They had gone into the study, and Jean had taken out her cheque book. Before Vicky realised it Jean had made out a cheque and signed it with that same pen, obviously her pen of choice. The cheque was for a thousand pounds.

'It's time they went further than Whitby. Why not take them to London on me?' said the old lady as she handed over the cheque, smiling brightly. Jean had a reputation for being careful with money, but those close to her knew her generosity.

Vicky now looked at this same pen as it sat so comfortably in her hand. It was obviously handmade and perfectly balanced. Clearly a one off made for the family. Stylish without being ostentatious. Then she noted the initials engraved into the barrel.

'Oh. My goodness. Monogrammed JM as well. But why? Why ever me?' said Vicky, more puzzled than ever.

Of course she had known Jean, but this was clearly a deeply personal item. Why give such an item away to other than a close friend or relative?

Brenda smiled, and took her daughter's hand.

'She knew she was dying Vicky. In one of her lucid moments she said I was to give it to you. She used to love you popping in with the girls.'

'Well that is so nice. But surely the family..'

Brenda interrupted, putting her hand over Vicky's.

'Don't worry about the family Vicky. There are two of these pens. I know who has the other, and so does Jean. Handing over that pen to me for my family was a very symbolic act on Jean's part. The final act of a long saga which she and I never spoke of right to the end, because it evoked painful memories for us both. That's what I need to talk to you about. There's quite a lot you don't know, and it's time you did.'

'Oh that's very mysterious,' said Vicky.

They left the library together, arm in arm. Vicky could see that her mother was still preoccupied. She'll tell me in her own good time thought Vicky. It's probably nothing to be concerned about. They parted at the front door, agreeing to meet up later. Vicky headed for work at the estate agent in town. Her boss was understanding. By lunchtime everybody knew. 'Local business leader Jean Murgatroyd passes away' and 'Town mourns one of its own' were the headlines on the news-stands outside Granville's newsagents on the High Street.

*   *   *

On the other side of the Atlantic the telephone rang in room 401 of the New Yorker Hotel. An older man, whose jet black hair defied his advancing years, struggled into consciousness, grappled with the bedside light and eventually picked up the receiver. The hotel operator was strangely cool and impersonal given the ungodly hour, and handed over the call from Millview Nursing Home. They broke the news of his mother's passing.

James was not too surprised. He had spoken to Carol, his

ex wife, only last week and she had commented that Jean had become more distant and confused than ever.

He got up, still suffering the effects of the huge steak he had consumed last evening, and the several Budweisers that he had imbibed with it. American portions still took some getting used to. He put on the kettle and poured himself a strong black coffee. He looked out and saw the glittering New York skyline with the unmistakable Empire State lit up in the darkness. He rang his wife Mandy on the hotel phone, but her phone went to voicemail, as it always did. Buried in her expensive handbag no doubt.

He struggled into wakefulness, but still felt out of sorts. He went into the bathroom and showered in spite of the hour. As he allowed piping hot water to sluice over his head and torso he began to revive. He put on a robe and went back into the room.

He needed time to assimilate the news, so he switched on the TV and idly flicked across the channels, settling on baseball. He liked baseball. Mandy found it boring.

The coffee and the shower had revived him, and he relaxed as he thought about his mother. In spite of his bitterness he recalled the good times they'd had when he was younger. At least she'd appreciated his efforts.

'Switch it off now James,' he snapped at himself. 'Stay positive. Onwards and upwards.'

What to do? The timing was awkward. The board meeting was today and he needed to explain a dip in third quarter sales, which doubtless Michael J Courtstein VP of Finance would have a lot to say about. In his experience accountants always did. They never had any targets to hit, they just set them. Parasites to a man.

He switched on his phone, and it advised him of five missed calls. Obviously the nursing home had been trying to get him. Another from his PA in the UK. Oops, they obviously had her mobile number as back up. That would cost him some flowers. His phone rang. Mandy.

'Hi babe, how's London?' he said.

'Rainy and wet. Got splashed by a bloody taxi so I'm soaked to the skin. It's the middle of the night your end isn't it? What's up?' said Mandy, the noise of a station announcer in the background indicating that she was at Kings Cross.

'Mum's died. In her sleep this morning. The nursing home rang.' James' voice was level, matter of fact.

'Oh. I'm so sorry darling. I know you'd tried to see her last time you were back up north. My fault.' Mandy replied.

'No worries. She only got grumpy with me last time I went.'

'Sad she died on her own in that old folk's home though. Deserved better than that. Anyone deserves better than that.'

'Oh she wasn't alone. Brenda was with her when she

died. Looking after her future I shouldn't wonder,' James murmured.

'Ah. I see. Well what will be will be. Do you want me to fix things this end? I can travel up later on today if you want? Make contact with the Funeral Directors?'

'Thanks. I'll get Jenkinson's to do it. The family ties go back generations. But yes, if you go tonight I'll meet you there as soon as I can and we can get things sorted. Gives us a chance to arrange the funeral and get the details of the will. I'd better write off next week entirely. There's quite a lot to do. Head of the family bit,' James added.

They rang off. James reflected briefly on his past. What was and what might have been. He opened the mini bar and picked out a miniature scotch. His mother's favourite. He drank a silent toast, and pondered his next move. He would get his PA to fix an evening flight home after the board meeting. It was time. Time to take on his role as head of the family. To arrange a suitable funeral for his mother in the community of her birth, to bury the hatchet and to put the past to rights. He slipped slowly into an uneasy sleep in his chair as the scotch warmed him through.

For her part Mandy had always quietly dreaded this day. Her mother in law Jean had seemed indestructible. She was sad for James but determined that he would not now rake over their past. James' life in Yorkshire was but a memory now, and they had built their lives in the south. James had made a separate life, so she didn't relish dealing with the Murgatroyd family baggage best forgotten.

*   *   *

For James' ex-wife Carol the news of her mother in law's death came with great sadness. Carol had been a regular visitor to Murgatroyd Hall. Her children, both in their thirties, seldom saw their father, and seemed to care even less. They had long since given up on any relationship with James, who could not even remember their birthdays. But they loved their grandmother and would doubtless come back for the funeral. They had spent many hours at the hall as children, with the tennis court a real draw. Jean had always looked out for Carol after her divorce from James, and had always taken her side. They didn't really discuss James, because they didn't really need to.

James' last visit was two years or so ago, when he arrived after Jean's last stroke. Mandy came too, but their children were conveniently away and Carol ensured that she was not at the Hall when James visited his mother. She was too old to deal with the emotional baggage it dragged up for her. She had moved on long ago. She was happy, and had a long standing boyfriend. He was solvent, and so was she, and they retained individual homes. James could do as he liked as far as Carol was concerned.

She wondered about the will of course. As an only child James would surely get the lot, but hopefully Jean would leave something for her grandchildren. Beneath the matriarchal northern bluff and bluster Jean Murgatroyd had a kind heart, and Carol would miss her.

She wondered what James would do with the family business. Although Carol had no business connection with the firm she was still regarded as being of the Murgatroyd clan, and kept her married name out of habit. As the town's only large employer the future of the Company was very important. If there were layoffs or strikes at Murgatroyd Pens the local economy always felt the pain.

*   *   *

Back at the factory Brenda Arkwright published a works notice, toured the shop floor, and closed the factory early as a mark of respect. The union flag which fluttered above the head office building alongside that of the Queen's award for export was lowered to half-mast.

Peter Dawson, the shop steward, heard the news of Jean's parting with particular regret. His father Derek had been at school with Jean, and they had worked together throughout their lives. Derek was a resident of Millview nursing home too, and Peter had decided to visit straight from work. Doubtless his father, still as sharp as ever in spite of his age, would recount many war stories of his time with Murgatroyds, of Jean, and Brenda, of Bill and James.

Much had changed in Murgatroyd since his father's day, but Peter still remembered things from his youth. The Easter eggs, the works outings and the Murgatroyd's Christmas party. An old fashioned family firm with family firm values. But he was worried too. The ownership position was now uncertain, and rumours of a sale were circulating already.

*   *   *

As a young reporter at the Gazette collated his story and dug through the archives for pictures of Jean Murgatroyd he became aware of the family saga which had gone on nearly a century. He'd only recently come to the town as a junior reporter, so the history lesson was fascinating. He learned that Josiah Murgatroyd's son William had started Murgatroyd Pens during world war one. His son Bill had succeeded him. Bill died in 1974, and Jean Murgatroyd who had died that morning was Bill's wife. He then learned that their son, James Murgatroyd, had left the business after a family row in the mid seventies. His ex wife Carol Murgatroyd still lived locally. Interesting. So who was this Brenda Arkwright, the current managing director? How did she fit in?

He penned a rather long piece for the following day's paper, but his editor cut most of it back. Mustn't rake over old enmities with rumour and speculation. Respect for the dead and all.

At Braceby and Atkins Solicitors, Martin Braceby heard the news just after lunch when his PA told him of a rumour concerning Jean Murgatroyd. A quick telephone call confirmed the news; Jean Murgatroyd had passed away.

Braceby's had been the Murgatroyd's solicitors for many years. They were also the executors of Jean's will. Martin's father had constructed the will of Jean's husband Bill Murgatroyd all those years previously. A will with somewhat unintended consequences for the ownership of Murgatroyd Pens. Martin knew what Jean's will contained, and was in a unique position. He and only he understood how the ownership position would wind up on Jean's death. It guaranteed that the next few weeks would be busy.

He had been contemplating a long awaited holiday with his wife, and the coffee table at home was covered in brochures. He sighed as he rang home. His wife picked up the call immediately.

'I've already heard the news. Our holiday's on hold I assume?'

2.

1916 – Humble beginnings

William Murgatroyd stood on the old mill site by the river. The building was run down, but not as derelict as he had anticipated, although wild flowers had begun to sprout through some of the long disused window frames.

The Murgatroyd family had amassed quite a fortune from wool, and from the waterways, and from the railways. Right place, right time, at least so far.

Old Josiah was big in wool, but it was his father, born and raised in the valley, who had built Murgatroyd mill. It was originally water powered, and had the classic features of a mill of its time. The remains of the now defunct water wheel and the mill pond built to control the flow of the river were still evident.

William had served king and country. One of the survivors of the seventy five thousand soldiers who General Haig had deployed in the battle of Loos in September 1915. As the big push commenced a bullet from a German sniper embedded itself in his left ankle, breaking the bone. He'd only travelled a few hundred yards when he was hit. He was lucky. Another eight and a half thousand of his friends and comrades had died that day.

He returned home in time for Christmas. His elder brother George did not. He died in a hail of German machine bullets in the futile attack on the notorious Hohenzollern redoubt on October 13th.

William was young, restless and ambitious. His father Josiah had plenty of money, but was close to retirement and both he and his wife Clarissa were left devastated and grieving. When William returned home they were relieved that he was safe if not unscathed.

His ankle healed, but he could only walk with the aid of a stick. To strengthen it in the spring of 1916 he walked extensively in the hills around their Yorkshire home. The old mill site had been their playground as a child. He remembered George swinging from the wooden beams as he dared his little brother to follow suit. He found their names still carved on one of the doors through which the raw wool had once travelled. A rook stood pecking at the ground close by, oblivious to his presence, and rabbits played happily in their adopted home. Nature had taken the site back for its own.

As he walked he hitched up his trousers once again, aware that he had lost weight. An observer would have seen a young man, square rather than tall, with jet black hair. The trademark Murgatroyd look.

He went around the back of the mill, to the yard. He pulled away the weeds from the wall, and found what he was seeking. The painted lines of three cricket stumps remained visible. He walked to the other end and picked up a small rock. He couldn't run of course, but bowled the rock in the direction of the stumps, and it hit the wall. He could visualise George at the other end defying his brother to get him out. Sadness welled up as the reminder of his loss returned.

He couldn't help but feel guilty that he had survived, and George had not. He had seen only a few days of live action, and now he was out. But at least he was alive, and could walk, albeit with a stick. He was determined not to waste the opportunity.

He sat for a while watching the water flow over the old weir, and took out a book. Isaac's notebook. They had been talking about America the day before the big push. They were planning their futures, trying to pretend that the war was nearly over. Trying to ignore the fact that tomorrow they might die.

Isaac had visited his rich American Uncle Benjamin in New York before the war and had seen a land of vibrancy and opportunity. His uncle was a jeweller and watch smith by trade. From their rat infested hole in France Isaac and William set about planning their future in business together. Isaac smiled and stood to stretch his legs, talking animatedly. The war was suddenly very far away from their thoughts.

Then suddenly a single shot rang out and pierced Isaac's skull. He fell back, eyes wide and mouth open as if poised to speak. A lone German sniper had added to his score. William cradled Isaac in his arms, but he was already dead. Isaac had been showing him his notebook, which was now lying in the mud at the foot of the trench and splattered with blood.

The events of that day came back to William as he sat by the weir. The only noise was that of running water. It was so peaceful after the western front. He shouldn't have kept the book he realised. But in it were sketches of pens. Drawings too. Beautiful fountain pens. Distinctive. And expensive. Isaac was adamant that after the war was over he would make these pens in England, and William had been trying to convince him that the old mill site would be perfect for a factory.

He looked at the designs. They were not Isaac's, but those of a young English designer and engineer called Thomas Camden. The Camden family had a small workshop in London, but were hardly rich. Thomas Camden needed a wealthy partner. The Schiff family had fitted the bill, now

William reasoned that he could offer Camden the finance and the factory that he needed instead.

William decided to go to London that very day. He slept for much of the train journey and arrived refreshed. The address on the drawings took him to Great Prescott Street. It might have been a fool's errand, but William had friends in London and time on his hands. He knew that Thomas Camden had also been in France, and could have either fallen victim to the carnage or still be serving his country.

William knocked on the front door of the modest looking terraced house, but there was no reply. A passer by stopped to assist.

'If it's Thomas you want he'll be in his workshop round the back. The man's obsessed if you ask me,' he said, then moved on.

William murmured his thanks, then went up a path next to the house. Behind it stood a workshop, from which came the sound of music. The Gondoliers he noted. He knocked on the part open door. No reply.

He entered an immaculate Aladdin's cave of a workshop. Tools were neatly filed on racks on the wall, and in spite of the whiff of engine oil there seemed to be an aura of obsessive tidiness. In one corner, working on a hand lathe, sat a rather thin looking man, a year or two younger than himself. The man was humming as he worked.

As William got closer the man looked up and paused.

'Can I help you?' he said politely.

'Thomas Camden?' said William, as Thomas arrested the gramophone, and carefully nurtured the record into its cover.

'Yes. Thomas Camden at your service,' he said, standing awkwardly as he did, reaching for his stick.

William introduced himself, and they shook hands.

'Come into the office,' said Thomas.

The office was more of a den. Two old but stout leather chairs stood in the corner. A small desk, with papers stacked neatly in regimented piles, and a table with an old primus stove upon which sat an old and well used kettle. Thomas reached for it.

'Tea?' he enquired politely of William. 'Do sit down if you will.'

William sat and watched as Thomas busied himself with the kettle and two china cups, rather incongruous in a workshop setting. As the kettle simmered he sat facing William.

'Now what can I do for you?' he said.

'I'm a friend of Isaac Schiff,' said William.

A look of great sorrow came over Thomas Camden's face.

'Was a friend. He died you know.'

'Yes. I know. I was with him when he died.'

Thomas paused a moment.

'Oh I see.'

He set down the tea in front of William, and sat.

'A real gentleman. You must tell me more of how he died. We had plans he and I. Until this bloody war intervened,' he said.

'Yes, I know. That's why I'm here,' said William, taking out the notebook and drawings.

'My word. I didn't expect to see those again,' said Thomas.

'We were discussing them when Isaac died. A sniper. A single shot. At least he didn't suffer,' said William.

'It seems that you and I were the lucky ones then. What happened to you?' asked Thomas.

'Ankle. Didn't get more than a couple of hundred yards. How about you?'

'I'm not sure if I'm honest. Bloody great big bang and I woke up with ringing in my ears and a few toes missing.'

They smiled at their shared good fortune, whilst at the same time mourning their friend.

Thomas was obviously interested in William's proposition. He had never been to Yorkshire in his life, but if this Murgatroyd family had money and an old mill then why wouldn't he explore the possibilities?

He turned to the desk, and pulled out a drawer. He took out three boxes, each containing a fountain pen. He handed each of them to William in turn.

'I made these up from the drawings,' he said.

William looked at each in turn. They were exquisite. It was exactly as Isaac had said. This quiet and unassuming Londoner was gifted for sure.

'Are they any good?' said Thomas. 'I couldn't quite get the finish right. Not sure if they're up to scratch.'

William looked up and smiled. Thomas was looking at him intently, as a pupil awaiting the verdict of his teacher.

'They're perfect Thomas. Just perfect.'

Later on that day William met with Isaac's mother Abigail. He shared his memories of his time with her son, and apologised for taking the notebook. Abigail was pleased that her son's dream would live on, and promised to write to Benjamin Schiff in New York to effect an introduction. William embraced the tearful Abigail and thanked her profusely.

The old mill was redundant, but William now had a plan for it. He was keen to build a business of his own, away from his father's shadow. He would produce high quality branded fountain pens for the post war consumer society that he sensed was coming.

He had a girlfriend, Anne, who was mad on the arts and crafts style, and loved the designs of Thomas Camden. She thought that they could capture the fashion of the day in the design of a fountain pen. William not only loved the diminutive dark haired beauty, but it was also a shrewd business move. Her father, Thomas Farley, owned the biggest retail chain across the north of England.

Thomas Camden visited the old mill site the following week. There was an obvious gulf in social class between the two men, and with hindsight William rather exploited the young Londoner. But Thomas Camden would never have a word said against William. William delivered on their vision, and never denied him the creative freedom he craved.

William shared his ideas with his mother. Although Clarissa had major doubts that he would convince his father Josiah, she wanted her precious only son to make his own way in the world.

She suggested that he talked to Charles Openshaw first, a family friend and banker. William's visit was fruitful. Charles was supportive of young Wiliam. The country would need young entrepreneurs. More than that Charles had a son, Gerald, who was a chartered accountant. Gerald had returned from the war blind in one eye, and was looking for a new opportunity.

Charles Openshaw was impressed by Thomas and William. A strangely ill matched pair and very young of course, but with complementary skills he thought, and of course Gerald Openshaw would keep a close eye on the money.

William proposed to Anne Farley and they were married

in the St Mary's parish church in the town in late 1916. They shared a desire to make their way in the new post war world.

The Murgatroyd Pen Company Limited was registered in May 1917, with William and Anne owning 90% of the shares, and Thomas Camden the rest. Thomas Farley placed the first order on the new company that same month, The old mill archway was freshly engraved with 'Murgatroyd Pen Company Limited - 1917'. The freshly painted gates swung open, and Anne Murgatroyd proudly cut the ribbon to declare the old mill back in business.

By the early Autumn William showed Thomas Farley two production pens for approval. Both had the distinctive 'M' monogram on the clip. He liked them both, and approved them for production. He noted that each were engraved with his name and that of his wife. A gift as the first customer. A nice touch he thought.

A workforce mainly consisting of injured ex-serviceman and women from the town somehow managed to fulfil the first order. They made the market in time for Christmas, and sold well for an unknown brand. Anne shamelessly bullied Farley's store managers into giving Murgatroyd pens prime locations in the shops. They knew better than to risk incurring the wrath of Mister Farley by disagreeing with his daughter.

Further orders were secured by Benjamin Schiff in New York, and William's friends who were now returning to their family businesses. As the war ended orders grew steadily, and Charles Openshaw saw that the bank's investment was safe.

William seldom left the mill until after nine in the evening, and the only day he had off was Sunday. Thomas Camden had been given the old mill manager's cottage next to the site to live in, and wrapped up as he was in his engineer's dream world he was content to toil in his workshop for nights on end. Anne Farley would take pity on the wiry Thomas from time to time, taking in food for him. She had more than once found him fast asleep in one of the old leather chairs he kept in his workshop.

In 1921 Anne gave birth to their first child, William junior. He was nicknamed Billy as a child, and the name stuck, becoming Bill in his adolescence.

*   *   *

A few years previously, in a rundown estate of back to back houses across town Margaret Adams had given birth to her first daughter Jean. Her husband left shortly after for the western front never to return. Life was extremely tough as a consequence, so later on Margaret became one of the first Murgatroyd employees, leaving her daughter with her mother.

Jean was an intelligent child, and went to the local school adjoining the terraced streets where they lived. Whilst not having a father was a disadvantage, it also spared Jean some of the expectations of a female child to become a wife and mother. Her mother encouraged her only daughter in her reading and schoolwork. Jean excelled in class, and was clearly ambitious.

One of her classmates was Derek Dawson. Derek was a very naughty child, and enjoyed a number of pranks at Jean's expense. He targeted Jean because she was top of the class, which Derek wasn't. Not that he wasn't bright; actually he was very bright. But he was lazy and just preferred to be bloody minded and awkward.

His father Alfred joined Murgatroyds after the war ended. He later tried to start a trade union at Murgatroyds, immediately singling him out as a troublemaker. He was given his cards when the depression hit.

As William and Gerald toiled to keep the business moving forward in the depression, Schiff came across an unknown Hungarian journalist called Ladislo Biro, who had invented and patented a crude version of the ball point pen. William seized the initiative and secured a licence from Biro to produce a ball point pen in England.

As world war two commenced Margaret Adam's daughter Jean joined her mother on the shop floor at Murgatroyds.

Due to William's disability and age, he was able to run the business throughout the war.

Bill meanwhile was an endearing child. His cheeky smile and dark curly locks got him out of many a scrape. And he was bright. At aged eleven he was sent to a prestigious grammar school near Leeds.

The competition brought the best out of Bill. He was as driven as his father, and took a keen interest in the family business. During school holidays he returned to Murgatroyd's to earn pocket money by working in the post room. He was fifteen when he first encountered a stunning seventeen year old girl called Jean Adams.

Jean was of course a worldly wise young woman, and was completely dismissive of the adolescent Bill, even though she knew he was the bosses' son. He asked her out once, but she made a polite excuse. Bill was old enough to recognise a brush off.

Jean's mother warned her off having anything to do with him.

'They're not for the likes of us those Murgatroyds. Don't you be getting ideas above your station, it will only turn out badly for you my dear.'

Time moved on, and when Bill was nineteen, war broke out. With a decent academic record he was accepted into the RAF as ground crew. He wanted to remain in engineering, and the RAF gave him that opportunity. He was posted to RAF Scampston in Lincolnshire, and spent the war working on heavy bombers.

He spent much of his leave in the business with William. This meant he encountered Jean once again. They were both in their twenties, and Bill was bright and quite dashing in his RAF uniform. In him she had found an intellectual match.

They dated in secret for a while. Bill knew that his family wouldn't approve. There were rumours that he might get posted overseas. Bill got a weekend pass and they managed to travel down to Burnham Market. A friend of Bill's had a holiday cottage there, and lent it to Bill for the weekend.

It was a blissfully romantic and illicit weekend, and at the end of it Bill was convinced. They were sat underneath a flowering Magnolia tree on the Sunday morning in bright sunshine, sharing the last precious minutes before the journey home.

'Time is short Jean. I'll try to get home before the posting, but I can't guarantee it,' he said.

'I know that Bill. Look. What will be will be,' said Jean, trying to be positive.

'We're going to win this war. Then I'm coming back to Murgatroyd's. I'm going to work with Mister Camden. Dad's agreed.'

'Yes. You said.'

'We need to sort things out. You and me I mean,' said Bill.

Jean stayed silent. She'd agreed to come for the weekend even though she'd wanted to wait. To share a bed with him that is. But you never knew what would happen next, not in wartime. Even having crossed that threshold she wasn't sure. She needed more time and so did Bill, but there wasn't any.

'I need you.... I want you to marry me Jean,' he said finally, taking both of her hands in his.

As she considered her answer he continued.

'I know the problems but there's no time. We've got to make decisions.'

Jean looked at Bill, a smile giving way to sadness.

'Your parents won't have me Bill. A girl from the typing pool marrying a Murgatroyd? And as for my mother well...'

'Times are changing Jean. The class divide is breaking down. They'll come around. They want what's best for me, and that's marrying you.'

Hearing him say these words, imploring her to say yes, Jean convinced herself that her mother was wrong. She was in love with Bill.

'I'd better say yes then. After all I've let you have your wicked way with me young Mister Murgatroyd. So I suppose you'd better make an honest woman of me.'

The threat of an overseas posting was lifted shortly after,

but Bill decided against advising his parents of this. Bill had made up his mind. He wanted to marry quickly. He told his Father of his intention to marry Jean Adams.

William reacted cautiously. To him Jean was a solidly dependable person and nobody's fool. Her mother was one of Murgatroyd's longest serving members of staff.

He saw absolutely no reason why these two consenting adults shouldn't marry. He knew too however that Anne Murgatroyd would have a problem coming to terms with it.

Bill was Anne's pride and joy, and she had tried to find suitable girls for him since he was a teenager. The Murgatroyd family were the pillars of this community. Anne was also a Farley, and expected her son to marry well after this desperately inconvenient war was over.

In the event Anne found it amusing that William had been unaware of the couples growing fondness for each other; It showed how wrapped up in Murgatroyd he had become. Jean was clearly a woman of great common sense and very well organised, something which at times Bill was not. Yes, thought Anne, young Jean was not ideal as to social class, but eminently more suitable than some of the well to do but rather air headed girls she had previously lined up.

The couple married in St Mary's Church a few months later. It was July 1944, with Bill being granted leave from his squadron. The next year Jean Murgatroyd gave birth to their first child, James. It was a long and complicated birth, and in the aftermath Jean was told that having further children was inadvisable. She was greatly saddened at the news, but elated at the birth of her son.

William and Anne were delighted grandparents, and as the end of the war approached the future looked bright for the Murgatroyd family. Bill and Jean lived in a cottage not far from Murgatroyd Hall, and after the war Bill joined Murgatroyd full time.

He was now in his mid-twenties, and ambitious. He undertook a degree in engineering in Leeds. He formed a strong bond with Thomas Camden, who by now was experimenting with improved ball point pens and roller balls.

During the summer recess William took his son to New York to meet Benjamin Schiff. Bill was awestruck by New York, with its bright lights and affluent consumers. The contrast with the austerity of post war Britain could not have been greater.

Schiff had made William and Bill aware of the new productivity improvements made by the likes of Ford by introducing continuous production lines, and Bill's first major project was to oversee a radical streamlining of the factory to make it more efficient.

Murgatroyd had in any event out grown the old mill, and

Bill eventually persuaded his father to build a new factory building on land adjoining the site which the family owned.

Schiff meanwhile encouraged William to establish a permanent presence in New York and Paris. William hired a Scotsman, Paul Munro, to lead the UK and Europe sales team and become Murgatroyd's first Sales Director.

Bill was excited by New York, and had a desire to travel. William knew that his son needed a mentor. After all, he reasoned, one day he would retire and hand the family business over to someone, and Bill was the obvious candidate.

A week later tragedy struck. William failed to return home from the factory one evening, and a worried Anne contacted Bill to ask if he had seen his father. Bill went to the factory and discovered William slumped on the floor in his office. A massive heart attack had taken him. He was just sixty, and Bill just thirty five.

3.

2000

Derek Dawson was in his room when he heard that his old school friend Jean Murgatroyd had died. He was increasingly struggling with his breathing, a legacy of his heavy smoking younger days. The oxygen was kept in his room to assist, but Derek still popped outside the French windows for a quick smoke even so. The carers despaired of ever getting him to stop. For this was Derek Dawson. The Derek Dawson. The formerly all powerful Trade Union Convenor of the United Penworker's Union no less.

Brenda Arkwright stopped by. She used to drop in from time to time, but this time she was clearly upset as she told him the sad news. She was by now the Managing Director of Murgatroyds, but to Derek she would always be young Brenda Lawrence. They had known each other since she had joined the Company as a youngster, and Derek had always found her a straight talking individual with an impish sense of humour.

Brenda saw a look of great sorrow in the older man's

deep blue eyes. In spite of the previous feuds between the Murgatroyds and the Dawsons, Derek had come to respect Jean Murgatroyd. During a previous era of them and us Jean had never forgotten her humble council estate roots.

'Another of the Murgatroyd dynasty passes on then Brenda,' he intoned.

He thought for a moment, and coughed repeatedly, his face turning crimson as he did. He reached for his handkerchief, and Brenda sighed.

'You should give up the fags Derek,' she chided,

He recovered from his spluttering. 'She'll be missed for sure. Did so much for this town. We had our moments but still....' his voice tailed off.

Brenda let the silence hang for a moment as she surveyed Derek's surroundings. A picture of his son and daughter and several of his grandchildren. A black and white picture of his late wife Edna, and another of Jean presenting him with his long service watch.

Derek looked across and smiled. He wasn't sure how many others knew the full story of the events of the early seventies, but he did. In her darkest hour Brenda had turned to Derek for advice.

'Vicky still doesn't know does she Brenda?' he said.

'No. But she'll have to know now Derek,' Brenda replied.

Derek looked up into her eyes. He was just as sharp as

ever Brenda thought. Hair now silver, with just a hint of grey left. He put his hand on hers to offer support, something he had always done.

'I'm surprised you've never told her Brenda. Vicky's pretty level headed like her mum. I'm sure she'd have been fine about things,' he smiled kindly.

'We'll soon know Derek. I've put it off long enough. I'll tell her this evening,' she said decisively. Derek nodded but was unconvinced.

But there was little more to say. Derek tried to get up as she left, but a coughing fit took over once more, and he gave up with a shrug. Brenda smiled, and kissed him on the cheek. She still had the same radiant smile.

After she left Derek dozed in his chair. He thought about Brenda and about Jean, about his dad Alf and his past with Murgatroyds. He still had his white union convenor's coat in the wardrobe, and wore his Penworkers Union tie clip and badge with his everyday clothes.

As Murgatroyd's grew many new people joined the firm, most of them locals. Derek joined after the war. A couple of years before William died young Brenda Lawrence started at Murgatroyd's as a school leaver. She was a bright child and was easy to like. She was cheerful and took every challenge on as a positive.

Derek recalled meeting her on her first nervous day on

the shop floor in the packing department. She was always a bit on the curvy side. Natural light brown hair and freckles. A typically pretty Yorkshire lass, Brenda's mother and father had moved to the town a few years before, and they lived in a brand new council house. Derek lived only a few streets away, so he saw her fairly regularly. Her father worked for the council in the Housing Department, and her mother found a part time job as a teaching assistant in the local secondary school.

As she entered her teens she enjoyed tennis and joined Murgatroyd's Sports & Social Club. The sports ground at Murgatroyd's had been Jean's idea. As the firm grew the Murgatroyd family should give something back to the community she had argued, and with Anne's support William had agreed. An area of ground next to the new factory was levelled. It had a club house, cricket and rugby pitches, and two grass tennis courts. The setting was quite beautiful as the club house stood next to the old mill pond.

Derek enjoyed the indoor activities. A few pints and a game of darts or dominoes after work was his thing. But in the summer he would sit outside with his wife Edith watching the cricket or whatever else was going on. He still recalled watching a fifteen year old Brenda win the girl's singles competition, and Jean Murgatroyd presenting her with the trophy. Brenda had taken on a girl a year older, who seemed the better player. But Brenda had kept the ball in play with incredible tenacity, and wore her opponent down in the end. It was clear that this girl Brenda didn't know how to lose. One for the future he'd told Edith later.

Derek was not the only one in a reflective mood. Later that afternoon, when the factory was empty, and the rain had given way to sunshine, Brenda was on her way home. As she walked out through the old gate, the Murgatroyd name proudly etched into the granite, she remembered the butterflies she had felt the first time she walked through them.

Murgatroyd's had been hiring as she was leaving school, and her father could probably have got her something in the council, but Brenda was independent.

She had walked through those gates as a fifteen year old and applied for a job in the packing department. Her mother had wanted better for her than shop floor factory work, but Brenda was determined to work her way up through the firm starting at the bottom. Ironically only a few months later she had been given a Murgatroyd Lady fountain pen as her prize for winning the tennis, and loved it. If Murgatroyd's made beautiful things then Brenda wanted to be a part of it.

Brenda walked past the Sports and Social Club, and stood at the old clubhouse entrance. It was a private club now, owned by the members. One of the many cost cuts she had needed to impose to keep the firm alive in the nineties. The tennis courts were still there, but they were hard courts now.

She remembered the day she had won that tennis title. Alongside Jean at the presentation that day stood Bill Murgatroyd. He shook her hand and made eye contact. Brenda noticed that he was a handsome man with beautiful eyes and warming smile. He was twice her age, so she didn't really give it a second thought at the time.

It was late afternoon and she wanted to think, so she skirted the cricket field and the old mill pond before cutting through into town. She went into St Mary's church and sat alone. The scene of so many ups and downs in her life she thought.

Brenda's family were active churchgoers, so when William died Brenda was in the choir at the funeral. She was nineteen. It was as close as the town came to a state occasion she reflected.

As she stood in the choir stalls not ten feet from where she now sat she'd seen the Murgatroyd family close at hand, grief stricken. She remembered Bill as one of the pallbearers. She remembered Jean, a natural blond in formal black save as for her trademark pearls, comforting a distraught Anne. As Bill took his seat at the front she could see the tears rolling down his cheeks.

It was the first funeral Brenda had attended and it affected her deeply. William had been respected at Murgatroyd. He had a fearsome temper, and getting the wrong side of him was a bad idea, a man of his time. Brenda had seen him visit the shop floor at times, often with Bill, but she was just on the packing line, so had not actually met him.

As she sat in the church now she found herself thinking back to those early days after she started with the firm. She remembered how shattered she was after a forty hour shift on piecework. Suddenly there were no long school holidays.

She'd only been there a month when she was asked to work overtime. The other girls had family responsibilities, the foreman said, and he needed an urgent order getting out. As she bent over to pick up a box she felt a hand on her bottom. She looked up to see the foreman's leering grin.

'Nice arse Brenda,' he said.

She was shocked, but said nothing and ignored it as best she could. She was traumatised and too scared to say anything. She confided in an older woman colleague.

'Oh him? He tries it on with all the girls. It's just a bit of fun. You'll get used to it,' she said.

As a young woman Brenda received more than her fair share of unwanted attention. Her blood still ran cold when she thought about it.

But Brenda was tougher than her years and took it all. She became a leading hand, supervising women twice her age. She was good with people. She looked up at the stained glass window which bore the crimson Murgatroyd logo, a donation by the firm. The sun now streamed through it as if in celebration of Jean's life.

Brenda allowed herself to dwell on her own history for a moment. She'd done pretty well hadn't she? In her forty plus years with Murgatroyd's she had risen from a shop floor packing assistant to managing director, in what was still a male dominated world. Some would doubtless criticise her for her attention to detail, implying micro management. But she had come from the shop floor and still felt comfortable there. Unlike many bosses she at least knew the names of most of the staff.

From her earliest days in management she could be one of the girls outside of work, but was respected too. Brenda did what she said she would do, and came to be regarded as a natural leader. When her girls complained that the food in the staff canteen was awful it was Brenda that raised it with the factory manager, who of course ate in the executive dining room.

She invited him to dine in the factory canteen one Tuesday, and he agreed, albeit reluctantly. He conceded that the food was a disgrace and sorted it out. She began to get mentioned more and more as one for the future.

Just after lunch, only two weeks after she joined, all of

her colleagues headed out into the yard. A bemused Brenda followed. A young and militant Derek Dawson addressed them through a megaphone. Brenda was stood near the back, barely able to hear. She caught snatches of what he said. Something about piecework rates and the erosion of differentials. It was a foreign language to Brenda. At the end of his diatribe everyone around her put their hands up. Her workmate next to her nudged her, so she did the same.

They went back into the factory, but only to get their things it seemed. She asked her chargehand what was happening.

'We're on strike love,' she said.

Looking back she found it incredible that there was such a huge gulf between so called blue collar factory workers and white collar people who were regarded as having 'staff status'. The distinction was bizarre, but meant you got sick pay, and of course there was a screened off area in the canteen dedicated to staff. Senior staff of above a certain grade ate in the executive dining room, with waitress service.

She increasingly found these class distinctions repugnant, and later in her career both divisive and unproductive. They were discriminatory and socially disgusting. A factory worker was seen as someone who could not be trusted and needed to be watched closely and controlled.

Early on in her working career Brenda could see ways that the process of boxing the pens could be speeded up, and made some suggestions to the charge hand. A couple of days later Derek Dawson asked her to pop into his office.

'Now then young Brenda, about these ideas of yours, what did you have in mind?' said Derek kindly.

Brenda explained her ideas. She reckoned it would reduce the packing time by around twenty percent.

'I see. But why exactly would we want to do that?' he enquired.

Brenda remembered being surprised by the question. It would make the Company more efficient she ventured?

'But then they'd want to put a man with a stop watch on the shopfloor to retime the new method, and the shop floor would be expected to work harder for the same money? Why would that benefit us?' he said.

Brenda took the point, although even as a youngster she sensed a flaw in his logic. But she couldn't articulate it at the time.

Derek nodded as she floundered.

'Look Brenda there are two sides in this factory. The workers and the management. They want their share of the cake and we want ours. That's why we have a union. If there's a better way to do the job it's for management to come up with it, not us. We just do the job, clock on and off and get paid. We don't need to do their job for them do we?'

Brenda thus realised early on that there was little incentive for the people who actually made the product to suggest improved ways of working. Under piecework there was no incentive to suggest more productive working methods, and if shop floor staff were treated as second rate citizens why should they care?

In those days business was done at long business lunches which continued on the golf course afterwards. The male middle aged managements became complacent and arrogant. The seeds of Britain's decline as a world manufacturing power were sown in the fifties, took root in the sixties, and came to a bitter harvest in the seventies and eighties.

There were many who believed that the overthrow of the class system in Britain was an entirely legitimate aim, and trade unions gave those people, Derek Dawson included, an opportunity to play a part in engineering social and political change.

'Penny for them Brenda,' said a kindly male voice sat in the pew behind her.

Brenda turned. Timothy Parry, the Rector of Saint Mary's, was smiling sympathetically. They had been at school together, so they had known each other a long time. His hair was thinning now she noticed. They were both at an age where you start reflecting on the past rather than the future. It was something that Brenda fought with herself about nearly every day. Look forward not back Brenda she kept telling herself.

'Oh just lost in the past Tim. Jean Murgatroyd died today, did you hear?'

'Yes Brenda, I did. I'm so sorry to hear that. What a wonderful woman she was. How are you feeling?'

'Okay. Just thinking back over things. Murgatroyd's, the family, life, you know. This church has been so important to me over the years. I was married here, buried my parents here. It feels like a safe haven.'

Tim Parry knew all this of course. In her darkest hours she had sought his advice and then sometimes ignored it, at least partially. But Tim was as much a friend as her Rector. He never judged, only supported her. He saw her tears starting, and sat by her, comforting her as she sobbed quietly. This was the real Brenda, not the power dressed managing director. She was not so much grieving for Jean he realised, but for herself.

'Come on Brenda. Time to deal with things. Put the past to bed at last,' he said. He gave her a hug as a friend.

'I know that Tim. I've been very selfish haven't I?' she said.

'Yes in a way I suppose. But you were in an impossible place at the time. Now you just need to deal with it. I'm sure young Vicky will cope.'

'I'm not looking forward to that bit I'll admit. But it's more the things I can't control.'

'Yes I can understand that. But Murgatroyd's is not your

problem. You've done a wonderful job there and whatever happens now you can hold your head up high.'

She looked up. The tears were gone. Her eyes were clear and intense. She was back in the zone. She was ready.

'We'll bloody well see what I can and can't do Tim. You just wait and see.' She kissed him on the cheek and headed for the door.

Tim Parry laughed. In another life he'd probably have married Brenda he thought. There was much to admire about this spirited good hearted lady who was quick to seek a solution to any problem large or small, and always did precisely what she said she would.

He began to think about the funeral which would be at St Mary's. The family plot no doubt. This would be his third Murgatroyd funeral, but his first as an ordained Minister. He remembered his first when he stood alongside Brenda in the choir. For the second he was the curate, and Brenda didn't attend. It was only a few days after the funeral when she had fled the churchyard in tears that he learned why.

4.

1956

Anne visited Thomas the day after the funeral at his nice little cottage not far from the factory. It was the cottage which William had acquired when they were first married, and which they had sold to Thomas later, when the mill site was redeveloped and he had needed to be moved from the mill manager's house.

It was Sunday, and as she walked up the hill she could see Thomas weeding the garden. It was a vegetable plot that she had tended herself when they were first married. William had cursed as he spent more than one hard earned Sunday digging it over to her exacting standards. This was the house where she had given birth to Bill, and poor Emily, her stillborn.

Thomas cleaned his hands and kissed her, and showed her to the veranda around the back of the house. Thomas brought tea, with his ever present biscuit tin. He sat in his favourite leather chair, and Anne sat in the other.

Thomas was a man of few words, unless of course one entered the workshop he had built when he bought the house. Immaculate of course. Spick and span, everything in its place. Then he was in a world where he was comfortable, and was able to speak his mind with authority. He was never comfortable about expressing an opinion without knowing all of the facts.

But Anne needed to ask him the most difficult of questions. They had both attended Wiliam's funeral days before, and it was now time. Time to try to look forward. She would talk to Gerald Openshaw and to Paul Munro of course. But she had always had a real fondness for Thomas. He had no ambition to be the boss, didn't do politics and led a simple life which he loved. Thomas would tell it straight.

They talked about William. They both needed to as part of moving on. He spoke of William's first visit to Great Prescott Street, and of Isaac's blood stained notebook. He recalled showing William his drawings of fountain pens, the ones which William had so kindly framed for him later on as a gift, and which were still hanging above his fireplace.

As he spoke Anne was struck that in spite of all these years in Yorkshire, Thomas still retained his cockney accent.

At length Anne came around to the subject of succession. What did Thomas think?

Thomas looked at her strangely. To him it was obvious. He thought about it for a moment and framed his words carefully.

'Well let's see now. Murgatroyd Pen has been my life and I love it as if it were my child. It's very precious to me. My life's work I suppose. But it's called Murgatroyd and should have a Murgatroyd in charge I reckon. Not some hired gun.'

His words were simple but powerful. She realised that Thomas hadn't really given it much thought. He saw the choice as obvious.

'Bill is only thirty five Thomas. He's very young don't you think?' she said.

Thomas laughed. He sipped his tea and set it down.

'Don't you think that Charles Openshaw thought that when William and I showed up? Me in a suit two sizes too big, reeking of engine oil, and William only just an adult?'

Anne smiled. She remembered the energy, the idealism and the excitement of it all in the early days. After a moment gathering his thoughts Thomas continued.

'I remember young Bill coming into my workshop when he was about nine. He was into everything. Every question started with a why. He called me Mister Camden and still does to this day. Then he comes back from the RAF and does his degree. He's shown me things recently that I never knew existed. He's only thirty five but he's lived and breathed Murgatroyd for nearly twenty years. How long an apprenticeship does a man need?'

Anne had the reassurance she needed.

'So you think my son's ready then?' she asked.

Thomas looked at her intently.

'Oh yes. He's ready. He's just like his dad,' he said.

Bill thus found himself heir apparent on William's untimely and unexpected death, and took on the reins after a grieving and desperate Anne had other conversations with Paul Munro and Gerald Openshaw. William was a much admired friend and each had a massive sense of personal loss. They could not think of personal ambition at such a time, and in any event each realised that young Bill Murgatroyd was a highly talented chip off the old block.

It was thus that Bill was appointed Managing Director of Murgatroyd's at thirty five. Anne Murgatroyd lived only eight months longer than her husband. She loved him deeply and never really came to terms with her loss. Bill inherited the entire share capital of Murgatroyds, and he, his wife Jean and young son James moved into Murgatroyd Hall.

Of course Murgatroyd was to be subjected to the national issues of the time. Virtually full employment, immigration and the growth of trade union power all had an impact on the fast growing company. After the war William had reluctantly agreed to trade union demands for recognition, and the United Pen Workers Union was created. The shop floor of Murgatroyd eventually became a closed shop. You were either in the trade union or you would be blacked and ostracised. In reality it meant that you couldn't work on the shop floor there without being a member.

Derek Dawson became Shop Steward and then Convenor of the trade union. Throughout the sixties trade union power grew nationally, and union officials were allowed time off for union duties at work. So by the mid-sixties Derek Dawson was a full time trade union official and extremely powerful.

Bill focussed on building the Murgatroyd business he inherited from his father. He and Paul Munro travelled widely, and by the end of the sixties they had grown a large and very profitable business reaching virtually every developed country.

Gerald Openshaw retired, and his younger brother Archie took over as Finance Director and Company Secretary. Archie joined the business having saved several businesses from oblivion. True, he had never completed his accountancy examinations in totality, but was worldly wise and tough. If Paul Munro was Bill's mentor in sales and marketing, Archie Openshaw was his mentor in finance.

Thomas Camden retired in 1962, but stayed on the board until the end of the decade. He became a governor at the local technical college, and remained active in recruiting the brightest and best designers to ensure that Murgatroyd products retained their reputation for style and quality.

Jean brought up James almost single handed. Bill was an

absent parent for all too much of the time. He had suddenly been thrust into the top job in his family business at thirty five. For Bill, making a success of his father's legacy bordered on obsession.

With hindsight Jean could see how it had happened. Bill should have developed a bond with his son. Of course he should have been at home more. But sacrifices had to be made.. She developed her own life of course, and was very much involved in local matters. She took on Anne's charitable work in the town, which had prospered from Murgatroyd's success. The high street showed new signs of affluence as Farleys opened a branch in the town, and one of those new fangled supermarkets opened too. A new estate grew up at the east end of the valley, and the house in which Jean grew up was demolished.

She appointed a younger woman, Marjorie Fisher, as a live in Housekeeper, and she became a close friend in the absence of Bill, who was abroad too much of the time. Marjorie had a sympathetic ear, and was uncomplaining.

As the sixties came to an end Murgatroyd's won its first Queens Award for Industry, and was given the royal warrant. As Prince Phillip walked up the receiving line and shook her hand Jean was reminded of those words of her mother all those year's back.

'Those Murgatroyds are not for the likes of us Jean.'

She smiled and thought about what her mother would have made of this day. The Murgatroyds that her mother worked for was so different to now. Bill stood showing the Prince around the factory, sharply dressed in a new made to measure suit bought for the occasion, his hair thinning on top but still slick and dark. He needs to watch his weight though thought Jean. Too much red meat and fried food.

Sadly James was away. Following one of his many rows with his father. Too much alike she thought. Both obstinate, both talented, both given to acerbic wit and arrogance. Jean had tried to foster greater understanding between them, but nothing worked with those two.

The reception party then headed into the boardroom for a presentation. Paul Munro, hair now steel grey and a profile that implied too many business lunches, led the way. He started with an introduction, but then handed over to young Brenda Lawrence.

Now thirty three, Brenda was Paul Munro's right hand woman. Sales Office Manager now, the most senior woman in the organisation. She had not lost her local accent, and Jean admired the way Brenda spoke with certainty and confidence. As the Prince asked a question she answered flawlessly. A class act thought Jean. Good for you girl.

But although Jean was happy to be there, and confident in her role in the family, she was now feeling unfulfilled. Bill was never home, and James was now married. It was just her and Marjorie most of the time. It didn't feel right. She was only in her early fifties; surely there was more to life than this?

Brenda on the other hand was feeling incredibly excited. It was only the previous week that Paul had given her the brief to make the Queen's Award presentation. She was also going to a major trade show in Florence with Bill in a few months' time. Paul Munro had been very helpful to her career thus far, and was trying to cut back on his travelling. Florence? The furthest she'd been in her life were holiday trips to Calais.

Life was looking up. There had been a string of boyfriends, some serious, but somehow, how could she put this? Not bright enough. Meat and two veg guys who had expectations of what a wife should be. Brenda wanted a career, and to travel. Feminism was coming and Brenda was up there with it, although never in an activist sense. Relationships came and went as the meat and two veg guys found what they were looking for elsewhere. Girlfriends warned her that time was passing; she'd be left on the shelf. She just laughed. She was having a great time. Besides she was at work far too much for boyfriends. And now she was meeting royalty and heading for Florence.

5.

1974

Jean Murgatroyd stood in the churchyard. It was raining. Actually it was pouring. Someone was holding an umbrella to shield her from the downpour. The shiny black coffin was glistening as it was being readied for lowering into the soaking earth.

She wasn't really functioning. She was being managed, and unusually for her she was content with that. It was a cliché but she felt numb, totally numb. Time had passed since it happened, but she'd lost all track of it . Where it had gone she didn't know, and actually didn't care. She didn't care about anything, truth be told.

She vaguely noted that Tim Parry was following the standard funeral text. She actually did have a religious belief, but now found the pomp and formality meaningless and irrelevant. Her husband was dead. That was the top and bottom of it. She was dreading the wake. The Rector talked of this ceremony being a celebration of Bill Murgatroyd's life. Celebration? What was there to celebrate? Fifty four years? Is that all he was entitled to? Was that all she was entitled to?

She was angry and bitter. After the last few turbulent years she thought they'd earned better than this. No Bill to share her life with, after all these years of playing second fiddle to the business. Yes she was being selfish she knew. It was Bill that had died after all.

Of course she had just heard an hour of people eulogising about him. They were saying wonderful things about her dear departed husband. They didn't know what she'd been through, or the few that did were not about to spoil the celebration of course. Celebration be buggered.

She knew the truth, and she would probably never really know who knew what of course, because people would never discuss what had passed, at least in her earshot.

She realised that it was Archie holding the umbrella. Honourable Archie. One of Bill's best friends, Archie fixed things when it all happened. One of the few people that knew everything. Ready to retire, but that would go on hold now of course. Paul Munro had already gone a year or so back. He was stood opposite, tanned from his sojourn in his villa in Spain. He didn't really seem to age thought Jean. He caught her eye briefly and smiled a thin smile of recognition and support.

Now Archie had something else to fix. Probably as big

as problem as the other one. Only very different, very very different.

Across the churchyard, Brenda, dressed in black, stood watching, well away from the gathered Murgatroyd family and their entourage. She couldn't possibly attend the funeral she thought. But she couldn't not come. Archie had cautioned her against it, but she had decided that she would come at the last minute.

She had married twelve months ago. She was already having doubts if she was honest with herself. Maybe Vicky, her new baby, would help her to settle down now. Her future career at Murgatroyd was now most uncertain. Looking back maybe she should have aborted the previous child when she became pregnant. It would have been so unfair, but it was a time for expediency. That child was very inconvenient. The Murgatroyds dealt well with things which were inconvenient. They were nothing if not efficient.

But Archie had sorted things. So she was spared and side-lined instead of disposed of. Dealt with quietly, discreetly and efficiently. But now things were different. Archie was soon to retire and Bill was dead.

She was back in her old job now, but no more foreign assignments, no more trade shows. James would presumably take charge permanently. He had told them almost as much yesterday.

She stood watching the coffin being lowered, from what she considered a decent distance away. She had not gone to the service. Too public and too close to the family. She owed them that much she thought. But she couldn't stay away completely. She had to come to say goodbye, albeit from a distance.

She had brought flowers but had no idea what to do with them now. She became aware that someone was alongside her, Edith Openshaw, Archie's wife.

'Shall I take those?' she asked kindly.

Brenda nodded and handed over the flowers. There was no card. That was too much Brenda had thought.

Edith took them and hugged her. Brenda was crying now, tears mixed with rain.

'I'll take care of these. Don't you worry. Archie sends his love,' said Edith as she headed off.

The churchyard gradually emptied. The family departed and the rain intensified. She heard the rain beating on her umbrella. She should go but would have to stay. At length the grave was unattended, and Brenda felt safe to venture down, and stood briefly by the grave.

'Goodbye Bill,' she said simply.

She went back to her car. The umbrella had only had a limited success. She was wet through in spite of it, and crying. Great sobs came forth, and she just let go. She switched the engine on to warm herself, and the radio came on. Costafine Town, a one hit wonder from a band called Splinter was playing.

'Costafine town it's a fine town, I'm coming home'

As it played its melancholy three minutes accompanied by the heavy rain beating on the roof of her car Brenda sat silently.

'I feel so lonely, I've been too long away'

I've never felt so lonely she thought. She couldn't discuss this at home with her husband she knew. She'd have to face this alone. Away too long? Well yes. This was her home town, where she belonged. Now she was back for good. And Murgatroyd's? Well yes that was her home too. She had known no other workplace after all.

'Nobody owns all the dirty old clothes that are lying in the rain, whistling loud the four thirty shift had gone'

Yes it was a dirty old industrial town. Yes it was a one horse town. But it was home. her home, and yes the four thirty shift at Murgatroyd's still clocked off to the sound of the old works hooter. Was it old fashioned? You bet it was she thought ruefully.

'Open pub doors where the working class goes at night'

Yes, and most of the workforce still headed down to the pubs and working men's clubs after work. Except when they were on a three day week as they had been recently, or on strike as they were all too frequently. Had much changed she thought? No, not much, she realised.

'Costafine town it's a fine town, I'm coming home, I wish I'd never made up my mind to stray'

As the song ended she somehow felt better. She drove out past the old primary school, the Murgatroyd factory, then along the valley towards home. The sun came out and she reckoned that she'd been given a message. This might be a dump of a town, but it's your home and Murgatroyd is where you belong. Don't give in. Let them fire you if they want to.

As the months went by she realised that she need not have worried about her job. Her career stagnated, but James made no move to fire her. Actually she was too good at her job and in any event too low in the new pecking order to be of interest. True James knew the facts of what had gone on, and he brought in new people over her with new ideas. But she was left in post as sales office manager in an open office next to James.

Jean became Chairman, but in reality that just meant a monthly board meeting. They had minimal contact, and there was civility. No warmth or any discussion beyond immediate business of course, but that was fine. The truce was uneasy but the situation was tenable.

Archie retired after a health scare, and a new man came

in. So her last ally was gone. Did she miss being at the heart of things? The foreign trips, the negotiations?

Of course she did. But after what had happened she knew that she had made her bed and must lie on it. Her tiny daughter Vicky was young and was a beautiful compensation for the business world that she missed. She was a respectable married woman now. Her husband loved her and provided her with much needed stability after the turmoil. He knew the full story, but had been a friend since secondary school and wasn't judgemental. Everyone makes mistakes. She loved him for that.

The trouble was that it wasn't enough for her. She was good at her job. In fact she had become pivotal to all that went on, without really realising it. She had also taken up night school and a correspondence course in business studies followed. She learned practical stuff like finance, economics and law, as well as sales and marketing. Whilst her husband headed to the Murgatroyd Social Club at night for snooker, darts or dominoes, and little Vicky was in bed, she studied hard and found business ever more fascinating.

But this was 1975, the era of James' bright young team with big ideas. They didn't need any input from the sales office manager. They moved to a new office block near the centre of town, and it had become a goldfish bowl, so remote, that it was as if the factory didn't exist.

Head Office got the orders and they were sent to the factory each day. That was the limit of James' interest. The factory just needed to produce the stuff, so any chasing up of late orders was down to Brenda.

And there were a lot of late orders. At the first sign of management pressure to increase productivity Derek Dawson took the workforce into the car park, and on a show of hands they headed for the gate. Brenda tried her best for her customers, but was fighting a losing battle. When she discussed late deliveries with James he said that it was her job to sort the orders out and deal with the flak from customers.

The more that problems emerged the more James blamed others, including Brenda, for the evident shortcomings of the business. She muddled through the chaos, but it was apparent to her that the business was becoming ungovernable. Yet James spent thousands on expensive rebranding and new-fangled marketing schemes.

Some of the investment in the factory was very necessary. Automated packing lines speeded up the boxing processes, but the kit was unreliable. And of course Derek Dawson was not about to accept reduced piece work rates which affected his member's earnings. As a consequence, much of the benefits of the investments made were lost.

Bill had not left the ship in pristine order when he died prematurely. As with most businessmen of his time he neglected investment in the factory, and ran the business as a cash cow. Old equipment was patched up and made to run for longer at much reduced efficiency and reliability rather than renewed. The mill was now over a hundred years old, and when it rained heavily the gutters couldn't cope, the roof leaked and buckets were deployed once more. Competitors in Germany, the United States and Japan would have laughed at the state of the factory. James wanted to address these shortcomings.

Then there were the wage negotiations. There were central government attempts to prevent excessive wage claims, but against a background of soaring inflation there were always productivity deals to be done with spurious targets and incentives. Such negotiations were time consuming and massively complicated to implement.

In the summer of 1975 James tried to take on the trade union, and Derek Dawson took the workforce out on strike for eight weeks. It was financially disastrous, and by the time James fudged a deal to end the strike the damage was done. Then the factory was put on full overtime at premium rates to try to catch up the backlog in orders.

Brenda never saw the figures, but it was obvious that order intake was dropping, particular from export markets. The cycle of poor quality and missed deliveries came to be known as the 'British disease', and it was taking firm hold.

Then one day she heard that the Finance Director Alan Caswell was gone, and James was taking control of finance as well. In reality that simply meant that she got the telephone calls as James and his new team were never in the office.

One snowy day James came out of his office and tossed a letter on her desk, before storming out of the door.

'See what's happened now? That shiny arsed book keeper at the bank is kicking off. Just give him a ring and sort it out will you? I need to leave now or I'm going to be late, this snow's getting bad,' he said, and he was gone.

Brenda read the letter, it didn't sound good.

Dear Mister Murgatroyd,

I refer to the banking facilities agreement provided by ourselves and negotiated with your Mister Caswell, who I gather has now left the Company.

As you will be aware the facilities agreement requires that monthly management accounts are provided to the bank within twenty one days of month end. I note that we have yet to receive accounts for two successive months, which is in breach of the agreement.

An analysis of the last figures actually supplied showed a material worsening of the Group's financial position, and in particular:

1) The overdraft has been rising throughout the last six months.

2) The debtor to overdraft ratio covenant, whilst still within the bounds of the agreement, is worsening such as to give us significant concerns that this may now have been breached.

I have tried to contact you to discuss this position, but unfortunately you have been unavailable. I'm sure that you will now understand the bank's concern, and request that the outstanding figures are provided by return, and that we arrange a meeting in the next seven days to discuss the matter further.

I look forward to your urgent response.

Yours Sincerely
Paul Whitehill
Manager

Brenda felt her stomach lurch. It confirmed her worst fears. But what to do about it? She doubted if James had much more of a grasp of the figures than she did.

She did the only practical thing she could. She had become accomplished at making excuses to customers, so she could probably bullshit her way through with Paul Whitehill. Archie had introduced her to him when he visited one day, so she did know him well enough to speak to him at least.

She spoke to Fiona, James' new so called Personal Assistant. Apparently it wasn't cool to be a Secretary any more. She identified three time slots for a meeting and agreed to note them in James' diary.

As she reached for the telephone she had misgivings as to why she was making the call at all. Surely this was James' job? He was a director after all, and she wasn't. But he'd told her to sort it.

In the event Whitehill was avuncular and simply happy to diarise the meeting. She promised that James would get the figures to him as soon as he returned from Brussels, even though she hadn't a clue if anyone knew where the figures were. She was lucky because at that time Paul Whitehill had significantly more say than he would in the years to come. Murgatroyd's were a long standing customer and Whitehill had a legal charge over the assets of the business. As such he was less vulnerable than Brenda realised, and the letter was simply a shot across the bows.

She replaced the receiver reasonably satisfied with the outcome, typed a memo to James advising what she had done and left it with Fiona. James made no reference to her memo when he saw her subsequently, so presumably the matter had been sorted.

But what Brenda didn't notice was that the letter was copied to Jean Murgatroyd.

Archie was taken ill six months after Bill died, having worked relentlessly with his new protégée, James Murgatroyd. The doctor simply warned him that he was overdoing things, and that he was not getting any younger. Archie was a heavy smoker and liked his whisky. He agreed to slow down and cut down on his two vices. His long suffering wife Edith, having seen what had taken place with Bill, made it clear that it was time for him to retire.

Archie reluctantly agreed, but had actually stayed on as part time Company Secretary after the appointment of Alan Caswell as his replacement.

When Jean received the letter from Whitehill her worst fears were realised. Things had slipped out of control, and with Caswell gone there was nobody to rein James in. She invited Archie to lunch.

Archie arrived at Murgatroyd Hall and kissed Jean on the cheek. The recent snow had made the garden a picture. It would soon be Christmas. The housekeeper, Marjorie, joined them for Sunday lunch as she and Jean had become close. Bill's picture seemed to be very much in evidence, as if Jean was trying to retain some vestige of his presence. She had done her best to move on, creating the Bill Murgatroyd Foundation to do charitable things in the town. Circumstances had meant that she had felt obliged to become Chair of Murgatroyd's, even though James was against it. He wanted free rein over the Company, but Jean knew that he was headstrong and reluctant to take advice. To make things worse James despised Archie and blamed him for the run down and dilapidated factory that Murgatroyd's had become. He had christened him 'Mister No', because of Archie's tendency to oppose the spending of money.

The lunch was excellent, and the conversation remained sociable in tone until Marjorie headed for the kitchen to wash up. Jean took Archie through to the sitting room and as they sat in front of a roaring fire she showed him the letter from the bank.

Archie was not surprised.

'Well it's a shot across the bows isn't it?' he said, handing the letter back.

Jean was surprised at his low key reaction, but Archie wasn't given to panic. He'd seen a lot worse in some places he'd worked before Murgatroyd's.

'It's a significant event which needs careful handling, but it's not unmanageable at this stage Jean. The bank is very well protected by the asset charge, and they do understand the impact of the strike. Provided James comes up with the figures and communicates with Whitehill on a proper and professional basis things will be fine.'

'Forgive me Archie but James seems reluctant even to talk to the man. Frankly he seems to want nothing to do with the nuts and bolts right now, and who do you think will provide the figures?'

Archie smiled. He was trying to be more reassuring than he actually felt. Jean was clearly all at sea, and he needed to keep her from giving James a piece of her mind. Getting a telling off from mummy was unlikely to get James to do what needed doing.

'I would agree that James' tendency to bury his head in the sand where the bank is concerned does need to change Jean. The loss of Alan Caswell is also a bit of a blow.'

Jean shook her head. 'James is adamant that a replacement isn't necessary. He said he can handle it. I spoke with him this morning.'

Jean was not equipped for this she knew, and the loss of Bill had left a gaping hole in her life. For all that Bill had been away so much of the time, and for all the trouble that there had been, she missed him massively. Bill was the anchor of her life. He ran Murgatroyd's and she could simply enjoy the trappings, going to whatever nice corporate gatherings which took place as she chose. Now she had ultimate responsibility for a substantial international business.

Archie read her mind.

'I told you when it happened you should have put in a chairman from outside Jean. You shouldn't have to deal with this. Family should never get in the way of business.'

Jean smiled a grim smile.

'James wouldn't hear of it. I did try.'

He took her hand to offer comfort.

'I know Jean, but things aren't getting better are they?'

She leaned forward intently. 'I need you to come back Archie. If you're fit enough that is. Just to get things straightened out.'

Archie smiled and shook his head.

'Me being well or not isn't the issue Jean. I left as much because James won't listen to me as for health reasons. In fact it was him not listening which probably caused my health problems if I'm honest. I'm not the solution, I'm a sticking plaster.'

Jean wasn't giving up.

'If a wound is bleeding you start with a sticking plaster Archie, and you are so much more than that.'

Archie nodded and carefully framed his reply.

'Well I suppose I'm prepared to have another go if you want, because I have some shares after all, and I've put in too many years at Murgatroyd's not to care. But James and I will never achieve the working relationship that Bill, Paul Munro and I had.'

Jean responded with a sigh.

'Yes it was special wasn't it. Now all we've got is James and his hired guns. No loyalty at all. Nobody to build a business around as you three did.'

Archie sipped his scotch.

'Well I agree to a point. The relationship was special. But there are strong managers still there. They just need leading,' he replied.

'Such as?'

Archie hesitated.

'Well since you mention it Brenda Arkwright-Lawrence is the most obvious example. Top class sales and marketeer trained by Paul Munro, and as loyal to Murgatroyd's as you'll get. Totally wasted as Sales Office Manager, and there are others too.'

Jean looked darkly into Archie's eyes.

'I'd rather you didn't mention her name in this house Archie. I'd have fired her for what she did if you hadn't intervened. I still can't stand seeing her sat in that office next to my Bill's.'

'I know you hate her Jean, and not without cause, but you need to understand that she is holding the ship together, not me. Not James or his cronies. It's Brenda juggling the balls now, because nobody else will take responsibility. She's at least prepared to get her hands dirty.'

Jean ignored him. He stayed silent having said his piece. She stood and walked to the fireplace. She looked at the picture of Bill smiling at her, setting her glass down on the mantelpiece next to his picture. Then she welled up, all resolve crumbling. It was all too much. There were times when Archie's analytical approach infuriated her, particularly when it involved that woman. She looked at Bill again, and it seemed as if he was mocking her. She thought for a moment and then swiped both the glass and Bill's picture from the mantelpiece. The glass shattered on the hearth. Archie saw the tears flow, and Marjorie appeared. She sat Jean down and knelt as she hugged her, the sobs continuing. Archie picked up the glass as she did so, and took it out to the kitchen.

As he returned Marjorie met him at the door.

'Don't you DARE mention that woman's name in this house. I've quite enough to contend with as it is,' she spat.

He had never seen Marjorie angry before. She moved passed him as she went into the kitchen.

As he entered the sitting room Jean had her head back and her eyes closed, but she had regained her composure. He sat, unsure as to what to do next. He let the silence continue, and at length Jean spoke.

'It was too soon for that Archie. Much too soon. I've not forgiven her and probably never will. She caused Bill's death. If she hadn't been around Bill would still be here.'

'I know you think that way, and I'm sorry I mentioned her. It was just, well, relevant? The point I was making is that there are a lot of loyal soldiers left at Murgatroyd's Jean. Very good people,' he said.

Jean looked up and smiled a weak smile.

'Yes, it was relevant Archie, and I over reacted. You touched a raw nerve. James isn't going to make it though is he? As managing director I mean?'

Archie looked across at the woman opposite, whom he had come to admire greatly over the years.

'Too early to say Jean. Much too early I suspect. Look I'll come back part time and we'll review things in the new year? How about that?'

They both got up and Jean kissed him on the cheek as they hugged, and she wiped away a tear.

'Thanks Archie. I'll tell James in the morning.'

6.

1976

Seven months after Archie's lunch with Jean, a Murgatroyd board meeting took place in the new boardroom at head-quarters, now a designer built office block in the centre of town. It was a hot summer's day and tempers were fraying. Jean Murgatroyd was trying to remain calm as she chaired the meeting. James Murgatroyd was on one side of the table, Archie Openshaw on the other. She noted the body language. James, face red with pent up aggression, leaning forward, fingers pointing across at Archie. Archie sat back, calm and analytical as always.

'Let Archie finish James. The figures are important. You'll get your turn,' snapped Jean.

'I'm sorry mother but this just gets a bit repetitive, and frankly a bit tedious. Board meetings are meant to be about strategy not detail,' said James, clicking irritably with his Excalibur ballpoint, the latest product in the range.

Archie interjected smoothly, as if the interruption had not taken place. 'As I was saying Chair, we are substantially below budget on almost every measure. The cash flow is particularly worrying.'

James bristled at Archie's smooth delivery. 'Well talk to your mate Whitehill then. It's up to the bank to provide the resources for the expansion project. They agreed to fund it after all.'

Archie remained cool as he responded. 'And of course it's up to you as managing director to remain within the banking covenants, which you will note we are in dangerous risk of breaching, for the second time in a year?'

'Archie has a point James,' said Jean. 'If we continue the way we have for the last three months the bank will get heavy and we'll be in real trouble with them once again. Won't you just listen to reason?'

'And where are Brian and Mandy?' said Archie. 'They are board members after all, and we need to review the order intake and the marketing plan.'

James was becoming even more irritable, 'I can't have my key sales staff off the job to sit in bloody meetings. A total waste of management time. We need to be getting orders, not talking about them.'

'Oh there we do agree. The sales and order figures are nothing short of abysmal,' said Archie, with a calculating stare.

Jean let the silence continue. She knew James of course. As only a mother would. People don't really change. Every nuance and insecurity built in during his childhood she had witnessed first-hand. James moved uncomfortably. It reminded Jean of the time she had caught him stealing chocolate from a secret tin she had. James was cornered. Archie was simply too experienced for James to bluff his way out. Archie was calm and analytical. James was highly strung and emotional. It wasn't an even contest. She took no pleasure from watching Archie tear James apart, but it was necessary. They had to do this.

James knew that Archie had a point, but he was still convinced that the expansion strategy just needed time to bed in. He had taken over a business where there had been little investment either in the buildings or the plant and machinery. Brand promotion was virtually nonexistent and the product looked like a fifties relic, even if it was still highly respectable and desirable.

Things were not helped by the fact that the middle managers were used to his father's 'hands on' management style. He had tried to get them to manage rather than keep coming to him all of the time as they had with his father. But they didn't seem be capable of changing.

He had thought that creating a new head office would help. It housed the organisation's sales, marketing and finance functions. It was of modern precast concrete with huge double glazed windows, and furnished throughout with the latest teak furnishings. Stylish silver block wallpaper in the reception epitomised the new Murgatroyd and was impressive to customers. James was proud of the up to date equipment. New Golfball typewriters, the latest Xerox photocopier, the brand new telex machine. His mother hated it all and old Archie the dinosaur fanned the flames.

He had brought in Mandy and Brian as directors to drive change through the business. He just needed time, and the support of his board of course. Fat chance of that with Archie on his case all the time.

He had had enough of this. He had the temper of his father, and he felt the rest mist descending.

'Of course if you'd let me sack that commie bastard union convenor maybe we'd ship some stuff. Just one bloody strike after another,' he said.

The 1974 miners' strike had taken down the Conservative government, and unions could and did engage in regular strike action. Union convenors and shop stewards could call a strike within hours of a problem, often via a show of hands in a car park. Three million days were lost to strikes, rising to over ten million in 1977. Commitments over deliveries were regularly broken, and as a result customers deserted UK manufacturers in droves. Murgatroyd were no exception. How could they get orders when previously promised deliveries had not been met?

Jean had heard all this before. This was yet another conditioned response of James when cornered.

'Alright, alright,' said Jean. 'You know fine well that the trade union position is very delicate. If you spent more time in the factory it would help. You need to keep a constant grip on labour relations James, not just sit in head office. Your father would…'

'Oh I was waiting to hear when my dear departed father would enter proceedings,' snapped James. 'How long is it now? Nearly three years if memory serves? Three years in which I've been trying to bring this Company into the latter part of the twentieth century from the sixties time warp my father left it in, in spite of Archie sabotaging every modernisation effort I make. Frankly Mother I think it's time you made up your mind who you want to run the business.'

'What do you mean by that?' enquired Archie.

James maintained his gaze at his mother, ignoring Archie completely. 'Well perhaps Archie fancies running it,' he sneered.

'You're the managing director. That is not for discussion.' Jean was trying to reduce the temperature of the meeting but failing miserably.

'Well it doesn't feel that way to me. Now if you'll excuse me I've got work to do,' said James, at which point he got up, gathered his papers and walked out of the door. Jean got up to follow but Archie stopped her.

'Leave him Jean. It's no use, he just won't listen.'

Jean slumped in her chair. 'I know Archie. He's just as stubborn as his father.'

'Actually his father did listen Jean. James just doesn't have the experience to know any better. I've tried to sit him down to discuss things, but he's just completely disinterested. Of course he has a point about modernisation, and God knows the trade union position in this country is killing our manufacturing base, but there are some fundamental business dynamics which you just have to grip. Cash flow being one.'

'Maybe when they do the proper launch of Excalibur things will be better?' said Jean.

'They'd better be. We've got a warehouse full of the damn things, that's what I wanted to ask Brian about, and the marketing costs are just horrific. You should see the bills.'

Archie had planned his retirement with his long suffering wife Edith in some detail, and they looked forward to spending time together. Then one terrible day four months ago, Edith suffered a stroke and was gone. Archie was devastated. He returned to work glad of the distraction and purpose it created.

The finances of the Company continued to fall away as James pursued rapid expansion plans, supported by increased bank lending.

When he returned to the business at Jean's behest Archie

was very uneasy. Why had Alan Caswell left? James said that Caswell was not up to the job, and was no loss. Archie was suspicious as he had vetted Caswell carefully before his appointment. Why would an experienced man with a track record of staying in a job for a long time suddenly quit?

He arranged to meet Caswell in Leeds. It was apparent from the conversation that as the financial position worsened, Caswell had been put under pressure to engage in what was becoming known as 'creative accounting'. In particular a small acquisition made by James, his first as managing director, was going very badly, and James had clearly over paid for the business. James was very precious about the acquisition, and would not face up to the realities of the position.

Archie subsequently approached James which resulted in a major row. Archie was meddling in things he no longer understood as far as James was concerned. Archie insisted that they seek an independent auditor's review of the books. Jean agreed, in spite of James' vehement objections to the cost. The auditor's report vindicated Archie's view. Later on that week Jean invited him around to Murgatroyd Hall for dinner. It was a warm evening and Jean served them both in the conservatory, with its view of the factory in the distance.

Jean waited until the coffee was poured and they sat out on the terrace as it got dark. 'Now,' she said, 'to business'. Archie sat back. He knew that this was not an ordinary social occasion. He'd dined at the hall before of course, as he had almost become a member of the family over time. But he knew that Jean was in an impossible place. She had to act but knew that James was not going to take it lying down.

'We said that we'd review things after three months, but it's now six months since you came back and the business is still struggling. I need you to come back full time, just until we get things back on track,' she said, sipping her coffee.

Archie was not surprised, and had admitted to himself that without Edith what did retirement have left for him? In a few weeks' time he was heading for Australia to visit family for three weeks. He needed a break for sure. But then what? Before he could respond Jean acted as if she had read his mind, and put her hand on his shoulder.

'I know it's a lot to ask. You've been through so much losing Edith, and you've not been well yourself, but we need you now. You stuck your neck out and the auditor's report is pretty damning even if I don't entirely understand accounting. Go to Australia, have your break, then stay on as finance director for another twelve months, to help us out?'

Jean looked into his eyes intently as she spoke. Archie smiled. How could he refuse?

'If things last that long Jean. I've warned you three months running. Things are getting worse month by month. I keep telling the bank that things will improve, that it's no more than growing pains caused by the new products we are developing, but my credibility is crumbling as well now,' said Archie gravely.

'So what am I to do? Sack my own son? I've suggested to him that we get some outside help from an experienced chief executive as a mentor but he won't have any of it.'

Archie stayed silent. He didn't need to tell Jean what she had to do. Jean just needed to come to the inevitable conclusion, painful though it was.

Jean sat back in her armchair, sipped her coffee once again, and set the cup down.

'Maybe I'll just have to sack him if things come to that. If there's no other way? I can't let him destroy the family business can I?'

*   *   *

Meanwhile at head office James Murgatroyd sat opposite the young and attractive Mandy Brice Cooper. They were watching a new TV advertisement which was the centrepiece of the Murgatroyd rebranding, designed to make the Company more of a household name.

The on screen action showed King Arthur's Camelot. The on screen Arthur was wielding his sword above his head in a demonstration of might and power. The voiceover was from a moonlighting RSC actor, adding gravitas. 'In Arthurian legend there was a sword which might only have been used by the true king. Its' name? Excalibur. Now Murgatroyd pens introduce the new Excalibur retractable. A major advance in pen design and precision engineered as only Murgatroyd's can. Available now at all good retailers. Because a Murgatroyd pen is a pen for life. Murgatroyd Excalibur – The King of pens.'

The image faded.

'What do you think James?' said Mandy.

'So that's the finalised version of the TV ad we saw last week?' he replied.

'Yes. It'll be just brilliant to get national TV exposure. Really puts us on the map for the first time.' Mandy was in selling mode.

James smiled. 'Archie will go ape at the cost though?'

Mandy stood and threw her hair back dismissively. 'Archie is typical of the old backward looking management that held this business back for so long. The Murgatroyd brand is brilliant James, the market research shows that we could turn it into a premium international brand, but we've got to promote the brand to build it.'

'I know Mandy,' said James wearily.

'What's up James?' Mandy was concerned. The ebullient James she knew had disappeared of late. He was ever more distant and haunted. She moved around his side of the table and sat, taking his hand in hers. James relaxed, and smiled.

'Oh I'm just sick to death of Archie. The board meeting was a nightmare.'

Mandy bristled immediately. 'I told you not to face them alone. I'd have given Archie a piece of my mind. He's just such a dinosaur. No idea about modern marketing techniques whatsoever.'

'I know Mandy,' James put his hands up defensively.

Mandy softened. 'Is there something else? You seem, well, preoccupied?'

James looked at her intently. 'I think Carol might suspect.'

'Oh. But how could she? We had separate rooms at the conference. We were so careful?'

'I know.'

'Not having second thoughts are we?'

'What? No, no way.'

Mandy was marshalling her thoughts, fingers steepled as was her habit. She looked up at James, hesitating.

'It was great for me too,' she said. 'Look James I don't make a habit of shagging the boss you know. You're special to me. You know that?'

James returned her gaze and pulled her to her feet, hands holding hands. 'Yes. I know. You're special to me too.'

She kissed him. They held each other for a while, taking

much needed comfort from each other. Then they each went their separate ways.

James drove home, but via Craven ridge, a local beauty spot. It was a sunny evening, and he wanted some time to think before he returned to his wife Carol and the girls.

Mandy was such a contrast to Carol he thought. Mandy believed in him totally. She was a bit younger, a little naive, and all the more attractive for it somehow.

As he sat alone on a bench overlooking the view he silently chided himself, and his late father.

'Of course things are going wrong. I'm not that stupid. It isn't easy being the managing director is it? Everybody expects you to have the answers. But they don't realise that I don't have all the answers.'

James' relationship with his father had been distant in more ways than one. Dad was wedded to Murgatroyd's, and a combination of long hours and business trips robbed James of his father's attention. The bond had never really been forged.

Of course his father said all the right things, paid for everything. But what James wanted was what any child wanted, parental approval. And in that regard Bill came up well short. Any parent knows the distractions brought by long hours and crushing tiredness. Family trivia is only trivial if you think that your work is more important, and indeed it is in some respects. But that isn't a child's perspective at all.

When James took part in a nativity play at six years old, his father was at a trade show in Germany. When James won his secondary school singles title at thirteen Bill had promised to show up, but then arrived too late. Bill was an absent parent.

In craving his father's attention and approval James over reached and made mistakes, if anything eroding any confidence which Bill might have had in him. James had a spell in the factory when he was seventeen, but hated it. As the boss's son he was the butt of all the jokes and innuendo.

He confided in his mother from time to time, but she knew that being a Murgatroyd it would just go with the territory. One evening in a local pub a Murgatroyd storekeeper, Tom Webster, mouthed off about Bill to his mates. James called him a luddite and a commie bastard to his face.

Webster was drunk, and when he got up and lurched in James' direction, James punched him, knocking Webster and a table full of glasses flying. James was banned by the landlord. Worse still he said nothing about what had happened when he got home. On Monday morning the trade union convenor, Derek Dawson, went to see Bill. Bill of course knew nothing. Dawson wanted James sacked for misconduct. Bill stood his ground. He would investigate, but the incident had taken place off company premises, so he would take no such action.

Though Dawson grudgingly accepted that Bill couldn't actually do anything Bill was furious. It led to a flaming family row, with Jean trying to play peacemaker. They were father and son, and both as obstinate as each other. A father calling his son a complete waste of space only ripped open a festering wound. The best that could be said was that they agreed on one thing; James thought whatever he did would never be good enough for his father, and his father confirmed it. Bill felt betrayed by his son for not telling him about the incident, and putting him in an embarrassing position. His son thought he had done the only thing he could do; stand up for the family. Jean reasoned that both sides had a point, but Bill had just bowled in through the front door and let rip at James, giving Jean no warning. She had no idea what was going on, or what the facts were. James stormed out, leaving Jean to pick up the pieces.

Although Jean spoke to both sides and tried to get them to talk things out the damage was done. Father and son never had a rapport from that day on, and both were too stubborn to make things up.

It did however have one positive effect. James resolved to go to university, and far far away in London. Previously rather lazy he now became driven, and his A level results even surprised his father. University followed, then business school. He accepted a scholarship with International Pen, or IPCO for short, and took up a sales role there. He came home from time to time, but generally when his father was away. Bill never even showed for his graduation.

He did fine at IPCO. He made Sales Manager and learned the business. He had done well. Even his father seemed pleased, and relations had become a little less frosty. Then Murgatroyd Sales Director Paul Munro advised Bill of his intention to retire. He and Bill were very close. Bill had realised that succession was an issue, and pondered options for the future.

Munro made the obvious point. 'Bill I know things haven't been great with your son, but you're not getting any younger, and if you want a family succession now is the time. Why not bring James in as Sales Director designate, and he can take over in twelve months' time, after I've shown him the ropes?'

Bill was not convinced. He mentioned it to Jean. She thought that the suggestion made sense. After much soul searching Bill went with the view that it was a good time to bring his son back into the family business, working for Paul Munro as he had previously. For his part Paul ensured that father and son had little day to day contact, and he found James bright and articulate.

Munro retired and James succeeded him as Sales Director as planned, reporting to his father. James' role was externally facing, and he had little to do with the day to day issues within the Company. The relationship was business-like, and it seemed to Jean that father and son had developed at least a level of mutual respect.

Then but a few months later the world changed. It was a damp Tuesday morning, and Jean was reading the paper as per her normal routine. The doorbell rang, and realising that it was Marjorie's day off she went to the door.

There at the door was an ashen faced factory foreman who she knew, but whose name escaped her.

'Sorry to trouble you Mrs Murgatroyd, but it's about Mister Murgatroyd. He's collapsed at work and he's on his way to hospital.'

Jean grabbed her coat and they drove to the hospital. The Doctor met her at the door to intensive care, and showed her into a typical hospital meeting room. James arrived moments later.

They sat for about half an hour. Then the doctor returned. 'I'm really sorry...'

Bill Murgatroyd had died five minutes previously of a massive heart attack. Jean remembered William dying in similar circumstances. History had repeated itself.

As James sat on the bench high above the town he

recalled coming here with his father as a child a couple of times. He'd come to realise how few times he and his father had actually talked as father and son should.

Two weeks after Bill's death James Murgatroyd succeeded his father as Managing Director of the family firm, and the slow financial decline began which came to a head in 1976, as James Murgatroyd sat on Craven's ridge searching for answers.

7.

1976

Six weeks after Jean's dinner with Archie it was business as usual at the Murgatroyd head office. Archie had just arrived home from his holiday, and was dreading what he would find on his return to work the next day. He had almost cancelled the trip, with the trading of Murgatroyds slipping still further, but Jean had insisted that he went.

As Archie flew back Brenda Arkwright was busy, very busy. In addition to her already impossible workload she had another problem; James' PA was on holiday, and the Office Junior, Debbie, was sick again. So she was in the office alone and had to pick up James' telephone. It was afternoon, and most afternoons James had meetings. Business lunches he called them. Frequently at the golf club.

She had just put the receiver down from one call when James' line lit up again. She answered it wearily.

Sales Director Brian Biggs was sat with his feet up on his desk, reading a series of car brochures. Actually the particular magazine he was reading at that moment was Playboy.

He could have tried to disguise this fact but couldn't be bothered. He was a director after all. And Brenda was only Brenda Arkwright, the Sales Office Manager.

Brenda answered with a business like 'Good afternoon Murgatroyds', and paused to listen.

'No I'm sorry Mr Whitehill, Mr Murgatroyd is out on business this afternoon. I'm sorry, I did give him your previous message. No Archie isn't here I'm afraid, he's flying back tonight I believe. Back in the office on Monday? Okay, I'll get James to call you urgently. Goodbye.'

She put the telephone down and sighed.

'On business my arse, gone off to play golf again,' said Brian, still looking at a well-built blond centrefold in Playboy.

Before she could fashion an answer the telephone rang again.

'Mr Bradley? Yes good afternoon. The cheque? Yes I'm sure it's been raised, I'll get James to sign it when he gets back.'

She listened. One more rant from one supplier amongst many.

'Oh I see. I appreciate you need to wait for the cheque but we really do need that delivery. Couldn't you just..."

She listened once more.

'Oh I see...... Okay, look I do understand. Leave it with me. I'll sort it out as soon as James is back. My apologies.'

This time Brenda paused as she replaced the receiver.

Brian looked up. 'Good line in bullshit that.'

Brenda replied wearily. 'I do not lie, it's in there with the others, and those from last week.'

'We going bust then?' said Brian, re-examining the blond in more detail.

'No. Just a bit of a cash flow problem.'

'Business bollocks for going bust that,' said Brian, 'I've heard that line from too many customers to fall for that crap.'

Brenda bristled. 'Maybe if you sold something it might help?'

Brian ignored the comment, picking up a car magazine.

'I'm busy planning the replacement of the company car fleet. Should I go for the Ford Granada, or the new Rover do you think?'

'And fiddling your expenses. You do take the mickey. Berni Inn on a Saturday night?' said Brenda reprovingly, handing back an expense claim packed with receipts.

'Business client love,' said Brian, lobbing the claim back to her.

'And the gift from Samuels. The diamond pendant?'

'A gift for the Saddleworth's buyer. You should approve. A woman buyer and all that.'

Brian was enjoying the banter. He could slap Brenda down any time he wanted. She was just an admin clerk to

Brian. A female dogsbody just like the other women. Good for making tea and a bit of fun.

'Well, well, a female buyer. Heaven's be praised,' said Brenda, getting up to get some copying done before the telephone rang again.

'Sign of the times Brenda, equal pay, spot of bra burning, women's rights. By the way did you know Mrs Pankhurst?' Brian smiled at his own joke. Brenda winced but smiled. No point in having a row with a director.

Suddenly the door opened and a tall middle aged man entered, dressed in a pristine white coat. Derek Dawson, convenor of the National Pen Workers Union. He had the air of someone who knew he was important. His lapel badge read 'Union Convenor' and he had his own office in the factory. He was a card carrying member of the Labour Party, and was clearly not in a mood to be messed with. For Derek to leave the factory and show up at head office was most unusual. Brenda smelled trouble.

'Good afternoon Brenda, I need to see Mister Murgatroyd urgently on official trade union business.'

Straight to the point as usual, thought Brenda. She needed to buy time, but Brian was not about to assist things.

'Union business? What about completing the Ledley's order if it's not too much trouble at 'tut' mill old chap?' said Brian, with a sarcastic northern twang.

Derek ignored the comment, addressing Brenda directly. 'Is Diane not in then?'

'On leave this week Derek. Look could I suggest that you pop back at 4pm. James is due back for a 4-30pm meeting?'

She was doing all she could to avoid inflaming the situation.

'Alright Brenda, but please let him know this is urgent.'

He turned around and left as swiftly as he had entered. He made no acknowledgement of Brian whatsoever.

'What a luddite. Twats like him are ruining this country,' said Brian.

'A luddite with a lot of power. Why didn't you see him? You're a director after all?' Brenda ventured.

'I just do sales darling. I don't do luddites.'

Brian liked to see Brenda getting wound up.

'You don't give a stuff do you? If we go bust your job goes too you know.'

'Oh I don't think that's a problem. A couple of head-hunters rang last week. Plenty of jobs for a top salesman like me.'

Brenda took the bait.

'Well several hundred jobs do depend on this Company in this town... including mine. Haven't you got anything more important to do? Here – file these mister director.'

Brenda dumped some sales invoices on Brian's desk and left the office.

Keep your knickers on darling, he thought. Actually scrub that remark. He liked a girl with spirit, and she wasn't half bad looking that Brenda. Nope. Self-imposed rule, don't play with staff. It comes back to haunt you.

He checked out the Samuel's box. Nice. She'll like that he thought. Tasteful. Better get off then. Sales meeting down south tomorrow away from this northern shithole, and an important meeting with the Saddleworth's buyer tonight. It could be a long meeting. It'll go on all night if she gets lucky. It's a tough job but someone's gotta do it.

Brenda seethed at Brian's attitude. A hired gun with no feelings for the Company. Fat expense account which he abused liberally, but James didn't give two hoots about that. Brenda did the sales and orders report every week. She knew the figures and they were dreadful. Almost as bad as the weekly finance report. She could guess what Mister Whitehill wanted to discuss. She left at four o'clock that day. She'd had enough. She tried the golf club but James wasn't there. She had no idea where he was.

Actually James was sleeping peacefully in room 95 of the Royal Oak Hotel. Curled up next to him was a sleeping Mandy. He awoke thirsty, still feeling the effects of the beer he'd downed at lunch, followed by a bottle of red wine he'd shared with Mandy.

He dressed quickly. He needed to get back to pick up

any messages. He also needed to ensure that he wasn't seen leaving. He felt guilty. Guilty for playing away with Mandy, and guilty for bunking off work for the afternoon. The fact was that he couldn't face any of it. He could feel the pressure of the walls coming in on all sides. His mother and Archie on one side, the banks on the other, his wife and kids at another.

He drove back to his office. He was way over the limit but didn't care. He made himself a black coffee and dozed at his desk. He wasn't winning on any of these fronts and he knew it. Mandy was a welcome and wonderful distraction.

Did he love Carol? Yes of course he did. But Carol and the kids were just part of the collective 'life as usual' pressure he was under. Mandy was his escape.

Suddenly he was rudely awoken from his thoughts by a loud knock at his office door, which then opened to reveal his worst nightmare, Derek Dawson.

'What the bloody hell?' said James with a start.

'Sorry for the intrusion Mister Murgatroyd, but we have an urgent matter to discuss concerning the treatment of my members.'

Dawson spoke as if in court, and puffed a pipe as he did so. Pompous twat, thought James, his blood pressure rising.

'Oh do go on then. Make my day,' said James.

'Well you see Mister Murgatroyd your factory manager

has gone too far this time. Foreclosing on a legitimate tea break without any discussion with the union convenor. Bullying and harassment of my members. I must insist that this is addressed on an urgent basis.'

Dawson had clearly rehearsed this speech.

'I don't suppose that would be because we're late in delivering Lendel Stores' order yet again would it?' said James tartly.

'I couldn't say. That is clearly a matter for management, all I can say is that this does not justify the conduct of your factory manager, and I must insist on his immediate suspension pending investigation of these formal grievances.'

Dawson was in his element.

James stood. He was a stocky well-built man and stood toe to toe with the figure in the perfectly white workshop coat. He stared straight into Derek's slate grey-blue eyes.

'And if I bloody don't? Maybe I should just sack the lazy bastards who failed to complete the order instead?'

Derek held his gaze for a moment. Then he looked away and resumed his pacing.

'Oh I don't think you'd want to do that Mister Murgatroyd. I mean we've only brought the factory out at this time, but I could get pickets to head office, and talk to my colleagues in the stores and get them to support us. Could get very ugly.'

James realised he was out of touch with recent events.

More reasons to feel guilty after his afternoon of escape. His stomach lurched.

'So you've got the whole factory out on strike, over nothing! Don't you see how stupid that is? We've lost enough customers over late deliveries as it is.' James shook his head with dismay as he spoke.

'As I said that is not my problem. I cannot have my members subjected to bully boy tactics. Now if you'll excuse me I need to contact the national officials, put them in the picture like. You may wish to schedule a meeting for later in the week, now let me see. I could suggest Friday if they can make it, although it could be difficult with ACAS.' Derek leafed through his tiny diary which he kept in his top pocket at all times.

'I don't believe this,' said James. 'Let's get this straight. You want me to suspend Handsworth and then you might be so kind as to get your members back to work?'

'Well we would be happy to consider it after the outcome of the investigation, and Handsworth gets his cards. Now perhaps we could discuss this as a follow on to the pay negotiations on the 19th?'

Derek's face betrayed no emotion. He had control of matters and he knew it.

James laughed bitterly.

'Pay increase negotiation? Oh yes. I see that you're

prepared to settle for a mere 25% this year. Generous I'm sure. Frankly just see yourself out. I'll not be bloody black-mailed over this matter or your bloody wage claim either!'

Dawson's next move was predictable. He wasn't about to let James take the initiative back.

'I see. Very regrettable. In the context of the inflation rate our claim is only reasonable. In the union we believe that these matters are best sorted out by full and frank negotia-tions but if you're ......'

'You mean one of those meetings where the union puts a gun to my head, holds me to ransom so I capitulate?' inter-rupted James.

Derek stared, and paused for effect. Then he said coldly 'I regret your confrontational attitude, but so be it. Good day Mister Murgatroyd.'

Derek opened the door and left it open as he marched out. The telephone rang. James answered it irritably. It was Brenda calling from home.

Brenda realised from his tone that James was in a foul mood, as he told her of his heated conversation with Dawson, but she had to press on regardless. She needed to get him to speak to the bank, and to sign the cheques he'd sat on all week.

She got nowhere. 'He can bloody wait, and the cheques too. I have meetings this evening. If he rings again tell him

I'll call him later on tomorrow. If Archie hadn't swanned off to Australia it would have helped. Do I have to do everybody's job around here?'

He rang off. Brenda was left listening to the dialling tone.

She put the telephone down and sat back in her armchair, closing her eyes wearily. Vicky was playing with her lego bricks, wonderfully oblivious in a world of her own. Well I think that does it she thought. The bank manager's on the phone, we're on stop with most of the suppliers, now the bloody factory's on strike. So the boss just buggers off to his floozy Mandy bloody Brice Cooper. My God. All my years at Murgatroyd's and it's come to this.

She picked up the telephone and dialled. Archie picked up after three rings. Brenda was relieved. He was obviously back. Day or night he said. You must tell me if things crop up which you can't handle while I'm away.

They talked for half an hour. Brenda was careful and diplomatic in what she said. She trusted Archie, but wasn't going to be the one accused of betrayal, especially by the Murgatroyds.

'The strike is probably the final straw. It's going to go over the edge isn't it? Possibly within a week or two,' she said.

Archie frowned. She was right of course. A strike would bleed them of the remaining cash, and his credibility with Whitehill was blown.

'I fear you could be right Brenda. Let me think things through. If James won't speak with Whitehill then I must,' he said.

'Derek left James' office in a foul mood. James has got 'appointments' or so he says. So he won't be calling the bank that's for sure.'

'Appointments? Does that mean what I think that means?' said Archie.

'That's none of my business Archie. I'm just the sales manager.'

'I could come over if it's convenient? We could chew things over?' Archie replied.

'Well alright. It's darts night so Ron's out this evening. Seven o'clock? I'll see you then.'

She put the phone down with a heavy heart. She had no idea how this would play out. She was in very dangerous territory she knew. But she was no company director and had no experience of insolvency. The Murgatroyd family had no love of Brenda Arkwright. That much she did know. If she was seen as disloyal then she'd be out of the door. No job in a one company town, and a young child to raise.

She sighed to herself. 'Well seven o'clock it is then Brenda. Bill Murgatroyd where are you now? How did it come to this?'

Meanwhile at 91 Railway Street Derek Dawson was

stood by the fireplace, pipe in hand, still in his work clothes, hands on lapels. He was in full flow. His wife Edna sat in her favourite chair by the fire, knitting away as her husband rattled off his diatribe. She interjected periodically. It broke the monotony, and she saw it as her duty to share her husband's interests. In another life, at another time, Edna would have been a career woman. She envied the young women of the day who were heading off to university to improve themselves. But she could still keep her husband on his toes.

'Must have had a good day love. Nothing like a good strike to make you happy.'

'Never seen the like of it. Diabolical management,' he replied grumpily.

'So it's all their fault then?'

'Diabolical management.'

'So it was diabolic management then?'

Derek puffed on his pipe. 'Diabolical. Dia-bleeding-bolical,' he said absentmindedly.

'James Murgatroyd's not like his dad then?'

Derek came back to earth, relaxed a little and sat down. Edna read the body language. Calmer pragmatic Derek, the Derek she loved, was taking over as he simmered down.

'Oh you could at least discuss things with old Bill. At least he came to the factory, showed an interest, not like his son. Stays in his head office ivory tower. Dia-bolical. Tory prick,' said Derek.

Edna pondered as she continued with her knitting.

'Well you can't blame Barry Handsworth for trying to get the orders out, he is the factory manager after all. It's his job isn't it? Brenda Arkwright said that the last time we missed the Lendel's order they threatened to cancel. Big customer Lendel's.'

'Not my concern. I've to look after the interests of my members. Intimidation…it's…'

'Diabolical?' Edna completed the sentence for him.

Derek looked at his watch, irritated by his wife's bating. 'Look am I ever going to get my tea? Branch meeting tonight. Can't be late.'

'Maybe I should come along. Stand for office. How do you fancy that?' Edna retaliated, determined that his put down would not deter her.

'A woman? No chance. Diabolical.'

'Why not? I pays me subs, same as the blokes. Might join the Working Men's Club too,' she smiled.

'A right little Barbara Castle aren't we?' he laughed.

'Our time is coming. Look at Shirley Williams, and there's that young Thatcher woman. Could be the next PM they reckon.'

'What? A woman Prime Minister? Don't make me laugh. Diabolical. Now what's for tea woman?'

'I thought we were going out for chicken in a basket at the Rose and Crown?' said Edna, raising the stakes.

'Don't be daft. I've got to be at the branch office at 6 o'clock.'

'Nice and early so that nobody will turn up as usual? And of course town are playing at home.'

Edna shook her head and headed towards the kitchen.

Derek tried his best to justify himself. 'Look this is a democratic union election. One man one vote. If people can't be bothered to turn up it's up to them. Now can I please have some tea?'

Edna smiled. She'd made her point. 'All right. I'll rustle up some egg and chips.'

'Bloody hell. Since the Equal Pay Act they think they own the place. Diabolical,' he said to himself.

Underneath the bluff and bluster though Derek was worried. He wasn't stupid. He read the signs. Without the firm leadership of Bill Murgatroyd the business was heading for the rocks. Whilst one part of him said that this wasn't the union's fault he realised that if Murgatroyds went bust the impact on the town would be too awful to contemplate.

Later on that evening he stood smiling in front of a hard core group of trade union activists in the function room of the Working Men's Club in the centre of town, receiving the applause following his re-election.

'Thank you brother Atkinson. I am delighted to be elected unopposed as Branch Convenor again this year, and I shall continue to represent this branch at the national congress. In these troubled economic times it is essential that we continue our struggle to prevent the erosion of our pay and conditions and hold management to account for their actions. Whilst we regret the current dispute at the Murgatroyd Pen Company Limited we will not accept the provocative and bullying behaviour of the management, who are clearly bent on adopting a typically macho management style. A sign of the times in my opinion'.

Members interjected as he spoke. Words like 'hear hear' and 'well said brother' and some polite applause. As he took the applause Derek was unaware that over the other side of town events were unfolding over which he had no control, but which were going to shape the future.

*   *   *

Archie was on the telephone to the bank.

'Yes I quite understand the bank's position Mr Whitehill, and I'm very sorry that Mr Murgatroyd has not returned your calls. I will certainly be discussing things with James tomorrow, and I'm sorry that you've had to call me from home. Look I fully understand the banking covenants. I helped negotiate them you may recall. Let me have a day or two and we can schedule a meeting. Obviously the costs of the new head office building has stretched the cash flow somewhat, and sales of the new Excalibur ball point have been slower to take off than we expected. Nothing we can't work through though.'

Archie was talking things up, trying to shore up what was left of Mister Whitehill's confidence. Archie needed to provide figures though. But facts and figures were in short supply right now. He couldn't get either James or Mandy to realise that you couldn't sell a pipe dream of marketing gobbledegook. It was about doing the bread and butter of getting orders and serving customers. It wasn't all business lunches and swanky entertaining.

As for Brian Biggs? Simply a crook. Archie had checked his expenses and made a few calls. Not very clever our Brian. Archie knew a few of the local hoteliers from Rotary. It didn't take much to work out that his stay overs on business were seldom without some floozy happy to dine out using the Murgatroyd American Express card.

He had collected quite enough on Biggs and knew that he could despatch him at a time of his choosing.

His same source also told him of James and Mandy's burgeoning affair. That was a real problem. At times he thought that he might have been able to talk James around, but

Mandy's interference and influence made reasoning impossible. Whether Jean Murgatroyd knew of the affair wasn't clear either, and Archie had always tried to keep family matters separate from company matters. No chance of that now listening to Whitehill droning on in his banking jargon, he thought sadly.

He waited for the right moment, and made his play. 'I quite understand your problem Paul, and I'm sure that we can work this through together. But in the meantime I need your help in meeting the payroll this week?'

He listened intently to the reply and gently coaxed the position along.

'Well look I'm sure you will understand that we need to meet that and the VAT? If we don't do those two things the balloon goes up and we damage the business. Can you do that for me?

He sweated on Whitehill's reply, then smiled with relief.

'Jolly good, very reasonable of you in the circumstances. Okay Paul. I'll come back to you with the figures. Many thanks, goodnight to you.'

Archie put down the phone and poured a slug of whisky. He was tired after his long flight and frustrated. He took a swig of the bitter liquid, sat down and put his head back for a moment, deep in thought. It was as if his holiday hadn't happened.

What a lot of bollocks he thought. What on earth is James thinking of? You can't bullshit these people. Didn't he learn anything from his father? What should he do now? Well whatever he did it would cause a bloody great row. Jean would be furious and James would be defensive. Not exactly happy families at the best of times. He wondered what young Brenda would have to say? Seemed to be the only one talking sense at the moment. The management team is in denial. Too full of business school bullshit to see the wood for the trees. And as for that Brian chap, devious cheating bastard, he wouldn't trust him an inch. He needed to speak to James. No choice. But where? His home? No he rather doubted it. The Royal Oak was more likely he suspected.

Archie rang the number, and the receptionist confirmed that James was there. Archie waited for him to come to the phone. An open reception with people talking. Hardly a good setting for a difficult conversation. He took another sip of his whisky as he waited. Eventually he heard the rustling of the receiver being picked up.

'Hi Archie, you're back then? What can I do for you? I'm having dinner you know?'

Archie filled him in as best he could.

'Oh Whitehill rang you? My God what a prick that guy is. Look Archie it's nothing to worry about I'll speak to him tomorrow afternoon. I'm in meetings first thing. What? Look Archie I'll handle it okay? You want figures for new Cashflow projections? Sorry old son not exactly my top priority, Excalibur promotion next week. Yes Brian is trying to shift the stock, he's meeting the buyer tonight as it happens. Look Archie I'd need to check the diary? Sometime next week, diary's chocka old man. Look I am the MD. I'll sort it. We can discuss it at next month's board if you're not happy.'

The usual bullshit thought Archie.

'James. Listen to me. We are now very close to him pulling the overdraft. I'm going to have to speak with the Chairman,' he said formally.

'Look if you want to ring mother that's up to you but it's not really helping is it? You need to trust me on this Archie. You must do what you think is right of course, now I really need to go. I must admit I think it's a bit of an overreaction, after all you've only just returned from leave.'

Archie wasn't about to back down.

'I'm going to call an emergency board meeting. This strike is likely to be the final straw.'

'Look if you want an emergency board meeting then call one, you're the Company Secretary after all. Now if you'll excuse me? Okay Archie. Goodnight.'

The telephone was put down. James was furious. Mandy came into reception to see what the call was about. She was wearing a stunning red dress, clearly a designer number. She looked gorgeous.

'Trouble at 'tut' mill old boy?' She said.

They hugged and kissed. James was clearly distracted.

'What's up James?' she asked.

'Archie. Bloody man,' said James bitterly.

'Oh not again. Didn't we retire him after Bill died? Silly old fart.'

'The bank has been on to him. Making trouble about the overdraft.'

'Well I told you to get rid of that silly local bank and go to a national player. They haven't got a clue about corporate finance. We need a bank that understands the strategy, the big picture, the business plan. One that thinks outside the box. These provincial oiks are okay for a few local farmers and the village shop but we're an international business shaping up for flotation. They simply don't understand.'

Mandy was animated and her blue eyes flashed as she spoke. She looked gorgeous, and James was minded to take her straight to any place where they could resume their lovemaking.

Mandy continued bitterly.

'I'll bet Brenda's been making trouble again. I told you to get rid when your Dad died and I came on board. It's so obvious she's Archie's informant.'

'She's bloody good with the customers or I would have.

Certainly not the time now, I've got enough on my plate. Brenda's the least of our worries right now.'

'Well whatever darling,' she said, placating him. 'Look, come back to the dinner, I'll take your mind off things later, unless you're going home to wifey tonight?'

She puts her arms around James protectively.

James smiled and kissed her. 'Nope. She knows I'm staying over. Drink driving and so forth.'

'Then we've got a good night ahead then? Worry about Archie and his flat cap crew tomorrow. God this is a tin pot pisshole of a place. It's a bloody shame we can't run it out of the London office. It would be much better.'

'You're right. Stuff Archie. Stuff the bloody bank.'

'That's the ticket. Look let me have a chat with Jeremy. He joined Barclays from uni. I'll bet he can fix the banking facilities. That'll fix the old fart. Bet he meets old Whitehill at the working men's club over a pint of mild and a bag of pork scratchings.'

'Steady on. I like pork scratchings,' said James in mock defence.

Mandy smiled. 'Never mind. I have completed your rehabilitation in most aspects. At least you know what a lasagne is now. I'm not sure about this Blue Nun though, but we have time.'

'You sound like my primary school teacher.'

'Trust me James. I can be anything you want me to be,' she smiled seductively while furtively sliding her hand down the front of his trousers.

'Dear me I seem to have a bigger problem to deal with now. Would you like to go back to the black forest gateau or have your just desserts upstairs?'

James smiled. It was no contest. James took her by the hand and they headed straight to bed.

Archie was left incredulous and angry by the phone conversation. Just because he got a degree or whatever in that bloody business school he thinks he's got all the answers. Typical son of a successful father. Read all the books but shit for brains. As for Mandy well.

He headed for Brenda's house, and she answered the door. Archie entered. He kissed her on both cheeks.

'Hi Archie. How are you?' said Brenda.

'Wishing I'd stayed in exile in Australia frankly.'

She took his coat and he continued. 'At least our problem gives me something to worry about. Otherwise I'd just drink myself to death.'

'Have a scotch Archie, join the club,' said Brenda. 'Make it large. I'll have another myself. We both need it.'

Archie laughed as they went through to the sitting room. Brenda handed a glass to Archie and they clinked them. Archie sat.

'I spoke with our friend Mister Whitehill, he rang me. He's not a happy bunny,' said Archie.

'I'm not at all surprised. I've fobbed him off too often. In his position what would you do?'

'Oh I think I'd write a letter beginning with 'The bank regrets to advise you'.'

Brenda looked concerned. 'And will he?'

Archie sipped his whisky and pondered. 'I'm not sure. Probably not. But rule number one is don't bullshit the bank, and certainly don't avoid their calls. If a bank trusts you then you have a chance. If not then frankly Brenda we are, as they say, buggered.'

'Mandy says get a better bank. One of the multi nationals?'

'Huh. Mandy Brice Cooper is a menace. Bright yes, but a little knowledge is in her case very dangerous. She lives in a marketing fairy dairy land where she is spending a serious fortune to get the Murgatroyd name known internationally, but unless sales increase to meet the cost … well.'

Brenda interrupted. 'The losses just get bigger and we buy stock we can't sell.'

'A perfect recipe for a good old fashioned cash flow problem. Especially if you build a plush head office building, and lease that gin palace flat in London.'

'I don't know what Bill would have said.'

Archie laughed. 'Oh I do, and it would have been unrepeatable in mixed company.'

Brenda laughed too. 'Yes. I'm quite sure it would be.'

Archie leant forward earnestly. 'So what do we do?' he said.

Brenda was surprised at the question. 'Why are you asking me?'

'Because you know the answers. Bill taught you a lot, and you have that HNC of course.'

'Yes, I know he did. I miss him. I know I shouldn't, but I do. Especially now. Every bloody day if I'm honest.'

'I know.'

The awkward pause found Brenda struggling for words. Archie smiled sympathetically.

'You loved him Brenda. It's still early days. I've lost Edith, and I still hold the door open for her, and put out two mugs for tea, and talk to her every day. I can give you the cliché about time healing the pain. But it doesn't seem to for me I'm afraid. Take it a day at a time? What bollocks if you forgive my French'. He was animated, but then he relaxed.

Brenda pondered. 'So back to our problem. What would Bill do? Let me think.'

'What was Bill's first rule?' Archie mused.

'Boss the cash. Yes. That's what he'd do.'

Archie nodded. He sat back looking for more.

Brenda became intense. 'Chase the debts for a start. Marshalls are overdue by two months, Anglams by three, although there is the warranty claim.'

'Which James hasn't closed out yet of course. Far too busy. What else?'

'Excalibur is killing us. Four shipments in the warehouse, all paid for. No sales.'

Archie laughed. 'Ah.... Our super salesman Mr Brian Biggs?'

'Don't get me started. Big ego, big car, big salary and the biggest bullshitter I've ever met.'

Archie darkened. 'And probably shagging the Saddleworths junior buyer as we speak. Still I expect she's over the age of consent, just.'

Brenda was incredulous. 'Junior buyer? But she won't be able to sign the order? Or negotiate the selling price. He assured me.'

'Precisely. Never mind perhaps our marketing guru Miss Brice Cooper has the solution?'

'Mrs Brice Cooper at that. Look Archie I'm not going to throw rocks in greenhouses, after all I was more than a bit ... well...'

Archie smiled. 'No okay. But suppose you were the managing director? What would you do?'

'Me? You're joking.'

Archie leant forward. 'Actually not. After all Bill was a great teacher?'

'Well yes.'

Archie shrugged and stayed silent.

Eventually she spoke, calmly and deliberately. 'Solve the cash flow problem to shut Whitehill up at all cost. So we flog the Excalibur stock at cost if necessary'.

'Okay. That buys us time. But then what? You're still running at a loss, so you just bleed to death more slowly.'

'Well okay. But if I look back we didn't have regional sales managers or the marketing director come to that. Get rid of them, and the posh office block in town.'

'Cut the breakeven point. Yes. Good.'

Brenda was puzzled. 'But that just puts things back to where things were when Bill died. It's not exactly progressive?'

Archie frowned, and signed: 'No. I agree. But not a bad start though. You gotta make a buck to get started.'

'But James would never agree.'

Archie responded with hesitation. 'I know. Yes that is a problem I agree. Jean would need to act.'

'Jean Murgatroyd act against the wishes of her only son, the managing director to boot? I can't see that Archie.'

'Neither can I if I'm honest. But let's face it Murgatroyd's is the town's only major employer and will be bust within a matter of weeks unless we do something. Jean's a tough lady.'

Brenda shook her head, unconvinced. 'You're forgetting the strike too. God knows what impact on cash that will have. Lendel's will close the account for sure. After last time's debacle I took the call from the buyer because James dodged it. We're definitely in the last chance saloon with them. I took a right going over. I gave him the usual assurances. Now I've been hung out to dry.'

'Well I'm afraid that's where we are as a nation. Strikes are killing us. No one believes that we'll deliver on time. But I agree that we need to sort our Mr Dawson. Another challenge for our Jean.'

'Why Jean?'

'Well they went to school together, and Jean never forgets where she came from. Neither does Derek, It just about gives her a chance'.

'I wish her luck with that. Frankly I think I'd rather talk to the Lendel's buyer than old Derek. Not much chance he's going to change.' She shook her head and sipped her scotch.

Archie pondered for a moment, then he leant forward and spoke intently. 'Trust me he will have to Brenda. Being honest I think that Whitehill will let us meet the payroll for a couple of weeks, that's all. We've got a fortnight to change the game. Or basically that's it. Sixty years of history straight down the drain'.

That bad?

'Yes Brenda, I fear so.'

'What are you going to do?'

'I need to talk to Jean. Between Jean and myself we have 51% of the shares, so we can do as we wish, James or no James.'

'But blood is thicker than water Archie.'

'But Jean is no fool either Brenda. Don't forget that she helped to build Murgatroyd's. Bill was a brilliant business man, but Jean always had a calming influence. Bill would listen to Jean.'

'Until I came along and wrecked their marriage,' Brenda said ruefully.

Archie smiled and took her hand. 'Don't beat yourself up. You were young and Bill fell head over heels in love with you. He made his own decisions. Nobody forced him, least of all you. You have an instinctive love of the business, as Bill did. Jean didn't have that. Their physical love had died years before. Trust me there is much you don't know, but that's for another day.'

'Thank Archie. I feel a bit better for that.' She looked up at him. 'So what now?'

Archie stood, and Brenda followed. 'I'm going home. You try to relax. Give my regards to little Vicky. I'm going to organise my thoughts and talk to Jean.'

8.

1976

Later on the following afternoon, Mandy came into James' office and closed the door. He was reading and deep in thought. He seemed oblivious to the world. He looked tired, she thought. He needs a holiday, but isn't going to get one any time soon.

She sat, and he looked up suddenly and smiled.

'I'm sorry I was miles away,' he said wearily.

'I noticed,' said Mandy. 'How did you get on with Whitehill?'

'A bit of luck. He wasn't in. I left a message. How about you?' James brightened slightly.

Mandy leant forward positively. 'Jeremy will give it a go for us with his city chums. They'll want five year cash flow projections, lots of talk of sensitivities, leverage and accounting gobbledygook. But I'm sure when we make the pitch we'll get the cash.'

James smiled. Sometimes Mandy found things rather more difficult to achieve than she originally thought, but would never admit it. Quietly he knew that if Whitehill cut up rough the chances of getting funding elsewhere wasn't that good, but it was worth a try.

As she spoke he reached into the filing cabinet and took out two glasses and a bottle of scotch. He poured two measures, and set them down between them. He pondered her words, sipped his whisky, and then spoke.

'I've had another interesting call though. IPCO might do a deal.'

Mandy looked at him in surprise. 'What?'

'International Pen. Biggest pen company in the world?'

'Yes I know that stupid. Gosh. That's a bit sudden.'

'They want a high end brand and Murgatroyd fits the bill. Typical yanks, tell them you got by appointment to her majesty and they fall over themselves,' James shrugged and sat back calmly.

Mandy hesitated. 'But that's fantastic isn't it? Big marketing budget, better package. Might get one of those new Jags – an XJS?'

James smiled, typical Mandy, not exactly cheap to run.

'But there's a problem.'

'So what is it?' said Mandy. 'It seems like a dream come true. No more bloody cash flow problems.'

James countered. 'They would shut the site here and move production to Hatfield.'

'So? Even better. Sticks it up that fucking union darling. I'd love to see that Dawson bloke's face when you give him the news.'

James laughed. 'Well I'll admit that had crossed my mind, but Murgatroyd is the town's only big employer. We have obligations.'

James had known that Mandy would react this way. She hated the whole place and would like nothing better than to go back south. But he also knew that it would represent a watershed in their affair, and he wasn't ready for that, any more than he looked forward to telling his mother about the IPCO deal.

Mandy responded as he expected. 'Oh God is that all. Honestly darling that's not our problem. If daddy Bill hadn't been such a tight fisted bastard he might have had a factory worth saving. This whole town would have benefited if the Luftwaffe had got their aim straight in the war. It's a complete dump.'

James responded calmly. 'But it's Murgatroyd's home. Mum won't like it, and as for Archie, well.'

'Oh stuff the pair of them James. They'll soon sell up when they see a big fat retirement cheque,' she snapped, getting to her feet.

James sipped his whisky once more. 'I'm not so sure. And if they don't, remember that I've only got a minority stake.'

'But you could sell your shares anyway?' Mandy walked to the window and looked out into the evening sunshine.

James smiled at her naivety. 'Why would IPCO buy a minority stake? And besides the covenants in dad's will forces a sale to existing shareholders first.'

'So we need mumsy to sell then?' said Mandy flatly.

James pondered wearily. He'd been mulling this over since the phone call. 'Whitehill might do us a favour. If he pulls the rug, mum will have to sell or get bugger all.'

'There you are then. Problem solved.' Mandy was clearly determined, but James wasn't ready to deal with the underlying issue, and he knew what was coming.

James wasn't clear about his feelings for Mandy, and the conflicting love for his wife and family. Life was moving at too fast a pace for him to take stock, and the IPCO offer wasn't going to make that any easier.

Carol and James were both eighteen when they met at the final high school dance. They knew of each other, but both were shy and uncomfortable in social situations. Carol was particularly troubled by her long frock and high heels that evening. She turned her ankle and fell towards James, who caught her. In doing so James wrapped his arms involuntarily around Carol's chest, and Carol inadvertently tipped her illicit glass of smuggled champagne down his dress shirt. Carol was embarrassed and blushed, but James was very kind, and they sat chatting for most of the evening. Carol's father was a local solicitor, so the two families approved of the relationship. As the eligible son of the Murgatroyd clan, in a small town, there were not too many such relationships which would have been deemed appropriate.

Unusually their relationship survived university, since they went to the same one. They married, and two children followed. To the outsider they were a perfect couple in a perfect house with two perfect children. They had nice holidays in nice hotels and nice sex in nice surroundings.

Things changed sometime later when James met Mandy by chance at a summer school. They were teamed together on an assignment, with Mandy as a highly competitive project lead. She clashed with James over the assignment, and insisted that she had her way. The team lost badly, and Mandy shouldered the blame.

James came down to the bar later on after dinner, and found Mandy sitting on her own.

'Billy no mates are we?' said James.

'I'm not Billy I'm Mandy,' she replied.

James bought her a drink, and they chatted about their backgrounds. At one in the morning they headed to their respective rooms, which were on the same floor. James kissed her on the cheek as they parted.

Ten minutes later there was a knock at James' door.

Mandy stood there smiling, with a bottle of champagne in her hand, and wearing a dressing gown.

'It's my birthday today,' she said. 'Would you like to help 'Mandy No Mates' celebrate?'

She allowed her gown to fall open. They were late for the first tutorial the following morning, and they stayed over on the Sunday night after the summer school had finished.

Carol was from his old life, but James was now the managing director of a high flying company, and Mandy was the fast car in the garage, whereas Carol was more the family saloon. But James had obligations to his family, and in particular to his two children whom he loved deeply. He saw them all too infrequently, but that only made the idea of a divorce worse.

Mandy was married too. But she'd had enough of her 'hooray Henry' husband and his drunken philandering ways.

Back in the present though James still hedged his way around the main issue.

'Mum won't want to see the factory go. Too many friends and too many memories.'

'But it would give us a chance? You could leave wifey. By the way what the hell was she wearing the other day?'

'Okay okay. Leave it Mandy.' James was irritable and on edge.

Mandy tried to help. She knew James well enough to

know that he was battling with himself over his conflicting loyalties.

She sat, and said quietly. 'I'm sorry James. I just want to be free of this shit heap, and for us to be together. I don't want a quickie after the staff have gone home, or sneak into your room at a conference. To me IPCO is our big chance. Do it for us.'

'I know it is. But don't think it's going to be easy. I'm seeing mum this evening for dinner. I'll get in first before Archie has his say.'

Although James didn't know it at that moment Archie had already arrived at Murgatroyd Hall to see Jean. He had visited many times, and knew that on a fine summer evening she would be in the garden, so he headed through the side gate.

He walked across the finely mown lawn towards the distant figure. The air was fragrant with flower blossom, the recent rain had been welcome. Jean looked up as he approached, she was wearing gardening clothes with smart wellies and a sleeveless waxed jacket.

'Hello Archie, how was Australia? Come into the conservatory, Marjorie just made tea,' she said, taking off her gloves. It was apparent to Archie that Jean was slightly on edge.

'My word the garden looks glorious this year Jean. You've worked wonders,' said Archie affably.

He wanted to keep this as friendly as he could. Sometimes you couldn't help mixing family and business. This was one such time, and Archie wasn't going to pull his punches.

'Yes it does doesn't it. It's a shame everything in the Murgatroyd garden isn't so rosy,' Jean replied.

They reached the conservatory in silence. Marjorie arrived and set down the tea. She left, and Jean poured it.

Eventually Jean spoke. 'Well Archie your telephone call wasn't a total surprise I'll admit.'

'I know. I'm afraid what Brenda had to say confirmed my worst fears,' said Archie gravely.

'Are you sure she's telling the truth though? You know what I think of her. Forgive me but well...' Jean's voice tailed off bitterly.

Archie expected this reaction, but equally knew that it had no relevance to the financial position of Murgatroyd's, and he needed to get this distraction out of the way fast.

He smiled and took her hand, and she became calmer. They had known each other a long time, and Bill had trusted Archie like the brother he never had.

'Jean trust me I understand your feelings. Really I do. But Brenda has worked her way up through the Company, and what she says always seems to check out with what others say. I don't expect you to like her, but I have no doubt that she is entirely correct as to the position. Things are really bad as I said. Whitehill's phone call was the clincher. He is deadly serious, because those above him would expect him to take action. He has no choice.'

'I'm sorry Archie. I just can't forgive her. I know Bill was as much to blame but she threw herself at him.'

Archie remained quiet. Jean was just about in control of herself.

'Yes. Look I really do understand. I know that Bill's death affected you very badly. Still at least you've got Marjorie,' he said, slightly changing tack.

Jean smiled thinly. 'Yes. She's been great. You too.'

Archie said nothing. Let's take our time with this he thought. She'll come back to the main event when she's ready.

She set her cup down and relaxed. Measuring her words she said 'Look Archie I'm over the Bill thing, I think. But don't expect me to forgive Brenda and I don't really want her in the Company to be honest, my Company after all.'

Time to act thought Archie. Time to lay my cards on the table.

'Well I think you know that I can't agree with you on that. I don't think that's fair treatment of her at all Jean. After all Brenda worked her way up through the ranks to where she is now on her own merits, not through Bill's patronage. Paul Munro rated her very highly, as did you I recall. She is very talented and a major asset to the business. She's well respected by the workforce and most crucially by the customers. That counts for everything right now.' Archie was blunt. He needed to get her over this hurdle.

'Okay okay,' said Jean. She raised her palm as a placating gesture. Good, thought Archie.

'Let's talk about Murgatroyd. I read your paper? I don't like any of it, but I read it.'

'And?'

Jean shrugged. 'Well you've diagnosed the illness doctor, but what's your prescription?'

Archie briefly marshalled his thoughts, he had rehearsed this several times after all, and wanted to punch the message home, but in a measured way.

'We've got to cut the overdraft quickly to keep Whitehill on side. Then we've got to get the cost base down and get the factory back to work fast, which means sorting Dawson out. Brian Biggs needs to go immediately. The man is a crook and is working for his own ends. As for Mandy Brice-Cooper that lady is a menace. She has expensive habits which Murgatroyd's can't afford and the results don't justify it. The expansion strategy is killing us. James' big dream isn't going to work, particularly not in the current climate.'

Jean looked up and stared. 'And James? I can't see him agreeing to any of this can you?'

Archie returned her stare. 'I agree.'

Jean decided to put her cards on the table too. 'Just to be clear I know that he's playing away with Mandy. He won't fire her.'

Archie nodded sadly. 'Yes.'

Jean became sanguine and depressed. 'I had Carol over the other day with the twins. She knows in her heart of hearts. Said so in as many words, but how do you tell your mother in law that her son is being a total bastard like his father was.'

'Well it is rather obvious. Common knowledge in the Company I gather. He's not exactly covering his tracks. Mandy stays at the Royal Oak during the week. It's just a bit too easy.'

'You haven't said it, but James has to go too,' she said flatly.

Archie nodded, his expression grim. 'I suspect that you're correct.'

Jean stood, and started fidgeting with one of the house plants, tidying away some dead leaves. Finally she turned and faced him.

'You don't need to humour me Archie. Family is family and Murgatroyd is Murgatroyd. Bill was always clear that whilst the business was ours we could not avoid our obligations to the town. The two are indivisible as far I am concerned. That for me is the problem. I must put Murgatroyd ahead of any family issue. If he isn't good enough he goes.'

Archie nodded. 'It's the only option really. As things stand your shares are probably worthless. It's going under and Whitehill knows it. A rudderless ship heading for the rocks.'

'Whilst the skipper is otherwise engaged with a floozy down below. It's scandalous,' said Jean bitterly.

Archie thought and nodded. 'Well yes it is I suppose. James needed five more years of his father's schooling. Then he might have made it, he's certainly bright enough. Just very opinionated and headstrong.'

'I'm not sure Archie. All through his life he's tried to better his father, rather than learn from him. I actually think that James hated his father by the end. He could never be as good as Bill wanted, it put him under an intolerable burden. The weight of constant expectation with the sure knowledge that if he got near to meeting those expectations the bar would be raised. I actually hoped that he wouldn't come back from IPCO, that he'd find his own way. But he was determined to prove himself in Murgatroyd's and when his Dad died what could we have done differently?'

Archie nodded. 'You could see it evolving but there was no way to stop it. I think we both tried.'

'Yes. You tried at work and I tried at home, all to no avail, They were both too bloody stubborn I suppose.' She smiled and then became sad. Archie said nothing.

'Look Archie I think I have the picture, painful though it may be. Brian and Mandy go. We cut back on spending and flog the stock. Do a deal with Dawson to get the union off our back. I get that. But what if James refuses? What if I have to sack my own son? We'll have sacked the entire board and be left with nobody running the business?'

It was clear to Archie that Jean had thought things through to the inevitable conclusion long before he had arrived.

'That is of course intolerable. I will have to give up on retirement to run it for the next two years or so for you, if that is what you want that is. Frankly since Edith died the days hang heavy, and I've had a long rest in Australia, so it won't be any hardship if that is what you want me to do. But the problem is that the other key player in my view is Brenda Arkwright. She will give the customers a warm feeling of continuity, and is very good with them too. She will need to be appointed as sales director. I know that is difficult for you, but I've considered this very seriously and think it is the right thing for the business'

There, he'd said it. To save the business you have to sack your own son and appoint your late husband's mistress as a director.

Jean's repost was immediate and as frosty as he had anticipated.

'Surely we should appoint a new sales director from outside, forget about Brenda Arkwright? Someone with more experience.'

Archie smiled. 'Who would come in the situation, and at what cost? And how long would it take to recruit them? The only way we retain bank support in this situation is to replace the existing team with one the bank trusts. I have the gravitas to anchor the business through the crisis, but we must have someone credible from a commercial standpoint. Brenda hosted Whitehill at the London trade show last year, and he was very impressed. I am going to completely ignore any issues between Brenda and the family. As you said yourself the needs of Murgatroyd's must come first.'

Jean remained silent. The whole scenario was becoming more absurd by the minute. She was struggling to develop an argument against it though.

Archie sensed that he was nearly there. One more push he thought.

'And you won't do better than Brenda. You may not like it Jean, but Brenda could succeed me in a few years' time. She's that good. Bill taught her well.'

Jean allowed herself a smile. 'A female managing director with a young child? Not many of those about. My God that would set tongues wagging.'

Archie knew that he had got his way. He relaxed. 'You

should be proud. Clarissa Murgatroyd was a pal of Mrs Pankhurst.'

'I was an activist in the women's movement too. Then I met Bill,' she said.

'He was quite a man Jean. Brilliant in his way,' said Archie.

Jean agreed. 'And thoroughly charming too. Nobody could believe it when I pulled the Murgatroyd boy. My lot didn't have two halfpennies to rub together. That's why I have my socialist roots. I'll never forget it even if young James does.'

'And neither should you Jean,' said Archie. 'Look I'm sorry if this is all horribly difficult for you. You need time to think it through. Let's speak in the morning. Then you can make a decision.'

He got up and they held hands for a moment. Jean looked into his eyes, still composed but not far from tears. 'Archie there is nothing to think about. You've spelt it out for me, and I thank you for doing so. I will do what needs doing. James wants to see me this evening for dinner. He has something he wants to discuss. It will give me the opportunity to have a heart to heart with him. I'll let you know the outcome in the morning.'

Archie hugged her. 'Thanks Jean. I'll see myself out'.

Meanwhile at the factory Derek Dawson was stood by the brazier as the sun went down. The signs were visible.

'Murgatroyd Official Picket Line' they said. He stood, megaphone in hand. Another lorry arrived and he stepped forward to talk to the driver, who stopped and wound down his window.

'Driver this an official picket of the National Pen Workers Union. You'll not want to cross an official picket line, so I invite you to turn your wagon around please,' said Derek officiously.

The driver knew that crossing a picket line wasn't an option. There was no police presence, and like as not if he tried to enter the factory the picket would turn ugly. He shrugged and turned his lorry around. No skin off my nose he thought. It was the third time he had done so that day. Different companies, same picket lines.

Derek applauded the driver as the lorry turned around, and there were cheers from the pickets. He would hand over to the shop steward at nine o'clock and drop into the club for a pint before he went home.

Archie, returning home past the factory, witnessed the proceeding with great sadness. His car radio ironically played the Strawbs hit record, Part of the Union. He reflected bitterly on some of the words.

Now I'm a union man. Amazed at what I am
I say what I think, that the Company stinks

Yes I'm a union man
When we meet in the local hall
I'll be voting with them all
With a hell of a shout, it's 'Out brothers, out!'
And the rise of the factory's fall
Oh, you don't get me, I'm part of the union
You don't get me, I'm part of the union
You don't get me, I'm part of the union
Til the day I die
Til the day I die

'When will they learn. When will they fucking learn,' he said aloud as he drove through town and away from the factory gates.

9.

1976

James drove up to the hall a little later that evening. He was feeling more relaxed after his discussion with Mandy and a couple of whiskies. He had spoken briefly with Carol, but she was hosting her bridge club, hence he was dining with his mother.

The hallway was beginning to look shabby he thought. It needed decorating, but he had no time to get involved, and his mother didn't seem worried. He entered the living room, and she got up to greet him.

'Good evening mum. Will dinner be long, I'm starving?

Jean smiled. 'No change there then. It won't be too long. How's things?'

They hugged, but James was concerned. His Mother was clearly on edge. Something on her mind. He decided to ignore it.

'I've been better. You've heard that lunatic Dawson's called a strike? Just because Handsworth cracked the whip for once,' he said.

Jean didn't rise to the bait.

'And how are Carol and the kids?' she said, sticking to small talk, for now at least.

'Oh they're fine. Carol's talking of taking them to the coast in a few weeks' time. Friends of hers have this bloody enormous place on the cliff top near Filey.'

Jean tried to be encouraging. 'Will you go? Take a bit of a break and spend some time with the kids?'

'I shouldn't think so. Mandy and I need to get the Excalibur launch right,' he said, grabbing the evening paper. He looked at the front page. No word of the strike. Good he thought.

James helped himself to a whisky, and handed his mother one. She drank and then spoke.

'Look James we need to have a chat, about the Company.'

James was immediately defensive. 'Oh yes. Has Archie been talking to you again? Swanned off the Australia whilst I'm working my rocks off, then pretends he has all the answers.'

'Well yes,' she conceded, 'he is the finance director after all.'

James retorted. 'Retired AND unqualified. A shiny arsed bookkeeper. Sorry, a formerly retired shiny arsed book keeper.'

Jean hesitated, trying to stay calm.. 'Your father...,' she started, but James interrupted.

'My late father's arse licking book keeper you mean?'

'James. Let's calm down and keep things rational. Let's sit down.'

She led James by the hand, and they both sat.

'The bank rang Archie because you ducked their calls. Not exactly a wise move on your part?' said Jean,

James was having none of it. He stood up. 'He only rang Archie because they do fucking Rotary together. The bloke hasn't got a clue.'

Jean had heard enough. She stood too. 'But he does control our overdraft which we are regularly breaching, not to mention the banking covenants.'

James ignored the point. 'When businesses expand they need working capital. Any rational banker would understand it. Anyway we'll be changing banks soon. Mandy knows people.'

Jean was surprised, and highly sceptical. James had made the mistake that children often make with parents. He forgot how well his mother knew him. He was lying, or at least being economical with the truth.

'Change banks? Is that wise or even possible? We've been with Arndale Bank since, well since we started I think,' said Jean.

James was sarcastic in his reply. 'God is Whitehill that old? Well maybe it's time for a change if they're going to wet their pants at the first sign of a cash flow problem?'

Jean tried a calmer approach. 'But James it isn't only the cash flow is it? The business is losing money, the management accounts show it. Four successive months.'

'That's inevitable mother. If you want to bring this Company into the seventies from the fifties where my father left it we've got to invest. We said that when dad died and I took over. The new management team was the fresh start we needed.'

She ploughed on. 'I hear that but we were making money then and we aren't now are we? We're not hitting the sales targets either are we? The overdraft is way over what we said it would be. The bank has every right to be concerned.'

'Well if you're bringing in new products and promoting the brand it takes time, Mandy says that ....'

Jean had heard enough. Mentioning Mandy was the red rag.

'Mandy says? Forgive me but the less said about her the better.'

Jean regretted the way the conversation was going, but it was too late now. James looked at her, clearly getting angry now. Just how much he looks like his father Jean thought.

'Oh. So we have a problem with Mandy now. My my Archie has been busy. What's he told you about Mandy from his little time warped three bed semi? Is he a graduate of the London Business School? Mandy and I are, in case you'd forgotten.'

'You're sleeping with her.'

The conversation stopped. The allegation caught James cold. He looked away, then recovered his equilibrium.

'So what if I am?' he said.

'What about Carol and the children?' she retorted.

'They're fine.'

'She'll find out James. It's just a matter of time in this town. What about your children James?'

'I said. They're fine.' James was cornered. Jean had seen it before when he was young. The same defensive stance, the same look. No eye contact.

'Are you in love with her? Mandy I mean?' said Jean.

James had had enough. Years of bitterness welled up inside him. It was time to have it out.

'I don't think I can really believe that I'm hearing this? Such amazing hypocrisy,' he laughed.

Jean was perplexed. 'I don't know what you mean?'

'Oh let me remind you. You think I don't know?' James had the upper hand.

Jean was floundering for a meaning. 'What? Know what? I don't understand.'

James was ready to twist the knife. He hadn't planned things to go like this, but too late to pull back now. Let her have it. Have it out. All of it.

'Well if I'm going to get a moral lecture, maybe my

moral decline started with my parents? Bill Murgatroyd, Worshipful Master of the lodge, pillar of the local community, well to the outside world anyway. But things were different indoors weren't they? How many beatings did you take? As many as I did?'

'It was once James. Just once. Things got out of hand. He was under so much pressure,' she replied.

They stood face to face. He glared into her eyes.

Jean was upset. She looked away.

'Oh no there's more! Then he's goes and shags Busty Brenda, the tart from the office,' he cried.

Jean slapped his face. She'd heard enough.

'That's enough James.'

'Oh no, I haven't finished. You were BOTH hypocrites weren't you? Long before Dad played away. Now let me see I was fifteen when I came home from school early and went upstairs. I heard a noise from your bedroom and went in. You were naked in bed with Marjorie. Far too busy to notice me. Do I need to say more?'

Jean was ashen faced and desperately embarrassed. She could say nothing. Her stomach churned. Nobody knew.

'So don't you dare lecture me about Mandy. I'll do what I wish. I've outgrown Carol I'm afraid. Mandy is intelligent and stunningly attractive. You probably fancy her yourself!'

Jean crumpled onto the settee. She was crushed and

speechless. She couldn't find any words. James saw that he had hurt his mother badly. She suddenly looked old and vulnerable. The alcohol had heightened his anger. He softened, but only a little.

'I'm sorry mother but it had to be said. I'm tired of the wonderful Bill lectures and sick to death of the shadow he cast over our lives, yours included. Mind you when you played the wronged woman after the event I found it rather amusing. No wonder he went to Brenda, he wasn't getting much at home after all.'

Jean looked up. Tears in her eyes. 'Have you finished?'

'Yes,' said James, pouring more scotch.

Jean composed herself, stood up, and when she spoke her voice was icy.

'Good. Thank you for pointing out the defects of your upbringing. I apologise for those failings. I'm sure your father and I are sorry that we sent you to such a good school too, and for funding business school. You now think you know it all and have no desire to listen to anything or anyone but Mandy Brice Cooper.'

James tried to respond but Jean was having none of it.

'Be quiet James. You've had your say. Now it's my turn.' She paused.

'Neither the bank, nor Archie, nor myself have any confidence in your management team.'

James opened his mouth to speak.

'Don't interrupt. I'm still the chairman of Murgatroyd's even if you don't think I know anything, and just to remind you that Archie and I have the controlling shares, so what we say goes.'

She looked into James' eyes. He stared back.

'By 5pm Monday you will dismiss Brian Biggs for misconduct, and terminate Mandy Brice Cooper's contract too. She has no employment rights. Just give them both one month's pay and get rid. Make sure that the cars are recovered without damage. You can't trust sales types,' said Jean.

James was incredulous. 'I don't believe I'm hearing this, I won't…….'

'I've not finished James. You will also prepare in conjunction with Archie a twelve month cash flow forecast, to be submitted for approval at a special board meeting Wednesday next. I will arrange for us to visit the bank to ensure that Mr Whitehill is content to continue lending to us so we avoid insolvency. The plan will include a cost saving strategy which will cut all promotional spending and arrange to sell the head office building and terminate the lease on the London property. You are authorised to dispose of the existing launch stock of Excalibur at cost to improve liquidity. I will chair a weekly board meeting to review performance, and Archie will return to his role of finance director on a permanent basis.'

'Oh is that all madam chairman?' James sneered, 'and suppose I refuse?'

'Don't put me in that position James,' she said.

He reflected and turned away. His mother was serious. Archie had done a good job on her.

'You said that you have no confidence in the management team. That means you have no confidence in me.'

'I believe you're inexperienced and need support as managing director. We'll bring in a part time executive chairman to support you,' Jean replied.

'Who will take over and undo all the things we've done in the past three years? No chance.'

Jean said nothing. Your move, James, she thought.

'Suppose I won't play along with this scheme?' he said.

'For goodness sake James I'm trying to get you to see that when something isn't working you change course.'

'Well I'm not changing course. Back me or sack me.'

'Do you mean that?' she replied.

James stood, hands on hips. 'Let's be clear. What happens if I won't go along with this?'

Jean steeled herself. She'd realised that she might need to do this, but the words were still sticking in her throat as she spoke.

'Then you're fired.'

James laughed out loud and applauded sarcastically.

'Oh that's great then, sacking the managing director and the entire management team, that's really going to boost sales isn't it? Who's going to run the business for you? Derek fucking Dawson? Mind you the unions already run the factory since dad abdicated control to the union bully boys. Oh I get it, dad runs it from beyond the grave. Even from there I'm sure that he can run it better than me.'

'That's enough James. This time, for once in your life, you will do as you are told.'

She regretted the choice of words straight away. Treating him as a child was not likely to help.

'Or what? Do I get sent to my room without my supper, or does dad give me another beating?'

Jean tried to calm things again. She still didn't want to fire him. James spoke before she could.

'No it's okay madam chairman. I've had my instructions. But there's one other item we need to discuss. This letter.'

He reached into his inside pocket, and handed over the letter from IPCO. As Jean started to read it he continued.

'It is a written offer for the purchase of the entire share capital of Murgatroyd Pen Company Ltd by International Pen, otherwise known as IPCO. It's a deal which Mandy and I have been working on. It will ensure that the business has the necessary liquidity to fund the expansion project through to fruition. Mr Whitehill can have his piffling little overdraft back. I won't be needing it.'

Jean read through the letter and looked up.

'Sell the business? You'd give up control of the family business?' she said.

'Well it works on every level. You get a large sum for your retirement, as do I, and I will take up a senior position in IPCO. Archie? Well dear old Archie can resume his retirement. Oh and just to makes thing sweeter for you busty Brenda will bite the bullet too like as not. That should please you.'

'And the staff of Murgatroyd's? What do they get? IPCO has a large manufacturing plant in Hatfield.'

'Derek Dawson and his sheep get what they deserve. A spell on the dole. Look at the bright side. They can strike for as long as they like.'

'So you don't care about the town then? Without Murgatroyd's the shops and pubs will shut. It'll be a ghost town.'

James laughed. 'Not my problem Madam Chairman. You employ me as managing director to boost shareholder value and that's what I'm doing. Don't tell me I'm in the firing line again? Don't tell me you care about the likes of Brenda Arkwright? Shagging her way to the top.'

Jean was at a loss. 'James .. I...' she started, but James interrupted.

'Put it on your board agenda for next week. I'm selling my shares irrespective. They want to complete within a month. A copy of the letter has been sent recorded delivery to Archie as Company secretary. Goodnight mother.'

James set down his glass and headed for the door.

'But your dinner James. come back.'

The front door slammed.

Jean slumped into her armchair. Tears welled up and she began to sob uncontrollably. It was all one big mess, and she was going to have to sort it out.

She looked at the letter. Perhaps selling the business was the answer? Perhaps she couldn't change destiny.

Marjorie came in from the kitchen, having heard the front door slam.

Jean looked up tearfully. 'One less for dinner.'

Marjorie sat and put her arm around her.

'He knows about us. Has done for years,' said Jean.

Marjorie shrugged. 'So? It's not illegal anymore and one day in more enlightened times nobody will care a jot.'

'I couldn't have got through it without you. You're my rock,' she allowed herself to be held and sobbed.

Marjorie held her. She was used to propping Jean up. Actually Bill had had several affairs, and each time he was found out Jean forgave him, with Marjorie picking up the pieces. She was suspicious about Brenda for a while, but actually found her very engaging and funny. Marjorie knew that Jean and Bill's marriage has become a bit of a sham. Bill was away a lot and with their son away too the house was empty and she and Jean could live a fairly contented life behind closed doors.

She did resent that she would never be more than Jean's lover, but had come to accept that this was how it had to be, and if it was a compromise then so be it. Then Bill revealed the affair with Brenda and all hell broke loose.

This affair was serious. This time Bill talked of leaving Jean. The facade threatened to be shattered. Jean only became aware later on that Brenda had borne Bill's child. Bill did love Jean, and didn't want to hurt her. In the end he broke it off with Brenda, and he reached a settlement over the child. Murgatroyd had an international operation, so Brenda was quietly seconded down to the London office. Bill remained with Jean. When Brenda gave birth to a daughter she had been quietly adopted. Jean had strongly objected to Brenda's return, but Bill said that it was not something he could avoid. She was needed in the business. The affair had been entirely his fault, and his alone. Brenda could not be blamed and had paid a high enough price already.

Throughout it Marjorie felt as if she was the silent victim. She was hurt by the way Jean battled to keep Bill, even though their affair was still going on. At times she thought

Jean hypocritical. In the end though, Marjorie was just a housekeeper with nowhere to go. She came to accept her lot, because she was just happy to hold on to her life and her job. When Brenda returned Marjorie quietly hoped that the affair might rekindle, and that this time Jean would finish her marriage with Bill. Instead Bill had died. Jean was devastated, but faithful Marjorie was there once more to pick up the pieces. Quietly she went about supporting her friend, in spite of her own pain.

Now as she sat holding Jean she could but think, here we are again. She had never really liked James. He was as arrogant as his father, without the charm. He could be obnoxious and boorish, treating her as a servant.

Jean had done her best to continue the Murgatroyd business. Now her son was carrying on like his father did, and ruining the business into the bargain. Marjorie recognised that, as little as she liked it, her own life and Murgatroyds were inextricably linked. For her to be happy Jean had to be happy too, and in spite of all that had gone on Marjorie still loved her very much.

She read the letter from IPCO, and later on they talked it through together. It was clear to Marjorie that Jean was in two minds. Although Marjorie could understand the dilemma she knew that Jean owed it to herself to sell the business, and said so.

James headed off for an evening with Mandy. They sat in the restaurant of the Royal Oak, eating a belated dinner. James had a pint and a chaser. They were both fairly drunk.

Mandy had been told the whole story by an emotional James, and they were now talking in circles. Mandy pulled him back to the point.

'Let's stay calm James. Actually I find it quite funny. She really expected you to fire Brian and I? The old girl's losing her marbles. Too much black pudding with her tripe and onions.'

James smiled. 'You should have seen her face when she saw the letter. It was a picture.'

'They will sell of course?' said Mandy, sipping her red wine.

James swallowed a piece of fillet steak and waved his fork for emphasis. 'They don't have a choice. If Whitehill's pulled the overdraft and they don't have anyone to run it anyway those shares are worthless. Archie will talk her around. His shares will pay for his tacky little semi, so he'll sell for sure and give us control anyway. Then IPCO can do what it wants. I'm actually looking forward to the meeting. We'll put this to bed once and for all.'

'VP Sales & Marketing IPCO UK. Not a bad title James,' Mandy said.

James was more relaxed now. 'And I get to pick my PA? Fancy the job darling?'

Mandy smiled. 'As long as you don't expect me to type, or file of course.'

'Perish the thought,' said James. 'Plenty of brand promotion and corporate events to organise, and no Archie snooping on the budget. They do Ascot, Henley and Wimbledon. Plenty of posh frocks for you to buy.'

'Oh I can't wait. Hats and shoes and fancy knickers. A bloody sight warmer than here too,' she ventured.

Mandy became serious as the conversation reached a lull.

She said quietly, 'When will you tell Carol you're leaving her?'

'As soon as the share sale is in the bag. I can't move any faster,' he said.

'Where will we live? Have you had any thoughts?'

'IPCO have a London flat we can use, until we decide.'

Mandy sighed 'I can't wait let me tell you. I'm fed up of this place for sure. I can't wait to escape south. I'm convinced I get vertigo north of Watford.'

James smiled. 'You'll have to go home soon any way. Your visa will be up. We don't let just anyone into Yorkshire you know.'

Mandy laughed. 'You could have fooled me.' Then she looked across the restaurant.

'Oh God James, Derek Dawson's just arrived. Hide. Oh it's too late.'

Derek wandered over, clearly without a care in the world, a pint of bitter in a jug handled glass in his right hand.

'Good evening Mr Murgatroyd, Miss Brice-Cooper,' he said, his faked deference apparent.

James responded in kind. 'Good evening Mister Dawson. Enjoy your day on 'tut' picket line?'

Derek ignored the bait, and was good humoured but dismissive. 'Oh we hardly need a picket at all Mr Murgatroyd. The strike's rock solid. Gone national too. I think you'll find our retail colleagues have blacked all Murgatroyd stock from today. You'll sell bugger all until you negotiate.'

James deliberately continued eating as if unconcerned at the news. 'Oh that's excellent. Not that it's going to matter much longer.'

Mandy was immediately concerned. The drink was talking. 'James. Don't…' she said

'Oh yes? Please enlighten me. I don't follow?' said Dawson.

James took a bite of his steak, thought for a moment, then tapped his nose knowingly.

'Well that's for me to know and you to find out, old boy.'

Derek laughed. 'Huh. As ballsy as your father, but no business brain at all. All wind and piss I think.'

James continued to eat, ignoring the insult. 'Ha. You hear that Mandy. The commie gobshite managed to string a sentence together.'

He looked up at Dawson, and got up as he spoke.

'Now let me make it very clear to you Mister Dawson. I don't negotiate with wrecking commie bastards like you, ever. May you and your rancid little union rot in your socialist cesspit!'

As he finished he was almost face to face with Dawson, who could smell the alcohol on his breath. He thought for a moment and backed off slightly. Then he threw his beer in James' face.

Mandy sat staring in shock. But James just smiled, and took out a handkerchief.

'It's okay Mandy. Mister Dawson just lost his cool, and his job. Common assault of a works colleague. Gross misconduct in any factory across the land. You're fired Mister Dawson. Your cards will be in the post,' he said, a smile spreading across his face.

He moved passed Dawson, bumping his shoulder as he did.

'I'd better let the police know I'll be making a formal complaint and sign up the witnesses. If you'll excuse me Mister Dawson.'

Mandy sat rooted to the spot. Dawson was gracious.

'Your boyfriend's got a big gob miss. Trouble is he hasn't a clue. Still wet behind the ears see. Wetter still now. Good evening Ma'am.' He touched his forelock and left.

10.

1976

Derek and Jean wandered through the garden of Murga-troyd Hall. It was the morning after the night before, and Jean was clearer in her mind. Marjorie had agreed to go to Derek's house to play intermediary, and he had returned in her car. Having dispensed the tea Marjorie left them to it. They continued the small talk. Neither of them wanting to give the game away. Derek had a good idea as to why he was here, but it was up to Murgatroyd's to make the first move.

Jean suggested a walk in the garden. The morning was warm and it looked like being another hot day in late summer. Both were relaxed in each other's company. They were old schoolmates after all.

Derek breathed in deeply and took in the glory of the garden. 'Well Jean it's been a while since I was here. The funeral if I remember?'

Jean pondered. 'Yes, it must have been. I haven't really entertained since Bill died.'

'A shame that. I remember the sixties with the garden

parties. The staff loved those. Queens Award for Industry and the Royal Warrant?'

Jean smiled. 'Yes I remember. Oh and the world cup too. Remember that?'

'Ay that's right. 1966. Bill had a red shirt on with number four on the back? Fancied himself as Nobby Styles.'

'That he did. You're exactly right.'

Derek sat on the bench by the pond, and Jean joined him.

'He were a funny guy your Bill. He was always the gaffer, but he had a good way with the staff. Knew their names, their families. Only little things, but they appreciated it on the shop floor,' Derek recalled.

'Until you negotiated the wages.'

Derek laughed once more. 'Ha. Now that's true enough. Then it was 'are you out of your fooking mind Mister Dawson?"

'Yes I'll admit I was treated to the odd rant when he got home.'

Derek lit his pipe.

'He was a good businessman too. Worked hard. He'd be in at the start of the early shift and his office light was also on when people clocked off at night. People respected him for that. In a good year or after a good job done, he'd drop a little bonus in the pay packet. Enough for a couple of beers. People like being treated as people Jean.'

Jean picked up the oblique point which Derek was making.

'And my son doesn't treat people as people,' she replied.

The formality returned. Derek stiffened and puffed his pipe in frustration.

'That's not for me to say Mrs Murgatroyd,' he said.

Jean put her hand on his arm. 'Keep it to Jean, Derek. We go back to infant school remember. No need for hidden agendas or words unspoken here.'

Derek looked up. 'Alright Jean. Will do. Now if I remember you were the register monitor at Westgate Primary. You always got the best jobs.'

Jean grinned. 'Oh I don't know, you were the milk monitor weren't you? An extra pint on the side?'

Derek raised his pipe in emphasis. 'There you go. Me a blue collar job lugging milk crates around whilst you....'

'Alright alright. The class struggle comes to Westgate Primary.'

'Well you haven't done bad Jean,' Derek replied, gesturing at the hall.

'Let's be honest I married well didn't I?' Jean was almost apologetic.

Derek pondered. 'Aye you did lass. But I don't resent you 'owt. Bill worked hard for what he got. Never had a problem with bosses making money if they worked hard and shared the cake with the rest of us. It's laziness and greed that I can't stand.'

Jean was ready for the main event. The time for small talk was over.

'And my son is lazy and greedy. Is that about it?'

Derek stiffened once more, and stood, ' As I say it's not….'

Jean interrupted him again, ' For you to say, yes yes I know. Look Derek we need to talk candidly about Murgatroyd's. Please?'

She motioned him to sit, but Derek stood his ground.

Derek looked at her gravely. 'No point in discussing Murgatroyd's with me Jean. I don't work there anymore. James sacked me last night.'

Jean was stunned.

'What? I don't…' Jean stammered.

'In the Royal Oak last night. He were a bit drunk like. Called me a commie gobshite amongst other pleasantries. He were with Mandy Brice-Cooper. I nearly hit him, but chucked me pint over him instead, cooled him down a little.'

Jean shook her head. Another of her plans was unravelling.

'What happened?'

Derek considered. 'He went to the landlord to call the police. One or two of the lads were with me, they thought it were funny to be honest. But he said I was fired for gross misconduct.'

Jean sat, shaking her head, lost for words.

Derek sat. He could see that she was struggling to hide her feelings.

'I'm sorry Jean. This won't make things any easier. Your lad's under pressure, I know that. But if he behaves like that with any of my lads they'll put him in casualty. You might have a word. As far as I'm concerned I'm fired unless I get a letter saying otherwise. National officials will be in touch with the Company on Monday.'

Jean sighed. Time to go for broke. Cards on the table.

'Okay Derek. Let's put that to one side, important though it is. It's just part of a wider problem isn't it? With James at the heart of it?'

Derek thought, then went on.

'Well quite bluntly yes it is Jean. I mean the strike is bloody stupid really. Barry Handsworth's a good bloke most of the time. He's a taskmaster, but okay with people. But you can't make stuff without bits can you? And we aren't paying our bills on time are we? So when the Lendel's order comes in we can't make it anyhow, so there's a big rush at the end. Then the boxes are late, after the lads worked overtime the previous night. The following day it was push, push, push. Then Handsworth cut the tea break and the lads had had enough. Can't say I blame them.'

'But the strike was irresponsible. We'll lose the account.'

Derek laughed ironically. 'Well that's what James will tell you, but actually he hadn't signed the purchase order for the new Murgatroyd box because Mandy hadn't signed off the design. It was one big bloody cock up if you ask me.'

Jean realised that she hadn't had the full story. 'So we couldn't have shipped the order anyway?'

'No chance. We had some old boxes the lads thought about using, but the new pen wouldn't fit properly so we were buggered.'

Jean sighed and looked at the ground. 'Managers aren't talking to each other are they?'

'Well they're never there Jean. Head office being offsite doesn't help. An expensive ivory tower if ever there was one. There's no face to face anymore. Things get missed which didn't when they were onsite at the factory.'

'Okay. But what about the pay claim Derek? It's obvious we aren't making any money so the pay claim is just unaffordable. You must concede that surely?'

Derek nodded. 'Well that may be true Jean. But all the lads see are the directors swanning around in posh new cars and spending money on a new headquarters building. Not a sign of a Company short of cash is it? Put yourself in their position with inflation running at 25%.'

'I see. Yes I can understand that causing resentment.'

Derek continued. 'Then they keep chopping and

changing the designs. This rebranding's costing a fortune. And what they come up with this week won't fit what they did last week. We've stock we can't use. Have you been in the warehouse lately? Chock-a-block with packaging. Inner and outer cartons. Cost a fortune they did.'

'And Is James aware of this?' Jean asked, already knowing the answer.

Derek laughed. 'Never comes to the factory. Last saw him there three months ago. That's why I went to head office to see him. Even then I barged in unannounced and he was none too pleased. Now I'll admit I were on me high horse a bit, but as I say your lad's under pressure and was rude. So I taught him a lesson. If you're reasonable people will be reasonable back; If not, then rude is as rude does in my book.'

'Alright Derek.'

Derek paused, looking at a koi carp in the pond.

'It's going under Derek. Murgatroyd's I mean.' Jean's voice cracked a little.

Derek looked up. "Oh,"

'The bank won't stand the losses any more. We can't pay our bills on time because we're over the overdraft limit.'

Derek sat. 'The strike. We'll be needing to resolve it quickly then?'

'Yes we do Derek. But that's not enough. The management team needs to change its attitude too. That much is clear.'

'Well I must admit if they did a full day's work it would help Jean. If you want James after lunch, try the golf course, and as for the Brian bloke, don't get me started.'

Jean looked straight at Derek. 'And Mandy?'

Derek thought about his answer. 'She's full of bright ideas. Trouble is we can't afford most of them. Walks around with a nasty smell under her nose too. It can't be right Jean.'

Jean shrugged. 'Alright Derek. I hear that, and all the other stuff. I've heard most of it already. But it's been helpful to have a view from the shop floor.'

Derek was suddenly very serious. Jean could see that he knew she wasn't bluffing.

'We can't let it go under Jean. I don't need to tell you that the effect on the town would be devastating. If the union can help then help we must. If we can help in any way with the bank I'm sure we'll do our best.'

Jean smiled and took his hand.

'Thank you Derek. There are two things I'm going to need you to do for me. You need to end the strike immediately. Barry Handsworth will apologise and that will be the end of the matter. But I also need a two year wage freeze, and I need that commitment tonight.'

'Bloody hell Jean.'

He stared, began to pace around, deep in thought. Jean waited. Your move Derek, she thought to herself.

Eventually he gathered himself, and looked directly in Jean's eyes.

'We can end the strike, but the pay freeze is a very big ask. With current rates of inflation that amounts to a really big pay cut for people. It's too much to ask Jean.'

'Archie's looked at the costings and it's what we need to get the business making money again. Without that whatever you do won't solve the problem.'

Derek was thinking on his feet. Jean could see he was rattled. Her late night chat with Archie had been worthwhile. As much as she understood what Derek was saying, he needed to take his share of the blame for where Murgatroyd's and so many other companies were.

Derek finally spoke, carefully, weighing his words. 'What about a productivity improvement agreement and a one year freeze? We'll add in some specific productivity commitments from the workforce?'

'Well it's a start Derek. We need to talk this all out with Archie of course. I'm happy to share the figures. We must have full transparency from now on.'

'But we'll only get that if we get some real changes in the management attitude. What about a work's council? Bill used to have something similar.'

Jean thought for a moment. 'Well yes, I'd like that. I think that's a good idea so we keep in touch with what's going on.

But what the customers need to know is that we will deliver on time. Why buy from us if we always deliver late, as we do? They can just go abroad, and trust me Derek they are. It's not rocket science. All we've got to do is give the customer what he wants on time. Doesn't seem much to ask does it?'

Derek nodded. 'Yes I suppose we don't really see things that way.'

'I need a no strike deal too, Derek.'

'Bloody hell Jean.'

Jean raised her hand. 'Derek I read the paper a lot and you know that I'm labour by instinct even if Bill never was. Day by day Johnny foreigner is gobbling us up. The car industry's going down the pan and if we don't do something we're going to lose our manufacturing base altogether.'

'Come on Jean it's not the unions fault. Managements are to blame. Too many of 'em bugger off to the golf club at the drop of a hat. You see the big cars lined up in that bloody car park, executives only. They eat in their executive dining rooms, crap in the executive toilet and pay themselves big bonuses that the business can't afford.'

'Right then Derek. Fair's fair. If you commit to a twelve month no strike deal we'll shut down the executive dining room and stop all the management perks. We'll have a staff bonus scheme which mirrors the bosses. We'll all eat fish and chips together on Wednesday. How about that?'

She stood, and thrust out her hand to shake on it.

Derek stood once more, and smiled. 'You'll throw in free mushy peas then?'

Jean smiled back 'Yep. With scraps too if they want it. Seriously Derek we're going to have to sort these 'them and us' issues or Murgatroyd's will go to the wall. Johnny foreigner's laughing at us. We're giving it all away.'

Derek nodded. 'I think you have a point Jean. We must get something done.'

They shook hands, and wandered back to the house. Marjorie was waiting in the driveway.

'Thanks for coming over Derek. I can rely on you to keep this quiet while I resolve matters, including your own situation?' said Jean as they reached the car.

'Of course Jean,' he said. 'Good luck to you. This is not going to be easy.'

'That's an understatement Derek. But thanks.'

She hesitated, then hugged him. Derek was surprised, but realised that she was close to tears. Marjorie realised that Derek too was moved to tears as she drove him back in silence.

Later on after Marjorie went to bed Jean confronted her other problem. Brenda Arkwright. She forced herself to relive the nightmare. The affair. The aftermath. Coping with Brenda still working with her husband. Seeing her in the next office to his. She had coped, because she wanted Bill back, and it was the deal they'd agreed. But now? Brenda was just one more reminder.

Later on in the morning, James entered Mandy's office as she sat reading a magazine. In addition to his briefcase he was carrying a large suitcase. James was late in and, unusually, had not advised his PA. Mandy had been puzzled, and the suitcase only added to the confusion.

'James, at last. I've been wondering where you were. God you look like shit. What's happened?'

He poured himself a coffee and sat. 'Carol threw me out. Confronted me about you.'

Mandy was suddenly frightened. 'What did you say?'

'I admitted the affair. No point in denying it.'

Mandy was indignant. 'Admitted the affair? So you're not proud of it? Not proud of us then? That puts me in my place in the pecking order doesn't it? The bit on the side.' She stood up and stared down at him.

James was defensive and clearly hadn't slept much.

'That's not what I meant Mandy. Look I'm just confused. I went home after I left you at the Royal Oak, and expected Carol to be in bed. It was after five in the morning by the time I got in. But she was up waiting for me. It was awful.'

'Well forgive me it's not exactly paradise for me either

I'm not going to be the bit on the side shagging the boss. I'm not Brenda Arkwright you know.'

'That's not what I said. I meant, oh whatever,' James put up his hands in surrender.

Mandy stood gazing out of the window. James put his head back, and closed his eyes in the hope that the world might stop for a moment if he did. He needed a time out to get his head around things. Too many things were coming together at once. Quiet descended. Both took stock and time passed.

Mandy was first to break the silence. 'Well at least it's out in the open now.'

'It's been local gossip for weeks Carol reckons. Bet that bastard Dawson told her. Petty bloody revenge. I should have taken him outside and given him a good hiding.'

Mandy shook her head. 'Come off it James. He didn't have time. This is a small town where everyone knows everyone's business, and the Murgatroyd's are the local celebrity family God help us. Pathetic lives with nothing to look forward to but Wednesday night bingo, Corry bloody nation street and a shag on Saturday night after going down the boozer.'

He sipped his coffee and said nothing.

'Sorry Mandy. This just hurts. It's not Carol. It's the kids' faces when I left. They were both sobbing.'

Mandy took his hands. 'I know James. It had to happen one day though didn't it?'

She let the silence stand for a moment, then felt her composure crumbling, and the words tumbling out, tears welling up.

'I'm in love with you you know? This isn't an affair to me. I'm in love. Probably for the first real time in my life. I know I don't do emotion. I was brought up by an ice queen to be an ice queen. I wasn't the daughter mummy wanted. She wanted someone she could dress in pink and marry off to a rich banker so she could keep up appearances. We might have been old money, but most of it was gone. I worked hard to get through business school. Mum never lifted a finger. I won a scholarship fair and square. There were parties, blokes she set me up with. Hooray Henry's in the main. I made the mistake of marrying one of them, so she got the posh wedding. Then I met you. A real bloke, with real emotions. I wanted you from the first moment I met you, but you were married. If you don't think that I don't feel guilt all the time I'm with you then you don't know me at all.'

He saw the tears and all the hurt bubbling up. He sat her down on the settee in the corner of the office and held her. This time he spoke with his voice cracking.

'I love you too. This isn't just sex Mandy. I married the local girl in the posh wedding and my parents were delighted.

Social event of the year. It's not that I don't care for her, I've just outgrown her. You are funny, sexy, bright, intelligent, prim, dirty and everything besides. I want to get the divorce done and marry you as soon as we can. It was awful this morning, but it was always going to be. I just wanted to do it my way.'

Mandy looked into his eyes and saw the tears. 'My poor love. Come here.'

They hugged and kissed. They held on to each other for a long time.

Mandy said into his ear. 'I've felt so lonely, but I'm not lonely anymore.'

James composed himself. He explained that having had the discussion with Carol he had packed a suitcase to leave immediately. He had explained to Carol that it wasn't an affair, and that he wanted a divorce. Carol had clearly had time to think things through, and they agreed it was probably for the best. The children had awoken and although too young to fully understand had reacted to their mother's tears.

He had rammed some clothes in a suitcase, and headed for the door, shutting it behind him, leaving his old life behind as he did so. Starting the car he decided to head straight to the solicitors. Barry Gregg was an old school friend, and started by 8am James knew.

He drove into town, and as he did so his legs turned to jelly. Is this what he really wanted? Fate had taken a hand,

and he was where he was. He liked to make his own decisions. He was the managing director. People did his bidding.
He controlled events. Nobody told James what to do anymore. That stopped when his father died.

Barry Gregg was just arriving when James pulled into the
car park. It was evident that something big was up. He'd got
a 9 am meeting, but this was James Murgatroyd. They were
friends, and a Murgatroyd was a Murgatroyd. He ushered
James into his office, and got his PA to give his nine o'clock
meeting to his Junior.

He got James a mug of black coffee. He looked ashen.
Barry remembered the look from primary school. The playground. Young James got picked on by the estate kids because
of his father. He'd become terrified by the playground, and
he wore the same expression now.

James poured his heart out for an hour. He was in tears
some of the time, but Barry just let him ramble. He knew of
the affair of course. It was obvious to anyone seeing James
and Mandy together.

His wife and Carol knew each other socially, and they
had been to James and Carol's for dinner. Classic growing
apart syndrome he thought. But he was a solicitor first of
course, and not given to allowing a client to do something
he might regret later. A James Murgatroyd divorce might
be messy and complex, and bloody expensive for James too.

He was content to let James talk, calm him down and send him away to think. He had a sense that events had forced James' hand, and that Mandy would win out in the end, but that was for later. However James seemed to become more resolved in his mind as they talked. He wanted a quick resolution, and to move on as fast as possible. A man in a hurry Barry thought. They discussed the IPCO offer, which seemed a bit too good to be true.

Eventually they agreed on the next steps, and he made sure that James would leave settlement discussions to him. Guilty husbands often gave away the store in guilt money, and James was an obvious candidate to get fleeced.

They parted two hours later, and James was in a better state of mind by then. Barry parked the notes for a day or two. Things would play out no doubt, and in the meantime do nothing. Events at Murgatroyd would take their course.

For Brenda it was obvious that something was up that morning. She had expected James to be in on time, to agree on who should speak to Lendel's. She also needed to get some cheques signed as suppliers were screaming. Finance wasn't really her job, but everybody knew Brenda. Practical Brenda they called her. If you want something done, then go to Brenda. Actually she quietly liked it.

She had a surprise when the telephone rang, and Jean Murgatroyd was on the line. They had never really spoken, since, well, before the 'thing'. She assumed that she had come through on the wrong line and wanted James.

'I'm sorry Mrs Murgatroyd, I haven't seen James this morning,' Brenda half stammered.

'Thank you Brenda, but it was actually you I wanted. Could you possibly come up to the hall? I'd like a chat, er if you could?' Jean's words were hesitant. Too hesitant really Brenda thought. She was the chair after all, and a request from her was a royal command.

'Er well of course Mrs Murgatroyd, what time would you like me to come?'

It was a 'come at once' of course, though very polite. Brenda got into her car. She was going to be fired, made redundant probably. Cost-cutting measure. But why Jean and not James? Perhaps it was Jean's revenge?

What would she do? To be honest she had expected to be got rid of after Bill died. Some pretext or other. Now it seemed that it was going to happen. How should I take it? Perhaps I should have cleared my desk? It was embarrassing to say goodbye, after all of these years at Murgatroyd's.

She decided that she would be dignified, hold it together. No tears. Don't give Jean the satisfaction of seeing you cry. Then sue her for everything you can. This is the seventies. You can't go around sacking your husband's girlfriend. Isn't that sex discrimination?

She drove out of town, up the hill past the school where she started her education, and then the Methodist hall where she first met Bill, giving out prizes at the talent competition. Brenda finished third, and won a box of black magic. She remembered Bill's smile, and him shaking her hand firmly.

Then she past the shop where she had her paper round as a girl. Then up the hill past Thomas Camden's old cottage. Perhaps she should go away far from here? Make a fresh start? Leave the past behind and start again.

All too soon she was at the hall. She drove through the gate, parked on the gravel drive and got out. Stiff upper lip Brenda, she thought, as she walked towards the imposing black front door.

But at that moment Jean appeared at the side gate, and motioned her into the garden. Their handshake was formal and business-like. Jean showed her into the conservatory.

Brenda sat, and Jean poured tea. They made awkward small talk. The weather, the garden, that sort of stuff. Get to the point Brenda thought.

'The house is beautiful, you have wonderful taste,' Brenda ventured.

'Marjorie is the style guru, she has a wonderful eye for colour,' Jean replied, trying to loosen up, but failing. 'Look, this isn't easy is it?'

'No, not for me either,' said Brenda, perhaps with a hint of defensiveness.

'No I erm suppose not. Look shall we start by being Jean and Brenda? I think that would be a start?'

'Yes, I'd prefer that, definitely.' Brenda was puzzled. What was this about?

'Okay that's fine then,' Jean said.

She smiled briefly, then became serious once more. 'Look Brenda, I can't forgive what happened, it's still far too soon, maybe one day, but not now.'

Brenda shook her head, unsure of anything now.

'Well I know that Mrs Murgatroyd, er Jean, I didn't ask to be forgiven and I don't expect you to. I'm sure I'd feel the same way in your shoes'

Jean was a little taken aback. She had a realisation that she didn't know Brenda all that well after all. Before she could continue Brenda brought her back to the main subject.

'Jean you said on the telephone that you wanted to discuss Murgatroyd's. That's, why I came.' she said.

Jean blanched a little at Brenda's directness.

'Yes. That's true. I just thought we should try to clear the air first,'

Brenda thought for a moment, then looked Jean directly in the eye. 'Well I'd love to, but that isn't realistic is it?'

Jean smiled once more. She found Brenda's directness at one with her own.

'No it's not, not really I suppose,' she said.

Brenda could see that Jean was deeply uncomfortable. She decided that Jean needed some thinking time. She sipped her tea.

Jean put her hands up, as if in surrender, then the words came out in a torrent.

'Oh Brenda this is ridiculous. I'm no good at this emotional stuff. Let's park the difficult stuff and talk about the current problems. I suspect we'll have more common ground?'

Brenda smiled. 'Well I hope so Jean.'

She thought for a moment, then picked her words with care.

'But don't think even that is easy for me Jean. Whatever you may think of me I've always been loyal to Murgatroyd's, and grateful too. I only spoke to Archie because I could see things couldn't remain as they were. But I don't want to be called disloyal.'

Jean put her hand on Brenda's. The first time they had touched.

Jean spoke confidently, the ice apparently broken. 'No one is, or has, suggested that Brenda. Sadly what you had to say just confirmed what Archie and I have thought for some time. To put it bluntly James has completely lost the plot. We're going to have to do something pretty quickly or we're going bust.'

'If that's your opinion then I agree with you entirely. I just didn't want to be the one to say it first. As I said I don't do disloyalty.'

'In this matter your behaviour is certainly beyond reproach Brenda. I thank you for having the courage to speak out. Family stuff is very complicated after all. But first of all the bank, let's start with them if you would.'

'You mean Mr Whitehill?'

'Yes, how many times did James duck his calls?'

Brenda considered a moment. She was still trying to understand where this was heading. 'Half a dozen or so. James just got ratty when I mentioned that he'd called.'

Jean moved on. 'I see. Not a very sensible approach. What about the Lendel's order? As I understand it you couldn't have made the product irrespective of the strike. Mandy screwed up and James didn't order the boxes. The strike was an easy excuse, for James' failure I gather?'

Brenda was taken aback. 'Yes. How did you know?'

Jean smiled ruefully. 'I didn't until it was too late. Forgive my French but it seems a complete balls up.'

Brenda shrugged. She wasn't going to tell tales, but Jean had most of the facts already. Obviously she had Archie, but he wasn't in the business day to day. The lady clearly had sources of her own in the factory.

Jean stood and looked out at the view towards the factory.

'If I can get the strike stopped can you save the account?' she said.

Brenda was surprised at the question. 'I don't have accounts any more. They were all taken off me by James. That's not to say that I don't still know the people to talk to though. Lendel's was the first account that I handled at Murgatroyd's.'

'I see. Well just suppose. Lendel's is a big account, the sort we need to retain. What can be done?'

Brenda thought for a moment before replying. 'Bill and Paul Lendel were very close as you know. But Brian Biggs went in and talked about exclusivity and rebate thresholds, the hard sell you know? When we started missing shipments and Paul Lendel started getting irate Brian and James went missing and I took the crap. He wasn't rude to me but said that there was no trust left. I'd give it a go, but I gave my word that we wouldn't let him down any more and we have. I'm not sure I've got any credibility either.'

Jean was getting to the heart of the matter. 'What do we need to do to secure confidence Brenda, I mean generally?'

'Stop wasting money and start doing the basics well.'

She paused to marshal her thoughts, then continued.

'Look I served my business apprenticeship with Paul Munro and Bill Murgatroyd. Their word was their bond. If they said they would do something they did. If Bill did a bad deal, and trust me he did from time to time, he would still honour it. People trusted him and we've got to get that back. That holds for customers, suppliers and the staff for that matter.'

'But what about the trade unions, and Derek Dawson in particular?'

Brenda shrugged. 'Well Bill always said you got the unions you deserved.'

Jean smiled. 'Yes… I do remember him saying that.'

Brenda explained. 'Derek's just a product of his upbringing. You know that better than I do. He's got a big chip on his shoulder because he could never achieve his potential because it wasn't what his generation did. You had to know your place. So he became a union rep, which gave him some power. He's a bit of a bully, but if you involve him and explain yourself clearly you can win him over.'

Jean interjected calmly, 'and James doesn't know how to manage him, in fact does he even bother to try?'

Brenda considered. 'No, not really. I've always got on well with Derek. In fact I don't think I'd have made it this far without Derek.'

'Oh? How do you mean?' said Jean intrigued.

'Well when I started at Murgatroyd's I did a spell on the assembly line. A foreman started touching me, pinching my bum and stuff. I didn't know what to do, because he was too clever to do it in public. He got me to work overtime, then it started. One evening he started his usual antics, but Derek had stayed behind and saw it all. A week later the foreman disappeared, dismissed they reckoned.'

'Allan Ferris?'

Brenda was surprised. 'Yes, how did you know?'

'You weren't alone Brenda. He always picked on the younger girls. Derek spoke to Bill, and he asked my advice. They set him up between them, then fired him.'

Brenda was surprised.

'I never knew that. Bill never spoke of it.'

'Well it was well before you and Bill, er knew each other.'

'Yes, I suppose. Bill and Derek were best friends and worst enemies weren't they?'

'Yes, actually I think you are probably right. In the end I think they both saw the other as someone you could do business with, even though they were poles apart politically. Unfortunately my son doesn't have the same subtlety.'

Brenda had a sense that to compare the two men was unfair. 'It's experience Jean. James is a very capable man and very bright. He just hasn't yet had enough experience to put what he's learnt into practice.'

Jean looked at her quizzically. 'Come on Brenda. Thus far you've been honest, but you don't actually believe that do you?'

'Well who am I to judge? I feel very sorry for him to be honest. Following in the footsteps of any father is tough, but when your father was Bill Murgatroyd well, he was a one off wasn't he?'

Jean paused. For a moment Brenda thought she had gone too far. Family was family after all. But Jean was determined that the raw pain of the affair would not get in the way of what needed to be done, and actually found Brenda rather down to earth and easy to like.

'Yes Brenda, he was. To be honest I had hoped that James would stay at IPCO, but he wanted to come back to the family business. He wanted to outshine his father, but nothing he did was good enough. Then Bill died and suddenly he gets his head, and whatever I say is ignored. I should have clamped down earlier, but I thought he'd earned a crack at it.'

It was obvious that Jean was struggling with a very difficult problem, whilst coming to terms with the hurt of the past. And Brenda was part of that hurt. She tried to make her reply compassionate.

'I think you were right. It seemed only fair. But Archie retiring was the big problem. Anything that didn't get done

Archie used to fix it. He was Bill's fixer, did the detail. With him gone it was a big gap. Big boots to fill.'

Jean moved on. 'And Mandy, what about her? I know about the affair incidentally.'

'Everyone knows about the affair. James isn't exactly hiding it. Actually I think that she's the right woman, but at the wrong time. Some of her ideas are great, but unless we're making money and can afford to fund them it just doesn't work. If it's any consolation he's deeply in love with her. They're made for each other. It's not a fling.'

Jean was suddenly tense. 'What if it wrecks a marriage?' she said.

'I'm sorry. That came out all wrong.'

Jean thought, then smiled grimly once again. 'It's okay. You're probably right. Carol is a lovely person and a great mother but Mandy is more James' type. I might as well accept that, although for the children well, who knows how things will end up? I'm just his mother and I've no idea anymore.'

Jean paused and looked out at a robin hopping across the rockery. She took out some seed, went just outside of the open conservatory door, and sprinkled some carefully nearby. The robin hopped ever closer, eventually reaching the seed. Both women looked on in silence. A timeout for them both. At length Jean looked back, but the telephone rang and interrupted her. She excused herself and went into the house to take the call.

Brenda sat in the warmth of the sunshine in the conservatory. She concluded that this was merely a fact finding mission on Jean's part. She was clearly a very shrewd lady, and Brenda was being used to confirm the state of play. What the game plan was wasn't clear, but Brenda had a sense that action had to take place very soon.

Jean returned, apologised for the interruption, and said simply, 'I suppose we'd better talk about the future?'

Brenda realised that this was the moment of truth. 'Do I have one Jean? To be honest I thought I was finished when Bill died. Many people in your position would have made it their business to get rid of me. If you'd done so I couldn't really have complained. I thank you for that.'

Jean shrugged 'It would have been vindictive and malicious, and whatever my faults I'm not built that way. I left it to Bill. It seemed fair to distance myself. I'm not exactly an objective judge of you am I?'

'No, I suppose not, but many would have.'

'Archie speaks well of you. That's good enough for me,' said Jean.

Brenda was flattered by the comment. 'Well I'd like to be part of Murgatroyds future. I'd like to build the Company that Bill always wanted. That might sound corny, but it's how I feel.'

Jean nodded her head. 'Amen for that. I have a feeling that we've talked enough for now. At least I think I know you a bit better, and it gives me what I need to make some decisions. Thank you for your honesty.'

They stood, and Brenda gathered her things.

'Thank you too Jean. It's good to get things out in the open at last.'

'You've a child of your own now? Vicky isn't it?' ventured Jean.

'Yes, she's nearly two now. Ron's a wonderful guy.'

'You're very lucky to have them. Do you ever think about, well, you know?'

Brenda felt the tears welling up. 'Pretty much every day. I only got to hold her once. I just feel an awful lingering pain. I have a feeling it's a life sentence for what I did. I deserved it I guess. I hope she's happy with her family, wherever she is.'

Jean put her hand on her shoulder as they reached the hall.

'I don't want revenge Brenda. Maybe when it first happened, but not now. It's Bill I miss. He just had the charm, the wit, the love of life.'

They reached the door. Jean opened it, then hesitated.

'Look, about that day, at the grave?'

'Three days after the funeral? Don't remind me,' said Brenda.

'I was evil to you. Taking those flowers from you and throwing them in the bin. The things I said. So very hurtful. I'm so sorry.' Jean was close to tears too.

Brenda stood for a moment, and took a deep breath before replying.

'Well I was distraught at the time. I just couldn't find any words. I thought running away was the best thing to do. I couldn't go to the funeral formally, obviously, but three days later I thought the coast would be clear. Bumping into you was the last thing I wanted to do.'

Jean said sadly. 'And you have visited since?'

'Yes. I go when I want to think sometimes, hoping for inspiration. But I don't leave flowers, I didn't want to cause further upset. I thought I'd done enough damage already.'

Jean shook her head. 'Well let's put that to rights here and now. You have every right to remember Bill your way. If you want to put flowers on the grave it's fine by me. If we meet at the grave it's fine by me. Life's too short Brenda, Bill found that out the hard way.'

'Thanks Jean. That's really kind,' said Brenda. They shook hands once more, and Brenda got into her car and drove away. She still had no clue as to what might happen next. But she was content that maybe they could both move on now.

She spontaneously stopped at Wilkes and bought a bouquet. She walked past the Parish Church, and through a side gate to the church yard. It was a glorious day, but as she got closer she started crying. She didn't attempt to stem the flow, just let the tears stream down her cheeks as she knelt by the gravestone, and unwrapped the flowers, carefully arranging them in a pot by the headstone. There was a single red rose in the pot on the other side. It was new.

As if on cue, the church bell tolled briefly.

She kissed her fingers and touched the headstone, squeezing it for comfort, lingering a little, then she left and went back to work.

A while later Jean came to the churchyard herself, saw the flowers, and smiled. She sat by the grave as she did each week when it was fine.

'So Brenda came then? I said she could. Not that she ever needed my permission. Thought it only right Bill. I didn't want to share you with her in life. But it's been long enough now. Time to move things on I think.'

She set another single rose next to Brenda's bouquet, and smiled once more.

'Er hem, I thought I'd find you here,' said Archie quietly.

Jean didn't look up. 'I often come. Just sit here for hours sometimes talking to a block of black marble. Silly isn't it?'

Archie smiled. 'So do I Jean, only my rock is in white marble.'

'Does she ever talk back to you?'

'Well I'm really not sure. But I do seem to find it a good way to resolve things in my mind. I'm not sure I believe in an afterlife as such, but I certainly feel better when I leave, so who knows? God moves and all that. Are you still stuck as to what to do?'

'Yes. Two possible options, both with appalling side effects.'

'How did it go with Brenda?'

'Well, I think. Difficult at first of course but it got better as we loosened up a bit and found some common ground. She's a talented woman as you said.'

'But James won't accept the executive chairman idea, even for a period while we sort things out?'

'No. I think that's a total non-starter. The man is as stubborn as his father. He just wants to sell up and move on and in with Mandy.'

'But sacking James?'

'It's almost unthinkable. Him and his children are all the family I have. But what would Bill have done?'

Archie shook his head. 'I don't think that helps you. Bill isn't around, and James is rather older and much more difficult these days.'

'He's his father's son. Well I don't have long to make my mind up. But at least I think I'm clearer about the options.'

'I need to discuss the bid document with you, now I've

had time to evaluate it. Can I take you to dinner and we'll discuss it?'

'I'd like that. Early to bed though I think. I'm just so drained by all this.'

'Completely understandable. I'll see you in the car then?'

He headed for the car, and Jean cried once more.

11.

1976

The following day there was an emergency board meeting at Murgatroyd head office. James arrived at 9am as usual. Brenda tried to act as normally as she could, and spent the morning fending off angry customers. There was nothing she could offer them, and order after order was cancelled.

At 10am Archie and Jean arrived. Brenda made herself scarce. They went into the board room, and made tea. James arrived shortly after. He was brisk and business-like. He seemed in control and surprisingly confident thought Archie.

They sat at the large boardroom table, with Jean at the head as chair, and James and Archie either side. There were no attempts at small talk.

'Can I ask why you've excluded Brian and Mandy? They are of course both directors of the Company,' asked James.

Jean replied simply. 'Because we are the shareholders, and I wanted to discuss the offer from IPCO.'

'Okay that's fine, but I have to say my mind's made up. I'm selling my shares.'

Archie was calm, but formal. 'May I point out that under the terms of the transfer of shares following Bill's death all shares must be made available to other shareholders based on a multiple of earnings?'

James laughed sarcastically. 'So you want to buy me out then? Didn't know you were that rich Archie?'

Archie ignored the insult. 'I think you may find that your interpretation of what IPCO's bid is worth is at odds with mine James. This is my assessment of the valuation.'

He handed over a set of figures, suggesting that James took a few minutes to study them. James did so, punching figures into his calculator and getting ever more puzzled. He looked up at Archie, and shook his head.

'But this is absurd. They've offered far more than this.'

Archie knew that this could all dissolve into a flaming row, so he had prepared a carefully scripted presentation, which he had shared with Jean the night before. He took them through the three typed sheets one by one.

Then he spoke, summing up. 'The offer is not in cash, but in IPCO shares. You obviously haven't read the latest about IPCO's share price? It plummeted 35% by Friday's close following a profits warning, and with the news coming out each day about the so called creative accounting practices my guess is that they will be worth even less by close of play today as well.'

James interjected tartly. 'But still a good deal for something you claim is worthless due to my bad management?'

Jean spoke up. 'Calm down now James. We'll keep these discussions at a professional level.'

James laughed. 'Professional level? When Archie's been going behind my back talking to staff and undermining my authority? That's a laugh.'

Archie remained calm. 'The bank rang me, I didn't ring them. I merely made some enquiries because you declined to do so, thereby putting the Company at risk. Now can we consider the other problems with the offer from IPCO?'

'I'm sure I'm all ears,' said James.

'James cut it out. Archie will have his say. Then you can have yours. Is that clear?' Jean slapped her hand down on the tabletop in frustration.

Archie continued smoothly, 'I have two further issues. The offer is based partly on an earn out based on the current and future profits of Murgatroyd's.'

'Which is quite normal for a transaction of this kind,' said James.

Archie was on his home turf and knew his stuff. 'Ah yes but their offer figure was based on the last two year's published statutory accounts profits. We have no chance of making a profit either this year or next in my view. It makes the earn out figure look very low.'

James stayed silent.

'Go on,' Jean prompted, 'you said you had two points?'

'Well yes. It seems that they are quoting a debt free figure.'

'I'm sorry I don't follow,' said James, beginning to sense trouble.

'Debt free assumes that we pay the overdraft off, out of what they pay us, cutting the value of the offer substantially.'

'Well I'm sure that's just an accounting nicety we can clean up in due diligence,' said James.

'Which I note we have to pay for, along with all legal costs. That could add up to another half a million pounds.'

James swept this aside. 'Well I'm sure when I've renegotiated these finer points we'll still get a deal better for the future of the Company. Present banking arrangements are clearly restricting my management team's ability to deliver the Company's growth plans.'

Archie looked up. 'I strongly disagree. In my view we need to act now to cut the overdraft and reduce our overhead costs. We cannot in my view make a profit with the business structured as it is. To retain bank support we need to provide the bank with projections which are credible and relatively risk free.'

'Thank you Doctor Doom,' said James.

Jean had heard enough.

'Do you have anything practical to say James? Archie's

figures seem to show that IPCO's bid is a nonstarter to me, leaving aside the impact on jobs in this town, a factor which I personally find difficult to ignore.'

James' hackles started to rise. What did she or Archie know? 'Archie's figures?' he said tartly. 'Are you going to let an accountant run this business? I don't remember dad having a good word to say about accountants.'

Jean remained calm. 'So that's a no then James? No constructive points to make?'

James shook his head. 'I can't believe I'm hearing this.'

Jean continued. 'I am rejecting IPCO's offer and invoking the sell on clause on the shares which will prevent you selling to them. I also want you to resign as managing director. I'm making a change.'

'Now you are joking.'

'No. I'm very serious James. The current results are not acceptable to me, and I see no realistic possibility that you or your team can turn this around. As you have indicated that you find the offer of support from an experienced chairman unacceptable, you leave me no choice. I'm prepared to pay up your full notice period as a compensation package subject to a legal agreement. I will be making Mandy redundant, and offering Brian the option of resignation or facing a disciplinary hearing for gross misconduct over systemic expenses fraud.'

James laughed. 'A clean sweep? Are you mad? Who's going to run it then? Sooty and Sweep? Or are you just going to let Derek Dawson and the union run it? Dig dad up maybe?'

'That's enough James,' said Jean 'It's not your concern any more. I'm sorry but as chairman I've concluded that it is in Murgatroyd's best interests that you step down.'

James shook his head. 'Mandy said you were losing your marbles. I didn't believe her until now.'

Jean stood. 'Go home now, wherever you call home. The Royal Oak I imagine. I want you offsite. I'll ring you later.'

James shook his head once more, but gathered his papers and left. Archie followed. Jean let her head drop back and closed her eyes for a few minutes. The look on James' face, a look of disbelief mixed with hatred was etched in her mind. She felt numb.

She composed herself and punched Brenda's internal number. Deep breath Jean, next item she thought.

'Brenda? Good morning it's Jean Murgatroyd. Can you spare me a moment? I'm in the boardroom. Thanks.'

Archie came back in.

'He's gone Jean. Chris will help him with his things and ensure that he leaves site. I'll deal with Mandy and Brian now.'

Jean nodded. 'Yes. That's fine. Brenda's on her way up.'

'Well done Jean. That took so much courage.'

There was a knock at the door and Brenda entered.

'Come in Brenda. Good morning. I'm just leaving,' said Archie, and headed out of the door.

'Was that James I just saw heading off? Only he has a meeting later on this morning?' replied Brenda.

'I'll explain. Take a seat if you will,' said Jean.

Jean got straight to business. There was no family talk today. 'I have just concluded a meeting with James in which I advised him that his services are no longer required. Archie is now going to tell Mandy and Brian that they are leaving too with immediate effect.'

Jean looked up at Brenda. There was no emotion in her eyes, just steely determination.

'My God.'

'Yes. It isn't easy sacking anyone, especially your own son. But as I see it I have an obligation to myself and the workforce that puts the interests of Murgatroyd's first. Ahead of any family loyalties.'

Brenda was taking stock as Jean continued.

'I have asked Archie to be managing director. He has already done a lot of work on a recovery plan. We are expecting to present the plan to the bank later on this week. Archie is reasonably confident that they will accept it and continue to support us, but there are no guarantees.'

'And the strike?'

Derek Dawson will call off the strike. He understands the trouble we are in, and the impact that failure will have on his members and the local community.'

Brenda smiled in surprise at the turn of events. 'Well I have to say you're not afraid of taking the bull by the horns.'

Jean shrugged. 'I don't think there's time to mess about. I've let this go too far hoping and praying that it would resolve itself. My mistake. The conversations and events of the last week have convinced me that that isn't going to happen.'

Brenda looked at the older woman with respect. 'I think you're amazingly brave. I hope it goes without saying that I will support you any way I can, if you want me to stay on that is.'

Jean nodded 'That is what I wanted to discuss. This letter offers you the position of Sales Director of Murgatroyd Pens, reporting to Archie.'

It was a very long day. Events at head office were dramatic, but the factory was on strike, so there was no real way to communicate the news. The post room photocopied a letter from Jean Murgatroyd, and it was sent first class to all employees. A press release was mailed in to local media, and handed in to the local office of the Gazette around lunchtime. For them it was too late to change the front page, but they tweaked the later edition, after a hasty visit to Archie.

Derek Dawson met Archie at noon, and took away copies of Jean's letter to the factory picket line. He summoned the workforce to a meeting the following morning.

Archie had a predetermined plan, and worked his way through it methodically. Dealing with Mandy and Brian had been difficult, but in his career Archie had done some tough things. He had been surprised when Jean had reached the decision she had. Firing your own son was difficult, but appointing your late husband's lover as sales director was more difficult still.

He admired Jean's determination to do what was right, and knew that the next few days would be critical. There was actually little more for her to do, so he sent her home after lunch. He arranged that Marjorie would take her out in the afternoon, to take her mind off things. She clearly needed time out. They agreed a meeting the following afternoon, so Jean could be brought up to speed. But Archie was in charge, and he was a man with a plan.

He picked up the telephone and dialled Paul Whitehill's number. He needed to speak to him urgently. He must hear the news from Archie before he heard it from elsewhere. The bank was a critical part of the solution, and must be treated with respect. Archie needed time.

'Good morning Archie. What can I do for you?'

The conversation took about half an hour. Archie had been working up his financial projections, but needed a couple of days to firm up his thinking. He would get his calculations done and typed up within forty eight hours.

He just needed to give Paul Whitehill enough top cover to be able to justify his actions to head office, and he was pretty confident he could do that. It did of course help that they knew each other socially. It also helped that Murgatroyd was one of Whitehill's bigger clients, and no bank wanted to lose a customer of their size unless they had to.

The issue was going to be pay day. They were also on stop with suppliers as they had failed to pay. In the short term the overdraft was going to increase, something which the bank wouldn't like. But Archie had a trump card.

'It's only fair to tell you that we've had a bid from IPCO Paul, but Jean and I consider that it very much under values the business. I'm going to talk with them of course, but I think that we've just got a bit ahead of ourselves, and with some strong management we can rebuild.'

He let Paul Whitehill have his say, starting with the standard bank platitudes, but becoming rather more down to earth and realistic.

'Well we want to support a long standing customer of course. We just need reassurance over the direction of travel, and have a plan that we can understand,' said Whitehill finally.

Of course you do thought Archie.

'That's reassuring Paul, but you will understand that we're going to need a short term increase in the facility to meet the payroll. I know that will be tough for you to get through your funding committee, but I hope that what I'm sending you this week will give you what you need.'

Paul hesitated slightly, as Archie knew he would. But he also knew that with bankers you under promised and over delivered, and it started with brutal honesty. Give them the worst and the only news from then on was good news. Provided of course you didn't scare them into pulling the overdraft entirely.

'I appreciate your honesty Archie, but obviously we've had alarm bells ringing from head office, and James dodging my calls didn't help me,' said Whitehill.

Now to play the trump card, thought Archie. 'I recognise that Paul. Jean and I can only apologise for the lack of communication, hence my phone call to you this morning. One bit of really good news is that the union is calling off the strike immediately and has agreed a twelve month wage freeze. They met with Jean yesterday to be appraised of the situation and are fully behind the rescue plan. I expect a full return to work in the morning.'

With inflation at over twenty percent a wage freeze was phenomenal, which is why Archie had insisted with Jean that Derek Dawson would need to swallow some pain.

Whitehill was pleased with the news, and Archie had his deal.

For Brenda the day went by in a blur. She was stunned by the size of the changes and staggered by her own appointment. But she was confident that she could do the job.

Her first task would be Lendel's. She pulled together a few people to discuss strategies, how best to get the deliveries out, and they quickly made a plan. Then she rang Paul Lendel.

'I know Mr Lendel. Look I can do no more than apologise. I agree that the recent track record of strikes is unacceptable, which is why Mrs Murgatroyd intervened personally to agree a new deal with the union with a robust arbitration mechanism and a no strike deal. As sales director I will have personal oversight of your account, and you can be assured that hitting delivery targets will be my top priority.'

Lendel was hostile at first. He'd heard all of her excuses before, and was surprised that both James and Brian had gone. But he had a grudging respect for Brenda, and she did her best to reassure him.

'Yes I understand that IPCO supply ex stock but with respect you know that the Murgatroyd product is a better brand and generates better margins for you. To fill the gap

I can offer you the new Excalibur ballpoint in a range of colours for immediate delivery at normal retail but with an introductory five percent bonus to compensate you for the problems we've caused.'

Lendel was impressed by Brenda's proposition. He countered with ten percent of course, but Brenda knew that she'd got what she wanted.

'Come on Paul are you trying to bleed me to death?' she countered. 'Look I'll go to 8% but I want double the standard volume and seven day terms?'

Paul Lendel laughed. 'Bill and I did a lot of business Brenda. So I'll go with that. Just this once mind. But will you make sure you bloody deliver in future? I've had it up to here with British firms that don't deliver. You don't have that problem with the Germans or the Japs.'

Brenda was relieved, and took it on the chin.

'Okay understood. That's great, Paul. Look I do appreciate your help. We'll pick the stock in the morning and get it to the stores starting tomorrow. I'll be down to see you next week.'

She put down the receiver and smiled. She'd shifted the stock, and Lendel's paid on the nail. Mister Whitehill would be pleased.

She sat back for a moment. She was not exactly sure what a 'robust arbitration mechanism' was when it was at home, but it worked with Lendel. My God what a day. Sales Director. Bill if you could see me now. Now what's next? Need to pick Vicky up at some point, get some shopping and make the tea. Then plan how on earth she could balance bringing up a family with a more than full time job. This is going to take some explaining to Ron she thought. It's going to be a more difficult negotiation than with Paul Lendel.

Archie addressed the head office staff, including those from the factory who were at work. Archie introduced Brenda as the new sales director, and Brenda was touched by the spontaneous applause. Archie pulled no punches. The business was in trouble and everyone needed to get stuck in and go the extra mile. He was more cagey about the deal with the Union. Let Derek have his day he thought.

As the day drew to a close Brenda and Archie met for a recap. Ron had picked Vicky up. It was six o'clock already. Fish and chips for tea she thought.

She had a sheaf of invoices, which she handed over to Archie. 'I've been going through the stuff in James' office. I thought that you should see these invoices.'

'My God, what are these?' he asked.

He was looking at the amounts with horror.

'Looks like a Mandy Brice Cooper project. A TV advert. You should see the draft advert, it had King Arthur, Guinevere the lot,' said Brenda.

Archie stared. 'A TV ad? You're surely joking?'

'Nope. I found quotes for repeated slots on ITV as well. Those are just the costs for producing the advert.'

'But that would blow the entire annual marketing budget twice over? What planet was she on?' said Archie.

'Exactly. Worse than that. They were trying to get a celebrity for the voiceover.'

Archie was askance. 'I assume you've shut the project down?'

'Yes, but there are still these invoices to pay. How many more of these are we going to find? I closed out the Wimbledon launch party, but I'm getting pestered by Royal Ascot,' said Brenda.

'I've seen some large hotel bills, not only for James, but also for our friend Brian Biggs. If I see any fraudulent ones I'm going to deduct them from his final pay packet. At least we got hold of his car. He'd have trashed it for sure,' said Archie flatly.

Brenda smiled. 'I'm having the reps together on Friday. Do you realise that they've not been given sales targets this year? They can forget about new cars as well. They're not earning the ones they've got now. One or two of them can follow Brian out of the door.'

Archie asked about Lendel's and was relieved at the answer. He needed upsides in his discussions with the bank.

They needed good news and plenty of it from now on, to restore confidence. Brenda had hit the ground running as he knew she would.

On her way home, Brenda got the fish and chips and with Vicky in bed she talked things through with Ron. Childminders weren't the best way to bring up a child but they had no choice. At least money wasn't a problem now. Ron tried to congratulate her, but it was clear to Brenda that being a second fiddle to his wife was not what Ron had signed up for.

At 7-30am the following morning Derek stood in the factory car park addressing his members with a megaphone, stood on a soapbox he kept for mass meetings.

'Fellow comrades I have here a statement from the Trade Union issued today, which follows on from one issued by the Company Chairman, Mrs Jean Murgatroyd. It reads as follows:

After detailed negotiations between Mr Archie Openshaw, Managing Director of Murgatroyd Pens Limited, and Derek Dawson, Works Convenor of the United Pen Workers Union it was agreed that there would be a full return to work. The Union noted the substantial change in the management structure of the organisation, and the Company statement in respect of its financial difficulties. The Union will actively assist the Company in its' negotiations with the bank to secure on-going financing facilities. Whilst redundancies are a possibility the Company has committed to work with the union to achieve any required staffing reductions by natural wastage as far as is practicable. We welcome the open and honest communication from the Company, and in particular their commitment to the establishment of a Works Council to give workers a say in the running of the business. We hope that this marks a new beginning in labour relations at Murgatroyds leading to a ground breaking no strike deal with profit related staff bonuses. Message ends.'

Derek set aside the note, then changed his tone, becoming less formal.

'Comrades these are clearly difficult times, and I have to say that Jean Murgatroyd, whom I have known for many years, has taken some very courageous steps in recent days, some which have doubtless been personally very difficult. It is incumbent on us to get behind her and offer her our full support. Let's gets back to work lads.'

There was a perfunctory show of hands, and the workforce of Murgatoyd Pens walked through the gates back to work.

The packing line packed the first consignments which left the gate for Lendel's by four o'clock. Ironically the staff worked through the afternoon tea break, with Derek and Barry working side by side on the line.

Jean visited in the morning and toured the factory. Her common touch had always gone down well with the staff, and she was at home on the shopfloor. At lunchtime, in a symbolic gesture to the new Murgatroyd's, she ate fish and chips in the canteen alongside Barry and Derek. The physical closure of the executive dining room took a while longer, but 'them and us' was gone for good.

Archie and Brenda stayed at head office, working their way through a hefty agenda. At five o'clock Archie's PA dropped a large envelope off at the bank as agreed. The 'For Sale' board would go up at head office the following day.

Archie waited until mid-afternoon the next day, and was just about to ring Paul Whitehill when his PA put through a call to him.

'Mr Whitehill? Good afternoon to you. You've received the Business Plan and the revised financial projections? Excellent. Yes, as we discussed we needed to make changes I'm afraid. Never pleasant but we needed to get a tight grip on what was going on in the Company, so the chairman asked me to return as managing director for my sins. As you see we have secured the full support from the trade unions and an immediate return to work took place this morning. As we said the next priority is to get both the overdraft and our costs under control.'

Whitehill had become very worried in the previous week,

but having sifted through the figures and the supporting plan he knew he could sell the proposition to his lords and masters, especially since the projections were somewhat better than Archie had implied previously. Nevertheless he was still going to make Archie jump through the hoops, and played hard to get.

Archie recognised the ritualistic dance and happily played along. 'Yes obviously you will need time to study the figures, I wondered if Mrs Murgatroyd and I could meet with you to discuss our proposals? The day after tomorrow would be fine, at Murgatroyd's, say ten a.m? That's great, it will give you an opportunity to meet Brenda Arkwright, our new Sales Director.'

*   *   *

James meanwhile had gotten over the shock of the events of the previous day. Mandy had been stunned when called in and summarily made redundant by Archie. He had been careful to pack James off site before he talked to her, in a carefully choreographed manoeuvre.

The sale to IPCO had been a certainty she had thought, and it offered both her and James a new life together. But now they were both unemployed. True they both had pay offs but were now uncertain of their personal futures. She headed south on the next available train. As far as she was concerned she would never set foot in that town ever again.

James met her in London the next day. She saw him walking across Kings Cross in jeans and polo neck sweater. They hugged for a long time, then headed for the Company flat, to which they had the only keys. Doubtless Archie would terminate the lease in his cost cutting plan, but in the meantime it was their bolt hole.

They sat on the balcony, and James opened a bottle of champagne. They clinked glasses.

'To our future,' said James.

'You've said your goodbyes then?' said Mandy.

'Yes.'

'How were the kids?'

'I couldn't face them.'

'And Carol?'

'Angry and in tears. Getting divorced from an unemployed husband. What do you expect?' James said, shrugging his shoulders.

'I'm sorry James. I've wrecked it all for you haven't I? You'd have been better off if I hadn't shown up.'

'Don't say that. I don't feel that way. I'll get divorced and marry you. I told you that and I mean it.'

They sipped their champagne in silence for a while.

Mandy smiled. 'So we're ready for the rest of our lives then? Two homeless unemployed lovers in London?'

James tried to smile, but he was clearly depressed and tired.

'Come on James. We're going to be fantastic together. Cheer up will you?' said Mandy, exasperated.

James thought for a moment. 'At Murgatroyd's I'm somebody. I'm James Murgatroyd, one of the Murgatroyd family. Down here in London I'm absolutely nobody. I've just lost the job I wanted. I'm Bill Murgatroyd's son. I succeeded Bill as Managing Director of the family firm. The best job. The only job for me to have. Archie made a total fool of me.'

'Forget Archie, James, he's a dinosaur. So is your mother.'

James shook his head. 'You don't understand Mandy. Archie's a bright guy. He's got the experience which I don't have. He sized up the IPCO deal and found all the holes. I just saw the pound signs. I've been a fool. I should have had him stay on longer when I took over, but I wanted all of dad's mates out of the way. A clean sweep. Big mistake.'

Mandy was concerned. 'You're not thinking of grovelling your way back in are you? Grovelling to Mummy like a naughty school boy?'

'Nope.'

'Then what?'

'I'm going to go away to learn Mandy. I'm going to be the best I can be. Better than my father.'

'What do you mean? I don't understand?'

'I spoke to IPCO. They've offered me a job in their new Far East operation. A new territory for them. They're going to teach me everything I need to know. Then I'm coming back to Murgatroyd and taking back what is rightly mine. I still have my shares and one day the rest will come to me. Five years or ten or fifteen I don't care. One day I will have my Company back.'

12.

New beginnings

The turnaround at Murgatroyd's became a case study of its time. A model for industrial relations. Both the Institute of Directors and the TUC were to incorporate Murgatroyd thinking in their future strategies, but it was too late for many companies.

But things at Murgatroyd's did not go swimmingly all of the time. In the early days there was a redundancy amongst the office staff at headquarters which had mushroomed under James. The sales and marketing team took a big hit, since it was apparent to Brenda that some of the salesman were little more than order takers.

She imposed sales targets, and earnings were heavily linked to performance. Previously bonuses were paid based on Brian's somewhat haphazard assessment system. Brenda now insisted on lower base salaries with much higher volume based commission. Brian had promised them new cars which she immediately cancelled, along with a team building golf tournament which Brian had arranged.

The sales team had no women, and the culture was macho male, reflecting not only Brian's management style, but also James'. She fired two within a month for expenses fiddles, and brought in weekly activity reporting, in which each salesman submitted a report by close of play each Friday, without fail.

A number left within months. Some joined James Murgatroyd, who had handed over a full list of telephone numbers and addresses to IPCO. James was not responsible for UK sales, but took every opportunity to take revenge.

Brenda replaced several with women. They became known as Brenda's babes, because they were not only female, but also young. Some failed of course, but several became the major players in the Murgatroyd sales force for years to come.

For Ron Arkwright however living with a woman who put her career ahead of being a housewife and mother was increasingly unacceptable. If Brenda was away he couldn't visit the working men's club as often after a hard day's work, unless he arranged a babysitter. He could of course have given up work, and let Brenda be the breadwinner, but that was unthinkable. Brenda was late most evenings, and she often collected young Vicky from school and took her back to work with her.

There were an increasing number of arguments, and

one day five years later Ron said he'd had enough. He told Brenda that he'd met someone else. Brenda was deeply saddened, but loved Ron and understood that this was not the life he had signed up for. They parted on good terms, and he remained a close friend of Brenda's and a good father to Vicky.

Archie was in his element and re-energised. He had nothing to go home to but an empty house, so his energies were entirely focussed on Murgatroyd's.

Paul Whitehill visited head office as arranged a few days after James was fired. He had a private meeting with Jean Murgatroyd in which she expressed her personal determination to turn the Company around. Few in the Company knew it but in order to secure the additional overdraft to see Murgatroyds through she accepted a bank charge on Murgatroyd Hall, effectively putting her home on the line. Archie had advised against it, saying that Murgatroyd's was in so much trouble that he couldn't allow her to take the risk, but Jean insisted.

She had grown up in this town, and Murgatroyd's had provided employment to both her and her mother. It had also provided her with a life that she could only have dreamt of as a little girl, and of course it gave her Bill, who in spite of everything she loved and missed every day. No brainer she thought. I have to do this if this is what it takes.

Murgatroyd's came back into the black in 1977, after a tough year of cost cutting and productivity improvements. Archie was visible on the shop floor on a daily basis. He would have an official tour every Monday morning with Barry Handsworth and Derek Dawson.

If Dawson had an issue he knew that he could raise it informally before anything got out of hand. Archie knew that an on-side Derek was a positive asset. If some shop floor barrack room lawyer emerged he would have to deal with Derek, who was not slow to exert his power. That is not to say that Archie found him easy, but trade disputes plummeted.

By 1980 Murgatroyd's was very profitable and a number of key markets were restored. It was growing once more, and although it suffered through the recession of the early eighties it was robust enough to survive and thrive.

The overdraft was paid down, and in the middle of nineteen eighty the bank removed the charge over Murgatroyd Hall, and Archie breathed easier. He doubted that James Murgatroyd would have appreciated that his mother had put his inheritance on the line. Actually he wasn't sure that Bill would have approved either.

13.

2000

It was late afternoon on the day of Jean Murgatroyd's death, and Vicky and Brenda were sitting in the living room of the family home where Vicky grew up. They were surrounded by the trappings of family, so the news which Brenda had imparted seemed all the more poignant. For Vicky it represented a major bombshell.

'I'm sorry Vicky. I've just been rambling on. I didn't really plan to tell you this way. I've meant to many times but somehow, well it never seemed the right time.'

'It's alright Mum. I think I'm okay about it, just shocked,' said Vicky, more stunned than she cared to admit.

'That you have an elder sister who you know nothing about, after your mother went to bed with her boss and screwed her way to the top?' Brenda said, close to tears.

'Well that's rubbish and you know it. You made it from apprentice to managing director, got the Queens Award for Export and an OBE. You didn't get that by shagging the boss. It's not like you to feel sorry for yourself,' said Vicky bluntly.

Brenda smiled a little. Like mother like daughter she thought.

'Oh I guess not. I'm just glad I found the courage to tell you at last. I could never find the words. You're right. I'm just feeling sorry for myself.'

'Does my father know? Is that why you split up?' said Vicky.

'Yes and no. I told him after we got together. It seemed only fair.'

'Then what caused the split?'

Brenda composed herself. She felt relieved that that the guilty secret was shared now.

'Murgatroyd's. I became managing director in 1980 when Archie finally retired. That was the final straw. Ron was a blue collar worker and could never stand playing second fiddle to Murgatroyd's. Thought I should have stayed at home and looked after you. In the end it just got one row too many after one late night too many. Do you remember?'

'A little. I remember him leaving. Gave me that big teddy bear. I've still got it.'

Brenda smiled. 'Yes, I remember him buying it.'

Vicky smiled back. 'When he rings me he always asks about you. Still got a soft spot for you I think.'

'I'm still very fond of him too,' said Brenda. 'I married him on the rebound from Bill. I was very selfish looking back. But he was very kind, a good man was Ron. Sadly we just outgrew each other.'

'I can see how it became complicated. It's remarkable that you and Jean became so close after what happened with Bill. I'm not sure I'd have been so forgiving if my husband played away.'

'Yes. It just happened that way. We were saving a Company together. She was an absolute tower of strength. We worked hand in glove with Archie. They were long days.'

'Did you ever discuss Bill?'

'Well sort of. We never formally buried the hatchet as such. But we got to the point of sharing reminiscences. And we used to go to the grave together. Do you remember that?'

Vicky laughed. 'Going to the churchyard with Auntie Jean, with a bar of chocolate afterwards? Of course.'

'And do you remember, after I split with your father, if I had to work late Jean picked you up from school?'

'Yes, she was so kind to me. And Carol too. Do you think she knows the full story?'

'I'm not sure to be honest. Probably.'

'So what happened to Mandy?'

'James and Mandy are still together. Married over 20 years now. No children though. She paints. Professionally I mean. She kept her maiden name, Mandy Brice Cooper. She was always gifted and bright. In a funny way I liked and envied her. She'd travelled, she was full of bright ideas. She was very refreshing in a small town. I can see what James found appealing.'

Vicky shrugged. 'People outgrow people don't they?'

Brenda sighed. 'Sadly yes they do. Small town Carol Murgatroyd against big city bright lights Mandy Brice Cooper. No contest I'm afraid.'

There was silence for a while as Vicky thought things through, absorbing the news. She was putting on a brave face, but underneath she was confused, lost and frankly pretty pissed off. When something like this happens you feel the foundations of your life shake a little. Surely her mother could have shared it with her sooner? But she felt sorry for her too. She had seldom seen her close to tears, but as the story came tumbling out the hurt and the raw emotions came with it. Then she began to see how pieces of the jigsaw fitted together.

'Now I know why you wanted to go to Florence with me,' she said.

'Well I said I'd been before. I didn't lie to you,' replied Brenda.

'I knew there was something. You cried after we'd seen the David? You were remembering the first time weren't you?' said Vicky gently.

Brenda shrugged. 'Yes of course. We were at an

international sales convention. The affair had only just started. You know what I mean? We were just so into each other, and Florence was stunning. It was Autumn so it was a bit less crowded. We did all the touristy things. It was like one of those long weekends you see in films. We had the freedom to be ourselves; we didn't have to worry about cover stories, or looking over our shoulders.'

'Didn't he think of leaving Jean?'

'Yes. He was terribly torn, particularly after he knew I was pregnant. But he couldn't bring himself to. I was massively, impossibly in love with him. It was so awful.'

Vicky was annoyed. 'What a rat. Surely you hated him after he ditched you and went back to Jean? I know I would have.'

'I tried to. I went on a secondment down south to the international division, had the baby and returned. There were suspicions within the Company, but no more than that.'

'Then you met dad, as you say on the rebound?'

'Yes. I'm guilty about Ron too. I never really gave up on Bill if I'm entirely honest. We worked together, and once or twice there was a split second. I thought he was going to take me in his arms again, but the moment passed and he didn't.'

'That must have been so hard. Surely you could have left town and made a fresh start? I think that's what I'd have done.'

'I thought about it, but this town is my life. And I loved the Company. I was in a well-paid job, especially for a woman, and of course I could work flexibly when you were little. A bit of a revelation at that time. When I see the support single parents get now, it gladdens my heart.'

Vicky smiled. 'I guess we do take that for granted nowadays. Overall it's been a good decision for you, and for us I suppose, in the end. You did your best. But what about the future? Who owns what, at Murgatroyd's I mean?'

'I was coming to that. The future's going to depend on James. He still owns a big stake in Murgatroyd's, but working for International Pen as he does, who knows. Assuming that Jean leaves her shares to James he can do as he likes. Archie left me his shares when he died. He was a lovely man. But it's all going to be down to Jean's will. Now that brings me to the pen.'

Vicky had been cradling the pen during the conversation. It was quite beautiful. Clearly hand made in the factory. 'Yes. You said there were two?' she said.

'They were made long before Bill died. Hand made in the factory by Thomas Camden, and individually monogrammed. The one marked JM has been given to you by Jean. But the other one was given by Bill to our child. It is the only link with her past.'

'Did Jean know about that?'

'I didn't think so at the time, but now I think she must have. When she told me to give her pen to you I was a bit surprised. But she said something like 'Vicky has to know sometime Brenda', with that certain twinkle in her eye, so maybe she understood.'

Vicky nodded. 'So you think that she gave me the pen so that both of your daughters would have a link to the Murgatroyd family?'

'I think that was what she had in mind, but as I say I didn't dwell on the matter. It's possible. Jean and I became quite close, but we both knew right to the end that there were bits in our past which were no go areas. Out of respect of the pain it would cause the other, we just kept off the subject.'

Vicky considered. 'A truce then? Rather than a true friendship?'

Brenda shook her head. 'No. That doesn't do the friendship justice. We had a great respect for each other as people. We had the same values.'

Vicky couldn't get her mind off her unknown sister. 'So somewhere out there is an older half-sister of mine called Jane, with a very expensive fountain pen marked WM? How old is she?' she asked, rolling her own pen between her fingers.

'She will be thirty this year. This month in fact,' said Brenda.

'So she got nothing from Bill but a bloody fountain pen?'

Brenda grimaced and hesitated. 'Well there is something else she gets when she turns thirty, and as things turn out it might complicate things.'

'Go on.'

'Her trust fund matures. She will then own nine percent of Murgatroyd's shares, to do with as she will. That's how Bill set it up.'

Vicky was shocked. How many more surprises? 'My God they're worth a fortune now aren't they?'

'Yes they are,' said Brenda. 'Bill wanted me to have the shares, but I refused. I wasn't going to be bought off with money.'

'Too right mum.'

'So we agreed to put it into trust for Jane until she reached thirty. Archie and I were two of the Trustees.'

Vicky suddenly understood the implications. 'So she is about to find out who she is then? The shares will tell her?'

'She's already been here. I know she has.'

'What? How do you know?'

'About a year ago someone visited the records office in the town saying she was researching Murgatroyd's history. I think it was her.'

'She could just have been a journalist? Who told you?'

'Pauline – my friend on the school governors.'

'The Murgatroyd unofficial archivist. Of course.'

Brenda continued. 'She shouldn't have told me of course. The girl was the right age. Drove a Golf GTI, so she must be doing okay for herself. Asked about the family, the Company, stuff like that.'

Vicky thought for a moment. 'Well it still doesn't prove that much. It could have been anybody.'

Brenda shook her head firmly. 'Except that a week later there was a single white rose on Bill's grave. There's never been flowers on Bill's grave other than those from Jean and myself.'

'Oh I see' said Vicky.

Brenda was convinced. 'Well we'll know soon enough. She will get a letter from Braceby's Solicitors any day telling her the details of her trust fund, and sealed letters from Bill and myself written thirty years ago.'

'So if she didn't know who her mother was last year she will later on this week?'

'Exactly.'

Vicky could see why her mother was so stressed. Telling her was difficult enough, now she would have Jean's funeral to deal with, and then the reading of the will which would decide her future. Then on top of all of that she had to deal with her long lost daughter.

'Oh Mum I wish you'd told me before. I could have

helped,' she said sadly, putting her arm around her mother's shoulder and giving a squeeze.

'I should have. No excuse. I kept putting it off. Then you got older and had the twins to look after, and darling Robert. Sorry. I've been pathetic. Look love I'm so sorry I didn't plan this well, you've had a terrible shock.'

'Don't worry Mum, I'll guess I'll get over it.'

They hugged again as they parted. Brenda headed into the office for a while. She went into the boardroom, and looked at Bill's portrait, an oil painting he commissioned before he died. He was smiling, and Brenda found herself talking to the picture. It wasn't the first time. When she had been lost for an answer she would quietly seek inspiration from the picture.

'It's funny how life goes Bill. I could never have guessed that your wife would die within a week of Jane finding out about her past. I wonder how she will react? What will she think of you and me? Did we do right by her? It was a convenient solution to the problem in having her adopted wasn't it? But looking back I think we took the easy way out didn't we? Well in any event I'm going to have to face the music aren't I?'

She allowed herself to revisit her memories of Florence. She had no inkling that Bill had any feelings for her up to that point. They worked very closely together, and laughed at the same things, but nothing more. They dealt with the major business on the first day, and had dinner together that evening in a good mood. They had secured another major account, and a possible partnership in Russia, almost unheard of in those days.

She dropped her fork and stooped to pick it up, but Bill caught it as it dropped. They were momentarily close, and she smelt his aftershave as he smiled and handed it back. Their hands touched. Bill talked about himself and his hopes for the family in a way he had not before. They compared notes on matters outside of work for the first time. Bill suggested a tour of the sights the following day, and Brenda readily agreed. It was her first real time abroad.

They toured the sights with Bill acting as her guide. He'd been before, but she was surprised at how much detail he'd picked up. She found herself drawn to this cultured and surprisingly funny man. They visited the David last, and Brenda was awestruck at the perfection of this huge work of art. Bill put his arm around her shoulder as they left, but she hardly noticed.

Later, after dinner, she thanked Bill for a wonderful day as they headed to their rooms. He smiled and looked at her intently, as if seeking permission. She took the initiative and kissed him first. She intended it as a thank you kiss between friends, but then found herself kissing him passionately.

'God you're beautiful,' he said simply.

She opened her door and invited him in. Bill wasn't Brenda's first, but here was man of depth with emotions and intelligence. Unlike her previous lovers he made love rather than simply taking pleasure from her. They awoke in the morning as the sun beamed in promising another wonderful day, and made love again. They were living a dream that would become a nightmare for them both, but as they held each other and talked and talked they had no thought for what might happen.

Now all those years later Bill's portrait smiled down at her. The anguish that the affair caused would live with her forever, and now had profound consequences for her children too. She remembered that in the weeks that followed Bill was prevaricating. Would he leave Jean for her or not? Then the bombshell. She was pregnant. Then the final rejection and damage limitation. The adoption, the legal agreements, the trust fund.

She felt herself welling up once more, but stopped herself. Stop feeling sorry for yourself she told herself. You invited him in that night. You made the first move. You were the younger woman who should have known better than to go to bed with a married older man, and your boss to boot.

At home, Vicky spent her evening reflecting and talking it over with her husband. He was as understanding as always.

She was shaken. She'd put on a brave face for her mother, but was in tears as she drove back. She couldn't believe the story. Her mother had been her rock throughout her life, and she felt suddenly unsteady.

She began to feel resentment towards her mother. Then she felt guilty for feeling that. She slept poorly, and awoke in a foul mood, chewing out Robert and the girls at breakfast. She got through her day at work, but after supper the next evening she burst into tears.

Robert held her for a while, until the sobs subsided.

'You've had an almighty shock. You have every right to be upset. Your mother has behaved shabbily, and she knows it. You'll work it out with her in time, because you love each other, but you are entirely justified in feeling betrayed,' he said finally.

Vicky wiped tears from her eyes, Robert donating his handkerchief. She blew her nose and composed herself.

'And Jane? What do I do about my sister, who I've never met?' she asked.

They sat down, and Robert went quiet, thinking. Vicky knew better than to interrupt. Robert thought things through, and wouldn't be rushed. She sometimes found it infuriating, but had come to respect that this was his way. Even more annoying was that he was almost always right when he came to an opinion.

'We should have tea,' he said. Then he headed for the kitchen. Vicky laughed. That too was in Robert's thought process.

Half an hour later, the tea was finished, and silence had taken over. Vicky had given up, and was reading a magazine when Robert spoke.

'You need to be strong for your mother, because the next few weeks are going to be hell. The funeral is going to be a sensitive occasion, and James will call the shots. Your mother likes to have control of a situation, and plans things meticulously. She will not be in control of things this time. She won't like that. James may want to settle old scores. Then of course she has to face the Jane position. Your mother has been good at running a business, and is generally good with people, but she has a side which she keeps hidden as we have seen. The emotions and memories are very raw and painful. She's been in management long enough to have seen it all. But dealing with these painful memories and realities will take her as far out of her comfort zone as it is possible to be.'

Vicky wasn't too reassured. 'So?' she said.

'So she can't fight battles on three fronts, nobody can. She needs to handle the ownership question as well as the emotional issue with Jane. Whatever entirely reasonable grievances you have you need to park those for the time being. She's going to need you in a way she never has before.'

Vicky nodded slowly.

'I know you're right. I've been telling myself similar things for the last twenty four hours. But do you really think James will take revenge? It's such a long time ago?'

Robert shrugged. 'Well I don't know him of course. But the Murgatroyds are a proud family, and being fired by his own mother will have left a deep scar I would have thought. It's bound to. Look I may be wrong, but I think you should prepare for the worst, and make sure that your mother does too. Frankly I don't think you'll need to though. Brenda is a tough lady, and very shrewd. She will understand the risks only too well. She won't necessarily share them with you though. She won't want to add to your distress.'

They left it there. Vicky came to the view that Robert's advice was a sensible basis to work from. She made her boss aware that things would need to be a bit fluid in the coming week or so, although as a local he didn't really need telling.

14.

2000

Brenda decided to write to James in her capacity as Managing Director of Murgatroyd's expressing sadness at Jean's passing, with suitable words about her contribution to both the Company, and the local community. She considered adding something about the desire of staff to attend the funeral, but decided against it.

She knew that the funeral would potentially drag up family issues. Jean's grandchildren would certainly want to come, as would Carol, who had seen far more of Jean than her absentee son.

But James was the next of kin of course. He would ultimately decide on how the funeral would play out, along with Mandy, who to Brenda's knowledge was last in the town on the day she was fired twenty odd years ago.

Brenda awaited a phone call from James, but none came. The funeral arrangements only became clear when Brenda's PA spotted the newspaper announcement. Even then it was unclear whether there was an open invitation to attend the service. It appeared that the service would be in the parish church, followed by burial in the churchyard. There was no more detail than that, and it seemed to Brenda that James' people skills hadn't improved. People kept asking her about the arrangements, but all Brenda could say was that she was unsure as it was a family matter.

As the day drew near she discussed it with Vicky. They decided that the safest route was via Carol. They decided to walk around to her house together that afternoon, and as luck would have it Carol was happy to see them.

Brenda explained her dilemma. Murgatroyd's wanted to pay their respects to Jean Murgatroyd, but she didn't want to re-open old wounds.

Carol didn't need to have it explained. James had given instructions to his PA, and made all of the arrangements, consulting her only on the choice of hymns and readings. She shared the plan for the service, which she had sorted out, James being more than happy to delegate that task. The wake would take place at the hall, and local caterers had been booked by James' PA. But as to who could or would attend either the service or the wake she was none the wiser. She had received a number of calls about it, and was becoming annoyed at the lack of communication. She had phoned James and left a message, but he had not returned the call.

They chewed over the options, and developed a solution.

As James had not arranged much for the service Carol would arrange for the funeral cortege to go via the factory. As James had not specified that people were unwelcome Brenda and older workers would attend as members of the general public and friends of Jean. In the absence of any invitations they would not attend the wake at the hall.

Brenda still had misgivings, but it seemed the best solution, and James could not accuse Brenda of interfering.

Then, one morning, Brenda took an unlikely call from her PA, saying that a Mandy Brice Cooper was on the line.

'Mandy, good morning,' said Brenda, rather at a loss as to how to tone the call.

'Brenda, good morning to you. How's things?' said Mandy cheerily.

'Well of course we are saddened by the news Mandy. How's James?'

'He's fine Brenda, same old James. He's back tonight from the US, the timing hasn't been great. He asked me to ring you to thank you for your letter.'

Brenda decided to just see where this was headed. Let Mandy make the running.

'Not at all Mandy, I'm sure that everyone at Murgatroyd's feels the same. Jean was a one off. I've been inundated with cards and letters. We're keeping them all, to hand over to the family of course.'

'That's fine. We've sorted the funeral arrangements, obviously with Carol's help. I gather the cortege will pass the factory? I'm sure Jean would have wanted that.'

'Yes, the staff want to pay their respects, and we've closed for the day of course. I've had a number of requests to attend the service. The parish church is quite large, would it be okay if they attended? I would want to attend as well, if that was alright with James and yourself?'

Brenda was treading on eggshells, but needed to get things straight.

'Brenda of course you must, and the staff too. We aren't a large family, so the more the merrier. James is catering for a hundred and fifty at the hall afterwards. Quite happy if you want to give out a few dozen invitations to staff who knew Jean. If you could handle that side it would be great. James and I aren't exactly in touch with the area any more are we?'

And thus the arrangements for the funeral were resolved. Brenda began to think that things might work out okay after all.

*   *   *

The day of the funeral dawned dry and quite sunny. As the cortege passed the factory, the staff warmly applauded. There were no tears. This was a person who had led a full life, and was respected. A tough cookie, but capable of touching generosity. The boss, but one of the people too.

The service reflected the woman, Brenda thought. It was particularly touching when the primary school choir sang. Jean had been both chair of governors and an ex-pupil. Ironic too that young Jamie Dawson, grandson of Derek Dawson, was singing. Derek was there too, with both his son and his carer from Millview. Brenda began to feel old, and her mind wandered. She loved her job, and the cut and thrust of business, but could feel herself tiring. Equipment bought using hard won finance in the early days was now old hat, and her team were in the process of ripping out plant which had cost a king's ransom. In her old office the old telex machine and electric typewriter had long gone, and computers were in the process of making the fax machine all but obsolete. She had drawn the line when they wanted to throw out her old Golfball typewriter. She no longer used it, but kept it in her study.

Funerals always make you face up to your own mortality Brenda reflected. In this case the uncertainty over future ownership made corporate mortality a more immediate concern. The early years had been a real battle for survival. There had been times in the recession of the eighties when it had been real backs to the wall stuff. Redundancies had come from time to time, yet the factory now produced far more product, with far less staff, than in 1976. They had reinvented the business several times. Was there anything new under the sun?

Previously so excited by new ideas, Brenda now had a sense that she had seen it all. She chided herself. If you feel that way, Brenda, then it's time to go. Murgatroyd deserves better. As the chief you never lose that feeling of responsibility to the staff. Or maybe that's just your social-ist streak coming out, she thought. Derek Dawson would have laughed at the very thought. Thatcher had broken the trade unions, at least in private sector. Union membership had plummeted, and the Pen Workers Union had long since been absorbed into a larger national union, losing its identity almost entirely. Large scale manufacturing had died in the UK, with millions of jobs shipped off shore. Tony Blair said that manufacturing was the past; we were a service economy now. The man's a bloody idiot thought Brenda.

Her thoughts were interrupted as the first hymn was sung. It had to be Jerusalem.

James then read a prayer, but not a eulogy. He looked much older. but his hair was still black, like his father. Almost too black thought Brenda, sensing artificial assis-tance. Mandy was still pretty. Although a healthy tan, dyed hair and very expensive facials could not entirely disguise the effects of aging.

Carol had arranged for several speakers to provide the

eulogy, including Brenda. She had been unsure as to whether it would be insensitive to the family, but Carol was insistent. Part way through she realised that she was crying. Clearing her throat she continued, tears streaming down her cheeks. The anecdotes and stories were well received, but Brenda realised that she couldn't say exactly what she wanted to say. How extraordinary it was that two people so polarised by an affair could become so close.

Jean had forgiven her without ever saying so specifically. Forgiving her for an affair which had caused her massive distress and heartache. Brenda had no idea about Marjorie of course. That secret was known only to James.

'And thine is the kingdom, the power and the glory, forever and ever... Amen,' intoned the Reverend Parry, bringing the service to an end.

The choir sang Hills of the North Rejoice as they took the coffin to the churchyard. How appropriate thought Brenda.

Vicky took Brenda's arm, and handed her a tissue.

'Well done mum. Nice stories.'

'Blubbering like an idiot,' said Brenda.

'Are you not going to the graveside?' said Vicky, as they turned right at the entrance, instead of heading for the churchyard.

'No. That's just a bridge too far,' Brenda said quietly as they headed to the car.

Vicky thought that her Mother was referring to upsetting the family. But in fact seeing Jean buried with Bill was just too much even now. James and Mandy left the churchyard after the internment. James had said little and shown no emotion throughout. Mandy tried to break the silence.

'This place hasn't changed much. Bit more run down I guess,' she ventured.

'North south divide widens every year. It's even lost its Woolworths now,' James replied.

More silence.

'She was a formidable lady,' Mandy tried again.

'Yes. She was.'

More silence.

'I never really met her in good times. Let's be honest she never really approved of me.'

More silence.

'Perhaps we should have forgiven and made it up when she was alive. Too late now.'

James stopped for a moment and looked intently at Mandy.

'She didn't exactly try did she? Didn't exactly make you welcome for starters.'

'No she didn't. But I bet she was proud of you really. Just couldn't say it. European Vice President of IPCO. Not bad really? Even your dad would have approved.'

They got into the car.

James grunted as he started the car. 'I'm not so convinced. I can't recall him ever having a good word to say about me. Never met his standards.'

'So what are you going to do now. With Murgatroyd's I mean? You should shortly own a controlling stake in the Company. You can do as you like then, daddy or no daddy. Mummy or no mummy. You can even have your old job back, though why you'd want it I don't know.'

'Oh yes, and you'd really want to come back here? I suppose you could paint some pretty northern landscapes. Goes down well with the tourists at fifty quid a time.'

'I think not,' said Mandy haughtily.

'I didn't think so. Look let's get this gig over with shall we. Then we can ponder the future'.

In the event the wake went okay, Mandy thought later. Could have been worse given that she knew so few people. She managed to find common ground with the owner of the local gallery who had heard of her work. Mandy had worked with James for a while at IPCO, but it was never a good fit. So she left and did an art degree in London.

She developed a unique style, assisted both by her tutor and an art group in Greenwich. She took a stall in a local market, much to James' amusement. They were both surprised that people bought her work. Then one day Jean

Jacques Desrantes showed up. He bought two pictures, then returned a fortnight later for two more. When he returned again he asked her to lunch. She said yes.

He was simply gorgeous, and cultured, and ran a gallery in central London. He said that he couldn't understand why she bothered with the market stall. He could sell her work for four times the price in his Bond Street gallery, and had indeed sold the four paintings he had bought in this way.

Mandy was stunned. They agreed to work together in a joint venture, with Mandy supplying the works, and Jean Jacques building the Brice Cooper brand. It had taken a number of years, but they had built a decent business together.

James was away so much with IPCO that she spent a lot of time with Jean Jacques. He was so different to James, who was intensely driven after his failure at Murgatroyd's, which burned inside him even now.

They had married, but she had kept her maiden name. Mandy Murgatroyd sounded too common, although she never said that to James. She wanted to achieve something on her own account. She didn't think that James understood how much being fired by Murgatroyd's hurt her too. It was all about family in his case, and bitterness towards his parents.

She still remembered that awful day when Archie had come into her office with the HR Manager and closed the door. She had not expected it to happen. Looking back she was incredibly young and naive. Archie was always charming and polite, but now this was a very formal Archie. Clinical, by the book.

She recalled her legs turning to jelly and her stomach churning as Archie outlined the position. She couldn't remember the words exactly. References to the need to restore profitability, reduction in overhead costs etc.

He left her with the HR Manager, and she fought off the tears. She remembered Archie shaking her hand, and covering the handshake with his second left hand, becoming fleetingly human again.

'I'm so very sorry Mandy. You are a talented woman who will do well in the future I'm sure. I can only wish you well,' he said.

Mandy had tried hard to despise Archie, but actually couldn't. He was in fact lovely company and a perfect gentleman.

But standing in Murgatroyd Hall she was back, and the ghosts of Jean and Archie were at rest. What now, she thought?

15.

2000

'Dear Jane,

I am the father you never knew. By the time you read this I may well be long gone, so I need to put these thoughts down on paper, as I know I owe you an explanation of my actions. You may think me a coward, for in many ways that is how I feel. A daughter who I would have loved to have cared for and raised as my own flesh and blood. How could I offer you up for adoption? My sin was to fall in love with two women. Jean is my wife of many years. I love her dearly and owe her a debt of loyalty which I regard as unbreakable. Then I met Brenda, your mother, and fell in love once again. She is a wonderful person. I agonised over my duty to Jean as my wife, and to Brenda and yourself. But I made the decision to remain with my wife. I do not attempt to justify my decision, and if you despise me for it I cannot complain. I can only hope that as you learn about Murgatroyd's you will come to love it as I have, and perhaps in time forgive me. I know that I will not see my daughter grow or share in those wonderful experiences

which a parent enjoys so much. I can only hope that I live long
enough to meet you one day and perhaps mend my fences. Jane
you will always be in my heart.

All my love
Bill Murgatroyd.'

As the train pulled into the station Jane put aside the letter,
stood and gathered her things. Why the train she thought?
Because she spent her life driving as she ran her burgeoning
IT Company, and had thought of this trip as a sort of holiday. She changed trains in Leeds, and took another rather
less comfortable train which reminded her of the ones
she had travelled on when she commuted into London.
Glorified cattle trucks. Referred to as sprinter trains, sprint
was something they did not do.

But the rest of the journey was at least more picturesque.
She had seen little of Yorkshire, having been brought up near
Maidenhead. She had visited the year before of course, but
she had driven up, and the train always offered you a different perspective, time to watch the countryside rolling past.

Her last trip had been a kind of reconnaissance mission.
She didn't have all of the pieces of the jigsaw. Only substantial fragments. Then she received a letter from a solicitor out
of the blue. With a full explanation of her parentage. Most of

this she knew. Her adopted parents Andrew and Charlotte Page had never sought to hide that she was adopted, although in the early part of her life she didn't really know what adopted was, and she had assumed that being adopted was completely normal and a completely everyday event.

What difference has it made to my life she thought? Mum and dad Page were her mum and dad, and she was Jane Page, and very happy with that. Jane Murgatroyd? I think not.

As she grew older though, it started to matter, because she began to wonder who she was. Every child has a natural curiosity about where they came from, and Jane was no exception.

Andrew Page worked in computers. Real computers. Ones that filled rooms, with magnetic tapes and lots of flashing lights. His degree in computer science was a first class honours, and they lived in the IT rich Thames Valley. He had worked for IBM and several other household names. So it was to an extent inevitable that she would be exposed to computers from an early age. She was given a pet when she was nine. A Commodore Pet computer. By then she was hooked.

Andrew and Charlotte had met at university, and married soon after. Charlotte was a teacher, and they settled in Maidenhead near their parents. They built their respective

careers, and bought a house well before the rampant inflation of the late seventies. They were comfortably off and
happy, except for one aspect.

Charlotte had miscarried early in their marriage, and
couldn't have children. She longed for a child, hence putting
their name down with the London adoption agency. They
waited years, but nothing happened. They tried to put the
matter to the back of their minds. When Charlotte became
anxious about it, Andrew just said just to be patient; things
would take care of themselves.

Then one day the agency called, saying that they had
a potential match. It took time, and several meetings. The
agency gave limited details, identifying the mother as a
Brenda Arkwright. They never met Brenda, but simply collected Jane from the agency near Green Park.

She later told Jane of that bright summer's day when they
collected her as a two week old baby, and pushed her through
the tourists of Green Park, to admiring glances. She recalled
being asked the baby's name and being lost for an answer.

'Jane Page' said Andrew quickly, sparing her blushes. It
was the first time she had heard the name said in public. This
was her very own child. Complete responsibility for this tiny
human being, and no instruction manual.

Charlotte often dressed Jane in pink. But from an early
age Jane did not conform. Gradually Charlotte relented;

Jane was always a jeans and t-shirt sort of girl. Her mother
soon gave up on pretty dresses.

But now many years on Jane would be dressed conser-
vatively in black. Four days after the first letter from the
Murgatroyd solicitor, another had arrived, explaining that a
major shareholder in Murgatroyd's, the wife of her late father,
had died. As this may involve her inheritance it invited her
to attend the reading of the will, or send a representative.

Jane decided to go. She realised that her shares were
worth a considerable amount, even in a private company,
which Murgatroyd's still was. Looking at its strong balance
sheet and sound profit record Jane was surprised that it had
not been floated in some way or another. Her advisors were
always telling her to float, or court a share sale. Dotcom mil-
lionaires were in vogue, and her company had double digit
growth. But Jane was driven and could see the potential
moving forward, and was not minded to sell her baby or
relinquish control.

She cradled a pen in her hand. The pen. She pondered
as she idly screwed and unscrewed the top. The mystery was
finally solved. On her thirtieth birthday she had received
the missing pieces to the jigsaw. The only previous clue was
this pen. WM. Bill Murgatroyd. So obvious that it was a
Murgatroyd pen and yet she didn't make the connection.
Then last year the visit to this run down northern town. But

she still couldn't be absolutely sure, and her mother was still a mystery to her. Now she had returned for the funeral of a stranger.

She did attend of course. She couldn't really stay away. She checked into the Station Hotel, as she was determined to immerse herself and make the connections with the past. She came up a couple of days before the funeral, and walked the run down streets. The High Street was dying, as so many were and would yet she thought. Her internet based company was going to hasten their demise, she thought ruefully.

She put on her faded jeans and university sweatshirt and walked for miles. She came upon the factory by accident, although it was clearly the only substantial company. A one horse town if ever there was one, she thought. Various Queens's award flags fluttered proudly in the stiff northern breeze. The old river frontage and mill race were derelict. The factory itself was a mixture of old and new. Given the run down area in which it sat, with the old terraced housing still much in evidence, the factory looked starkly modern. The office block in what had clearly been the old mill had been refurbished too.

The branding was also new. Gone was the old Murgatroyd monogram from the pen which she had, replaced by something very contemporary and stylish, yet classy too.

She walked up the hill past Murgatroyd Hall. A marquee

was being put up in the grounds, so she got a sneaky peek through the gates. A stylish house, but of its time, and looking slightly run down. And the garden beyond, once lovingly managed, was showing signs of neglect. Mowers were doing a rush job to tart the place up ahead of the funeral she noted.

She walked further around the hillside, noticing a blue plaque on a cottage advising that Thomas Camden, the co-founder of Murgatroyd's, had lived there. She stopped at the Star Inn for lunch. The same Star Inn where William and Thomas had shaken hands on the deal which had created Murgatroyd's all those years ago. An event recorded on a similar plaque on the front of the pub. The sun was out, so she sat outside. She looked back towards the hall. She imagined young Bill playing in the garden.

Two men joined her outside. They were clearly working on the grounds. She caught odd snatches of their conversation.

From the sounds of it, Jean Murgatroyd had been both respected and feared. Both men had worked at the factory and had known her. They recounted the Christmas parties that Jean attended, and the good works she had done locally. There was a fleeting reference to James, and it became clear that this related to her half brother. He had arrived that morning apparently, and had given them instructions as to what he wanted doing. The absence of the word please seemed to irk them somewhat.

When she left, she headed down past the school, and noted the inevitable extension. The tablet on the wall noted the involvement of the Murgatroyd foundation in its' construction. As she passed by it was playtime, and the children filed out into the sunshine excitedly. Jane smiled. One day. If she ever had time she thought.

Then, as she headed back into town, she cut through the park and saw the bandstand. The Murgatroyd bandstand she noted. The garden was immaculate. A workman was erecting a sign naming it the Jean Murgatroyd memorial garden. He looked up.

'Did you know her love?' he said.

'Er no... no.. not at all.'

'A one off she was. Gave me my certificate when I completed my apprenticeship. Lovely lady,' he said in reply.

Jane smiled and walked on to the church. She had visited the churchyard last time. She took a picture of the grave, but it was now cordoned off. They were readying it for the funeral. So Jean would be buried with her cheating husband she thought bitterly.

The rector saw her standing there, and smiled.

'A big day for the town tomorrow,' he said kindly.

'Yes. I imagine so,' she replied.

'The church is open if you wish,' he said.

'Thanks. It's quite beautiful I recall.'

'Ah, so you've been before then. The Reverend Tim Parry by the way,' he said holding out his hand.

Jane shook it. She didn't really want to open the conversation up, but still found herself yearning for the full picture.

So it was that she went around the church in his company, as his guest. They talked about the church, and the town, and the family. He never asked who she was. What her connection was to the Murgatroyds. Anything like that. He had been there man and boy, although he'd had a spell in Africa, where he'd been a minister in a remote settlement. As they parted he smiled and took her hand in both of his in a gesture of friendship.

'I hope that you find what you are looking for Jane. You would be most welcome at the funeral should you wish. The town is saying goodbye to an old friend tomorrow, and I think you remind me of someone,' he said. Then he turned and went back into his church.

His comment spooked Jane. Did he know who she was? Was he a Murgatroyd spy?

Later that evening she dined alone at her hotel. Fine dining it was not, and the wine list wasn't extensive, although not London prices either. She slept fitfully, her mind churning things over.

In the morning she decided to go. The rector had said it

was a public event, so why not? She put on her black trousers and jacket. As she entered the church, Tim Parry smiled at her and ensured that she was seated rather closer to the front than her status warranted. Again she felt strange, as if she was being managed.

Eventually the service started, and the church was full. Along with those dressed for a funeral there were people in working clothes. Some with the Murgatroyd logo. The Murgatroyd Brass Band played during the service.

'I should now like to invite Mrs Brenda Arkwright, Managing Director of the Murgatroyd Group, to share her memories of Jean with us,' said the Reverend Parry.

A woman had already stood up at the end of an aisle several rows in front, and was walking to the lectern. She knew it immediately, before she heard the name. The resemblance was unmistakeable. Her mother.

She spoke with a northern accent, but not as strong as some. She was a capable public speaker, as you would expect. But she was emotional. Jane was close enough that she could see the tears on her cheeks, running down uncontrolled.

'Jean Murgatroyd was a friend of Murgatroyd's, a friend of this town, and I'm proud to say my friend. Murgatroyd's will miss her, the town she loved so much will miss her, and I will miss her,' she said finally as she collected her notes and walked back to her seat.

As she got there a woman next to her stood and hugged her. A daughter. It must be.

Afterwards as they got up to go, Jane felt emotional. She found herself glad that she had come. She had learned so much about the Murgatroyd side of her family and a little, just a little, about her mother's side.

But she found herself confused too. Her mother had given a eulogy about a person for whom she clearly had a close affection and respect, and yet she had sought to steal her husband and had given birth to a love child. Had Jean known about the affair? Had it all been hushed up, with Jean Murgatroyd unaware of her husband's adultery?

She sat a little too long thinking about these contradictions, and left with the last few mourners. Inevitably Tim Parry saw her.

'A touching service I thought Jane. I'm sorry to use your first name, you didn't mention your surname,' he ventured.

'Page. Jane Page,' she said haltingly, 'and yes it was a lovely service. She was obviously quite a lady.'

'Then Ms Page I hope that you have enjoyed your visit and found it worthwhile.'

'I have indeed. Thanks for making me so welcome,' said Jane, as she shook his hand and walked away. She headed up the gravel path, then realised that she had left her scarf. Damn.

She headed back into the church. As she entered, the Reverend Parry was walking up the aisle. He handed her the scarf.

'Thanks,' she said. Jane paused momentarily.

'Was there something else Ms Page?' said Reverend Parry.

'No. Well yes, well sort of.'

'The answer is yes I do know who you are. One of the few that do I assure you. My goodness you do look like your father,' he said smiling.

16.

2000

The reading of the will was set for 2pm the following day, so Jane had little choice but to stay a further night.

The following morning she went back to the cemetery, with some flowers. She stopped dead in her tracks. There, by the grave, looking at the messages, stood Brenda Arkwright. Next to her was Jane's half-sister, who she now knew was called Vicky. Her two daughters were stood too, looking rather bored with proceedings.

They left shortly after, and she managed to avoid contact.

She was minded to leave her flowers with the others. The headstone had been removed, doubtless for the name to be added. She thought about her visit. She was far from home, and yet much of what was her was actually rooted where she stood, as alien as it might appear.

Now at least I know who my real mother is she thought, and unlike my father she is very much alive. How would she deal with that? The solicitor had made it clear that Mrs Arkwright would like to meet with her, but Jane couldn't face it.

She had re read her mother's letter of explanation last night in the hotel, and had cried. Only now had she begun to realise the carnage that a single love affair had caused.

'Dear Jane,

I am Brenda Lawrence, your natural mother. As you read this I will be approaching retirement, God willing. I hope that we will be in a position to meet and have a relationship in later life, but realise that it may not be possible for you to accept the decision over your future which I have decided that I must make. Your father Bill Murgatroyd and I fell in love. I would not wish you to think that you were the product of a tawdry one night stand. We are I believe still in love, but our relationship is not sustainable.

As I am alone, and wish to remain financially independent, I do not believe that at this time I am emotionally capable of bringing up a young child. I have not sought any financial support from Bill for me, only for you.

I have been a fool but having made my bed I will lie on it and deal with it. I honestly believe that in the circumstances your interests are best served by offering you up for adoption, much as it breaks my heart to do so. I will never forget your birth, and holding you, however brief the time we shared was. Bill has made appropriate financial provision for you, and the accompanying letter will outline these provisions. You will note that I have contributed too, to the extent of my own resources. I wouldn't have it any other way.

Although I may change my view over time, I am resolved that after adoption any further attempts by me to contact you would be wrong. Whether you decide you would like to know me or not, that is your choice and yours alone.

I earnestly hope that when you read this letter you will feel able to contact me, and give me an opportunity to know you, and you me, and your natural father. I will think of you, and pray for you, every day of my life.

All my love.
Brenda Lawrence.'

Brenda Lawrence? Yes of course she later married and became Arkwright, thought Jane as she folded the letter once more. She looked at the freshly dug grave. Then she spoke aloud to her dead father.

'Hi dad. So about these share certificates you gave me? Nine percent of a company which I know nothing about, and still less about the family that I suddenly inherited. Obviously you're well to do you Murgatroyds. You thought I'd need these shares. Paying your dues to me in penance I suppose. Well I've got news for you. I may be only thirty but I have my own IT company and I don't really need the shares. Thanks, but no thanks. I don't want to be a Murgatroyd.'

She turned. Tears flooding down her cheeks once again. She only realised when she got to the gate that she forgot to leave the flowers.

She arrived at the offices of Braceby's Solicitors on time.

She couldn't really understand how the reading of the will was relevant to her, but Mister Braceby had requested that she did attend, and would explain why afterwards. She did not intend to hang around for long either before or after the meeting. She had an open ticket, and would travel back first class to London that evening.

She had spoken to Alex last night. They were booked into the Savoy that evening, and would spend the weekend chilling out in London. Alex always knew what to do.

She was shown into what was clearly the boardroom, and Martin Braceby introduced her to both James Murgatroyd and Brenda Arkwright. James seemed devoid of any real emotion. He seemed to be treating it as simply another business meeting, one of many so to speak, and handed her his business card.

Brenda in contrast seemed tired and preoccupied. The Reverend Perry was correct. Jane looked at Brenda. The forehead, the lips, even the styling of her hair, although coloured very differently, seemed similar.

Jane was very dark however, like her father. As dark as James was before his hairline receded.

Brenda had been sick that morning. She hadn't eaten since the funeral and hadn't slept much either. As she sat there now she wished she had been able to eat some breakfast. Meeting her daughter for the first time since she had given her up was too much on an empty stomach, particularly when she shook Jane's hand, sensing a mood of truculence and indifference in her daughter.

Jane could see that Brenda was struggling to control her emotions, but that was not her problem. Let her look at me, thought Jane. Let her make the first move.

Her thoughts were interrupted by Martin Braceby, bringing the meeting to order.

'Good afternoon everyone. To complete formalities I am Martin Braceby, senior partner of the firm. I believe we're all here? If so I'll proceed.'

'Is Carol not attending?' said James.

Braceby looked up. 'She advised me yesterday that she wouldn't be attending. I'll communicate anything relevant by letter.'

'Oh I see. Fair enough then,' said James, mildly surprised.

Braceby anticipated a follow up. Why had he invited Jane Page to attend?

'I have also invited Jane to attend as she is a blood relative of the Murgatroyd family, and her trust fund has relevance to the shareholding of the Company which is impacted by the will.'

James thought for a moment, but then nodded. Brenda didn't move, just sat with her head lowered, quiet. Braceby started to read at a measured pace, ensuring that the impact of the will was clearly understood.

'This is the last will and testament of Jean Murgatroyd, executed 15th March 1998. I will skip the formalities and read her instructions as follows:

The task which I believe that I need to perform in my will is to look after not only my family interests, but also those of the Murgatroyd Pen Company Limited, its employees and the wider community it serves. As the people of this town helped Murgatroyd's become what it is today I cannot ignore what is for me a significant obligation. I recognise that some will disagree with this perceived obligation, but I am content that my late husband Bill would have concurred.

I will start with some smaller bequests. I have been involved in a number of small charities...'

As Braceby continued Brenda heard some familiar names. St Mary's Church, the primary school, the local Brownie pack. Then the brass band which Jean loved so much.

'And I now turn to the substantive points of my will. In doing this may I first of all say that I am proud of the achievements of my son, James Murgatroyd, and believe that his father would have been likewise. James, I regret that my decision taken years ago has been a major barrier in our relationship. I want you to know how much I regret that. You are my son and I love you. I still however believe that the decision was right at the time that I made it. Your father taught me that you had to make tough decisions, and what I did was as tough as they get. I do however regret the hurt and pain that it caused both yourself and Mandy.

Having considered the matter carefully I leave Murgatroyd Hall and the contents thereof to Carol Murgatroyd. She has lived a difficult solo life, and brought up my two adorable grandchildren alone. I believe that she is entitled to a reward for her sacrifice, and hope that she will use these resources wisely. In addition Carol and each grandchild will receive seventy five thousand pounds.

To my son James Murgatroyd I leave the remainder of my estate, save as for the shareholding in Murgatroyd's. The Murgatroyd shareholding is of key concern to me. James has never accepted the principal that the shareholders have an obligation to the town and community it serves. I cannot therefore hand over a controlling interest to him. I am also of the view that irrespective of previous differences between us Brenda Arkwright has never been adequately financially rewarded for her outstanding contribution to the resurrection of the Company from near bankruptcy and the subsequent on-going development of the business. I believe that it is a fair assessment that without Brenda Arkwright there would not be a Murgatroyd's today. Beyond her salary Mrs Arkwright has never sought nor received any bonus or reward. I therefore bequeath my entire Murgatroyd shareholding to her.'

Braceby stopped, and looked up. There was silence. Stunned silence. Brenda seemed hardly to have heard what was said, her expression was blank.

'To her? She's given the shares to her? My father's lover? That is outrageous,' said James. He gathered his papers and stood glaring at Martin Braceby.

Brenda sat impassively, looking straight ahead. Unable to speak.

'Mr Murgatroyd please take a seat. I have not completed the reading of your mother's will,' said Braceby.

'I won't take this lying down. I'll take this to the high court,' said James.

'That is of course your choice Mr Murgatroyd. Shall I continue, or would you rather we adjourned for a few minutes for you to take advice?' said Braceby levelly.

James sat once more and said nothing.

Braceby continued. 'Thank you. Now er yes, I therefore bequeath my entire Murgatroyd shareholding to her. I believe that in doing so I am honouring my commitment to the town, knowing as I do that Mrs Arkwright is as committed to the above principals as I am. I am of course aware that the shareholding is now held such that no party has overall control. I urge all parties to work together to ensure a vibrant future for the Company and therefore the town.

In closing I wish to pay tribute to my late husband Bill, who was a very special man. Everyone has faults. He was certainly no paragon of virtue. But he was a loving, caring intelligent man with a big heart who I loved dearly. With God's will I hope that we will meet again. Signed Jean Murgatroyd.

Ladies and gentleman that completes the reading of the last will and testament of Jean Murgatroyd. Are there any questions?'

James stood and headed for the door. 'Not at this time. My solicitor will be in touch. Good afternoon Mr Braceby, Ms Page.'

At that he left, closing the door behind him.

Jane stood too. She was embarrassed and confused. Now she was being embroiled in a full scale family feud which had nothing to do with her.

'Ms Page, it would be helpful if I could give you a more detailed briefing of the position, so if I could ask Carla to show you into my office I'll be in shortly.'

She realised that Martin Braceby was trying to pick his

way through the Murgatroyd minefield, rather as she was, and nodded. His PA showed her into another old fashioned office, which overlooked the park. It was now raining hard, and storm clouds were gathering. The Murgatroyd flag over the bandstand drooped in the rain. As she left the office she murmured a rather formal goodbye to Brenda, who was watching her with watery eyes. Brenda attempted a smile.

'Mrs Arkwright? Are you alright?' said Martin Braceby kindly.

'What? Oh, erm, yes,' she said, and took a sip of her coffee.

'Bit of a shock, would you like some water?' he asked.

'Thank you.'

'Take your time Mrs Arkwright.'

Brenda waited for him to pour a tumbler of iced water, then she drank most of it down, taking her time to think. She looked up at Martin Braceby.

'He will hate me more than ever now. This will be total war,' she said.

Martin shrugged. 'Yes, I fear it will, and Jean was aware of that. But her options were not good if she was to achieve her stated aims. With hindsight her decision to put 5% of the shares into an employee share fund may be regrettable, laudable though it was.'

'Because as of now I have 46% to James 40%, with 5% in employee hands.'

'With the balance held by Jane Page, your daughter.'

'So if James buys the employees out and Jane as well he can do as he likes.'

Martin nodded. 'Yes I fear that he can. But take some comfort that his bluster over the will is just that. Jean Murgatroyd was sound in mind and body. He has in my view no legitimate right of challenge to the will. Even if you lose control you are likely to be a very wealthy woman. Some consolation to you surely?'

Brenda laughed. 'Well I guess that's true. Thank you Martin. It should be I agree, but I've never been particularly materialistic. Good news for Vicky I guess. Has Jane said anything to you? Oh look I'm sorry, you couldn't tell me even if she had could you?'

Martin smiled again. 'Yes that's correct of course, but in any event she hasn't given any indication as to her intentions. Bear in mind that she's had a double shock poor woman. Now I need to explain to her the issue we discussed, so that she is clear as to the position. I invited her to attend the reading of the will so you could both meet her, and she can reflect on what is to come. I have simply arranged to meet her after she inherited as per the original arrangements agreed between Bill and yourself.'

'Thank you Martin, I will leave it in your capable hands. It's been quite a week.'

Martin Braceby saw Brenda out. She looked vulnerable. Not the Brenda Arkwright he knew so well.

He went to his office to explain the situation to Jane. In doing it he needed to put his preferences to one side. She needed the facts. He would leave the awkward emotional stuff to her to deal with. He had thought that she might have sought to meet her Mother in private prior to the meeting, but his suggestion was rebuffed by Jane out of hand, even when he indicated that Brenda would have welcomed the opportunity.

He read Jane Page as a tough cookie who kept her emotions well out of sight. Her track record in business was frankly staggering, as was the way of IT companies which hit on the right solution first in a fast moving industry. For most, an inheritance of nine percent of a profitable company like Murgatroyds, was a life changing windfall. But not to Jane Page. She didn't need the money, or frankly the hassle of a family feud either.

He entered his office and sat down. 'My apologies for keeping you waiting. I gather you live in Henley, Ms Page. I don't suppose you know our little town?' he said, to break the ice.

'I visited last year Mr Braceby. I had tried to find out about my natural parents for some time, but I didn't have much to go on. Just a pen which I have had since I was born. Your letter was very specific and filled in the gaps. My thanks to you for that.'

Braceby nodded.

'I should explain that my late father made the arrangements with Bill and Brenda at the time. I am carrying through on their instructions, and of course I handled Jean's affairs too, hence the invitation to you to attend today.'

'I understand that. So where should we begin?'

Martin reviewed his notes. 'Well I gather your natural parents realised that this day would come, and attempted to envisage how this might be handled in as sensitive a manner as possible. Alas Bill Murgatroyd died only a few years after you were born. A heart attack.'

'Yes. I'm aware of that, I visited the grave last time I was here.'

'Whereas your mother...'

'Is alive and well and the current Managing Director of Murgatroyds?'

'Well yes, obviously. You are well briefed I guess. Apologies.'

Jane shrugged. 'I'm in business. It's how I do things.'

'I understand. Mrs Arkwright is keen to meet you, if that is your wish?'

Jane felt herself tense. 'I am considering that Mr Braceby. But first I would like to understand how things work around here, and in particular the shareholding position within Murgatroyd's. You should be aware that I have already received a substantial offer for my shares from International Pen Company Limited. I understand that James Murgatroyd, my half-brother, is also a major shareholder, and that he is a senior executive at International Pen. Obviously I have no real interest in the town, so I was minded to simply accept his offer. I have my own business, so managing a small minority shareholding is of no interest to me.'

Jane left later on that afternoon, thinking back over her trip. She couldn't exactly say she had enjoyed it, but at least she had some answers. And she had seen her mother in the flesh. She would take advice on the valuation of course. US companies would always try to screw you, especially as a minority shareholder. But it seemed James Murgatroyd had a burning desire to win back his family name, and he would get the same price as her. She dozed off reasonably happy that this distraction could be sorted, and that she would have no reason to visit again.

Brenda spent the evening alone. She drank too much, and realised that being made wealthy by the bequest couldn't make her happy. She wanted so desperately to hold her daughter and make it up to her. To get to know her as she did Vicky. They had met only fleetingly, and she was so cold. No sign of any desire for contact. She had hoped that eventually the self-imposed sentence of giving her up for adoption would end, and that Jane would forgive. But there was no eye contact. No warmth at all. Brenda detected resentment and distrust. She left without saying goodbye, and might never visit again. The awful realisation came to her that she might never again see her first born child.

Vicky dropped in later, having completed the inevitable evening ritual that a young family requires. Brenda had phoned earlier with the news. Vicky was as surprised as her mother at the news of the shares, but was horrified that Jane had not chosen to meet her own natural mother, outside of a clinical business meeting. Her anger towards her mother lessened, as she saw how awful she was feeling.

Later on she pondered this in bed with Robert. He couldn't make sense of it either. Finally he said 'but that's women for you,' and turned on one side, snoring peacefully.

Some bloody use you are, she thought, then turned out the light.

17.

2000

'My God. When did this arrive?' said Vicky looking up from the letter.

Brenda sighed. 'This morning. Just three days after his mother's funeral.'

'And he wants to buy out every employee in the share scheme?'

Brenda nodded. 'Every employee. I'm not sure how he got the names without me knowing. The phone hasn't stopped ringing and the local paper has the story. I've just had a call from the Post as well.'

'My God he has gone to town.'

'Just as I feared. It's all-out war.'

Vicky was weighing the implications. 'But it's no use to him without Jane's shares?'

'She left town after the reading of the will. Martin said she was minded to sell her shares to IPCO. Didn't need the hassle. I suppose you can understand that from her perspective.'

'So she hasn't got in touch then?

'Martin says that he suggested it to her, but she hasn't followed up. What she did do was meet James. He met her briefly at the station before she got on the train. My spies have their uses.'

'I can see why you're worried now, what are you going to do?'

Brenda stood and started to clean the kitchen worktop, contemplating for a moment before speaking.

'I don't know what I can do. At the moment I feel totally powerless. I've got a ton of work piling up and I just can't get to any of it. I'm also tired out. I just can't sleep. I'll spend the rest of the day dealing with the press and concerned employees. I've taken the phone of the hook and told head office I'm out of town. James knows exactly what he's doing. He doesn't have a problem in the world. He's running rings around me and is probably enjoying it.'

'But surely when the employees know what he's up to they won't sell?' said Vicky, but as she said the words she realised how dumb she sounded.

'Huh. You might think so, but HR have been plagued with enquiries and the Company secretary reckons he's already had some forms back accepting the offer. People have bills to pay Vicky. Most will take the money and run. There's not much I can do. I'll go on the local telly and do my King Canute bit, but no one will listen to me.'

'I think it's time you got out of town, just for a few days. Why not go to the coast? Just get away? Get some sleep at least?'

'No Vicky it wouldn't work. I'd simply be worrying about the shambles building up in the office. No I just have to tough it out. I've had worse in the early days following James' sacking let me tell you.'

Vicky was unconvinced. 'Mum, you're nearly sixty, you were younger then. You're not superwoman. Take it easy or there'll be trouble. Do I make myself clear?'

Brenda smiled, and took her in her arms. 'Yes my dear, crystal clear.'

* * *

Brenda stood outside the factory, with an ear piece in place. The TV crew had finished the final tweaks, and they were all set. We don't often make the telly, thought Brenda. Would her appearing do any good? Appealing to people's better nature when James had offered each a king's ransom for their shares? She was too old not to be cynical, but she had to try her best.

'This is Graham Symonds reporting on the big local news story of the week. A matter of days after the funeral of Murgatroyd matriarch Jean Murgatroyd we have learned of a takeover bid for the Company by the American giant International Pen Company Limited. Union officials have requested talks with the Company to allay fears that the takeover might lead to the closure of the Murgatroyd pen factory. I have with us Brenda Arkwright, the Managing Director of the Company. Mrs Arkwright do you share the union's concern? Would IPCO's takeover result in the closure of Murgatroyd's?'

He thrust his microphone under Brenda's nose. The disarming chap with whom she had chatted pleasantly ahead of the interview was gone, and had been replaced by the hardnosed investigative reporter.

Brenda had decided ahead of the interview that all she could do was to be honest and up front. 'Well first of all Graham thank you for the opportunity to discuss this crucial matter. I am a major shareholder of the Company, and can confirm that IPCO has made a hostile bid for the Company, but I for one will not be selling, and I urge employee shareholders to follow my lead. An IPCO takeover would I believe lead to the eventual closure of the Murgatroyd site, and be disastrous for the town.'

Symonds took out a paper which he had not shared with her previously. 'But we have a statement from James Murgatroyd, who is the European Vice President of IPCO, and a major shareholder of Murgatroyd's. He says that the

Company is in a shambolic state following the death of his mother, and that he believes that IPCO would bring in, quoting him directly 'Professional management to bring the Company into the 21st century.' Would you care to comment?'

Brenda was furious at the slur. As if Jean had had anything to do with the running of the Company.

'Mr Murgatroyd is mistaken. By any analysis, our financial performance has been outstanding, I would remind you that only last year we received our second Queen's Award for Industry based on our outstanding export performance.'

But Symonds wasn't done.

'Mr Murgatroyd also said that he is launching legal action against you personally relating to a recent acquisition of Murgatroyd shares? He claimed that there were irregularities in these transactions, and that you stood to benefit substantially from these dealings?'

Brenda was stunned. Of all the underhand tactics. Bullshit and innuendo.

'I can only assume that he is referring to the bequest in Mrs Murgatroyd's will of a significant quantity of Murgatroyd shares to myself. If Mr Murgatroyd wishes to take legal action then let him do so. I have nothing to hide and such an action will be vigorously defended. I have always acted in the interests of Murgatroyd's and the wider interest of the town. I will continue to do so. I suggest you seek assurances from Mr Murgatroyd about the future of the Murgatroyd factory.'

'We understand that another substantial shareholder is in negotiations to sell her shareholding to IPCO? Mr Murgatroyd is saying that he expects IPCO to have effective control of the business by next weekend. It looks like it's a done deal.'

'All I can tell you Mr Symonds is that I am a major shareholder and I will not be selling, end of story.'

'So there you have it. However you look at it there are question marks over the future of Murgatroyd's tonight, with James Murgatroyd looking to recover the family business built by his father, Bill Murgatroyd. Mr Murgatroyd said 'I believe that we can restore the business to family ownership and am working with family members to make this happen. I aim to secure major investment from IPCO to restore Murgatroyd's to its former glory, and build a business of which my late father Bill Murgatroyd would be proud.'

*   *   *

Brenda went back inside to her office. She was angry and emotional, but had managed to hold herself in check during the interview. Charlotte her longstanding PA hugged her as she arrived, and made her a strong black coffee. It was as bitter as the taste she already had in her mouth.

How dare he? Scuttles off down south straight after the funeral, then spits out all this drivel and venom in a press release. Bloody coward.

But he was going to win. She knew that and was powerless to prevent it. In the coming days the share sales would trickle through, and control of the Company would bleed away from her towards James.

He would get the Americans to splash a bit of PR cash at the local school, the council, and the hospital. They would schmooze the trade union, which was a shadow of that which Derek Dawson led. IPCO would move production abroad for sure, and simply protect the brand through marketing. A brand which Bill had created, and she had enhanced.

Charlotte reminded her that it was the long service awards lunch that day, an event which she usually looked forward to. In former years she had compèred the ceremony, and Jean had done the presentations. But no Jean this year she reflected sadly.

She addressed the staff during lunchtime in the canteen, presenting the awards afterwards. As she shook each hand she was conscious that many of the recipients had arrived after the change, and had never even met Bill Murgatroyd.

Some of the older members of staff told her that they

would never sell their shares, and backed her stand 100%. But she knew it wouldn't be enough.

Day by day the selling of shares continued, and it was clear that James' generous offer was being accepted in droves.

Lemmings to the cliff edge thought Brenda. She thought about contacting Jane Page directly. She discussed it both with her lawyers and with Vicky, but was struggling to come to terms with Jane's attitude. Surely an adopted child would want to come to know her natural Mother? If only just to understand the situation and heal the wounds.

She kept telling herself that the question of the ownership of Murgatroyd's and her relationship with Jane were completely separate. Yet she couldn't bring herself to pick up the telephone.

18.

2000

Vicky couldn't believe that her elder half-sister had not made any contact with her northern family. Surely she wanted to put things to rights and understand her natural mother's point of view?

She had discussed it with Robert but he was of no help. He said that evidently Jane Page had built her own life and created a company from her own efforts. It was likely that she regarded Murgatroyd's as a closed chapter in her life.

Vicky could not accept that view. Even though she knew that he was probably right. She had a mother to think about too. One who had confronted her demons in the last few days, and was paying a heavy emotional price.

But what to do? She tried to put herself in Jane's position, but it was all too alien to her. She wanted to take more time, but there was no time. The shares were bleeding away to James, and within a week it would all be over.

So she needed to put up or shut up. She didn't ask Robert's advice, she just told him what she was going to do.

And now she was standing outside of the posh office block near Henley, debating whether to go in or not. Eventually she squared her shoulders and strode into the building. She ignored reception and got straight into the lift. She reached the top floor, and asked the first person she met for directions. Adrenaline pumping she reached the door bearing the name, and entered.

Jane was working her way through emails as the intercom buzzed. She didn't want the interruption.

'Yes Misra?' she said, annoyed.

'Hi Jane. Sorry to bother you, but I have a Vicky Bromwell in reception to see you. She doesn't have an appointment?' said a flustered Misra.

'Who? I don't know anybody called...' Jane started.

'Excuse me. No Ms Page can't be disturbed Look you can't just walk in,' she heard Misra say, clearly even more flustered.

She looked up and at that moment a woman arrived in her office, dressed in blue jeans and a smart purple top. Jane stood up to deal with this unknown, and yet strangely familiar visitor.

'Can I help you? Only I don't normally expect people to barge passed my PA,' said Jane, not trying to disguise her displeasure.

'I'm Vicky Bromwell, formally Vicky Arkwright. We've

never met,' said Vicky, thrusting her hand out, determined to be business-like.

Jane shook her hand, the truth slowly dawning.

'So you are?' Jane said, the realisation slowly dawning.

'Your younger half-sister. Brenda Arkwright is our mother,' said Vicky.

'My mother's surname is Page,' said Jane.

Jane didn't expect this. In her own mind she had decided to sell her shares and box off her Murgatroyd family history, which after all she had done perfectly well without. She didn't count on the stubborn northern grit of the Arkwright clan.

Vicky's blood was up, and she had decided that the only option was to attack.

'Well that bit's true of course. You've never met your natural mum have you, not properly anyway,' she said.

'No. She dumped me at birth,' she replied.

'No Jane, that's simply not the case. She was the one that was dumped. She fell in love but Bill Murgatroyd dumped her. He decided to go back to his wife, leaving mum high and dry and pregnant.'

'That's not what...' Jane started.

'What James Murgatroyd told you,' said Vicky, interrupting.

'Yes' said Jane.

She motioned Vicky to sit, but she stood her ground. Jane

admired the guts it took to march into a stranger's office. Vicky started calmly. 'James Murgatroyd only tells you what is in James Murgatroyd's interest. He's a pretty compelling liar, I'll give him that. He's currently launching a disgusting smear campaign against my, well our mother. Have you seen the papers?'

'Look I don't look at the papers, and I'm afraid I have a meeting in ten minutes.'

Vicky was incensed. 'Ten minutes? Forgive my French but ten fucking minutes for a saga that goes back thirty years? I thought you were, to quote Hello magazine, 'One of the brightest business minds of her generation'.'

'Look I don't have to take this shit from you. You come bursting into my office without an appointment and proceed to lecture me when you don't have a clue how I feel.'

'Don't come the big sister crap with me. Do me a favour. Don't you normally get both sides of the story before you make a decision? Isn't that what one of the brightest business minds of her generation would do?' Vicky stood defiantly.

'Yes.'

'Then why not cancel that meeting and give me the chance to explain?' said Vicky arms folded.

Jane shrugged and conceded. 'I guess you have a point. Look, take a seat. I'll get Misra to make coffee.'

'Could I have tea. With milk and two sugars please?' said

Vicky, not meaning for it to come out like that, but her blood was still up.

Jane smiled. 'Tea, with two sugars. Of course.'

Tea arrived, with double chocolate chip cookies. One of Jane's vices. As they sat talking Jane realised that they were somewhat alike physically. Both on the plump side, but comfortable in their skin. Same brown eyes. But Jane was a Murgatroyd. Jet black hair, whereas Vicky was fair like their mother. Vicky told the whole story as she knew it. It took some time, but Jane listened well. By the time Vicky was finished she felt drained.

'So you see it's a very long and complicated story. The top and bottom of it is that James never forgave his mother for sacking him and appointing first Archie then mum in his place, and now he has the chance for revenge he is determined to take it, whatever the damage to the Company or the town.' Vicky sighed and took a sip of her tea.

Jane nodded. 'Okay. I see all that.'

She paused to reflect. Then continued.

'But see my point of view too. This is none of my business. I have a block of shares I don't need, in a company I don't know, and I've been made an offer which on any analysis of the figures is extremely generous, and I'm so damned busy with this place I can't even think about a holiday, let alone anything else.'

Vicky laughed, the tension between them easing a little as they munched the cookies.

'Now you sound like mum. She hasn't had a holiday since I turned sixteen. I've just given up. She's a control freak, has massive to do lists which drive you nuts and she gets involved in every detail of the business. I found her re-arranging the flowers in reception last week. She drives the staff bonkers.'

''Ah, well...' said Jane haltingly.

Vicky laughed one more. 'Come on big sister... fess up!'

Jane smiled. 'Misra says I drive people nuts too. Well I am getting a little better. I did at least get a break last year. I came up to your place as a matter of fact.'

'Mum knew. You put flowers on the grave. She guessed,' said Vicky.

There was an uncomfortable pause.

Vicky spoke softly. The bitterness of an hour ago was now gone.

'It must have been rotten Jane. When mum broke up with dad it was rotten. It must be so much worse not know-ing who your parents were.'

Jane smiled. 'Yes. As much as my adopted parents have been fantastic, there's always been the nagging question. Last year I decided to do something about it. But I just didn't have much to go on. Just this pen, and a place of birth.'

She held up the Murgatroyd pen which took pride of

place on her desk, just in front of a picture. The only adornments on an otherwise empty desk.

Vicky took out the other from her handbag. 'Snap,' she said.

'My God. Where did you get that?' said Jane.

'Jean Murgatroyd left it to me as a gift when she died,' said Vicky.

Jane placed them side by side. They were identical, save as for the initials. She looked up at Vicky.

'So there were two then. His and hers. Bill and Jean. They are absolutely beautiful aren't they, the enamelling is exquisite.'

'Individually made in the factory workshop. Thomas Camden was William Murgatroyd's partner. He made the pens for Bill and Jean I understand. I was so touched that Jean gave it to me, and mum was moved too. It was like the final healing of the rift, the final forgiveness of the affair between Bill and mum.'

Vicky went for a tissue. Seeing the two pens side by side was somehow too much.

Jane was puzzled. 'But surely they'd sorted that out previously, years ago?'

'No. It seems not. When Jean fired James she just agreed with Mum that business was business, and Murgatroyd meant so much to both of them that they parked their differences and worked together. It seems they did precisely that. There was an unspoken truce which meant that they never discussed the hurt which Jean felt and mum had caused.'

'So they just had common cause and worked together? Extraordinary. I'm not sure that I could have been that forgiving, on either side?'

Vicky smiled. 'Both Jean and mum are, or were, extraordinary people. Women so much ahead of their time. I must admit it seemed strange to me at first. How do you become friends with your late husband's lover? It makes no sense.'

Jane thought for a moment. 'I suppose if you work so closely with someone over a long period it becomes like a marriage.'

'Well that's why mum and Bill got together. Worked together, played together...'

'Then slept together,' interjected Jane.

'Fell in love. True. But there is one significant thing you don't know. Jean was bisexual apparently, she had a female housekeeper Marjorie. She had an affair too.'

'A lesbian relationship? My word.' said Jane surprised.

'Yes. It was a closely guarded secret. Mother only knew because Bill told her when he was trying to justify his behaviour. We're a bit more liberal these days. But then, well. So Jean couldn't hold too much of a grudge about Bill playing away could she?'

'But it was still a tawdry affair between a boss and one of his managers,' said Jane.

'It wasn't so tawdry Jane. I notice you went to Florence last year? Says so in one of the magazine articles I read?'

'Yes, a trade show. Loved it.'

'So did Bill and mum. It was where they fell in love. Both away from home, in one of the world's most romantic places? Some free time to take in the sights? I'm not condoning it, but don't think it was a fling with the boss. Mum loved Bill and wanted to be with him. Bill agonised when mum became pregnant, but decided to stay with Jean. It was devastating for mum. It wasn't only her life, but also her career was on the line.'

Jane was moved by the story, but couldn't entirely let go of her anger. Knowing the facts didn't change what happened.

'Look Vicky I haven't found this whole thing very easy, as you'll imagine. This Murgatroyd thing is a lot of hassle which doesn't concern me and I just don't need it. My life's complicated enough right now. But obviously this bloody shareholding I've inherited means a lot more to Murgatroyd's than it means to me.'

Vicky put her hand on that of her sister. The first physical contact between the two.

'I can understand that you don't want to get involved. But

I'm surprised you didn't want to meet mum. You went to a lot of trouble to find your parents last year. Now you have the opportunity to finally put the matter to rest and you left town without seeing her? I don't get that bit?'

Jane smiled, and wiped away a tear, messing up her mascara. Vicky smiled back.

'I chickened out,' said Jane, blowing her nose.

Vicky laughed. 'Chickened out? You don't strike me as the type to chicken out on anything? 'One of the brightest business minds of her generation' doesn't chicken out.'

Jane flared. 'Don't keep throwing that at me. Frankly that article did me no favours.'

'But was that really the reason?'

Jane pondered her answer. 'Well in truth it was because I'm really angry with both of them. The letters, the whole way they structured my future, all so regimented and clinically planned so that they got what they wanted. Bill kept his position in the community, dodged the high profile scandal in the town and kept his wife.'

'And mum? What do you think she got out of the deal?' said Vicky.

'She got rid of an inconvenient child. She got to do what she wanted. She put herself first. Ahead of me. That's plain selfish and very hard to take.'

'She would agree with you.'

Jane looked up. 'What?'

'Look she only told me about you when Jean died. So you're not the only one coming to terms with what went on thirty years ago. She told me the whole story. She takes exactly the view you take.'

'Oh…I….'

'And she's as guilt ridden as hell about it. She's lived with that guilt for thirty years, and has been desperate to sit you down and tell you so. Now she's in bits because you didn't give her the opportunity. It's not about Murgatroyd's, this whole sorry business. Yes it would break her heart to lose her job, after all she has achieved over the years, but actually it's you she wants, actually needs, to make peace with.'

Jane shook her head. 'Well I don't let people off that easily I'm afraid. I'm sorry. Why the hell should I?'

'I think I can understand that. But you should put yourself in her shoes. It's 1969 and she is as old as you are now, and she falls in love with her charismatic boss, with whom she works very closely. They've gone away to Florence, a wonderfully romantic city, and she thinks that she has everything she wants. You're a small town girl who started as an apprentice, and now you're a senior manager at the height of your career. In 1969 that's a real rarity, you're ahead of your time. Woman are thinking of burning their bras, but haven't lit the match yet.'

Vicky continued, dabbing her eyes with a tissue as she did so.

'And you're in love, very much in love, with a married man whose wife is sexually disinterested. You believe it's meant to be. You expect him to return from Florence and leave his wife. Then it all goes wrong. You find you're pregnant and he won't leave his wife. You are suddenly so alone, having been so much in love days before. Bill stood by mum as regards her job, but put her in a position where she pretty much stood to lose everything.'

'A long way to fall I'll admit.' said Jane sadly.

'Exactly. To be fair to Bill, mum said that he never once threatened her career, never urged her to leave, but the sentence she has served for her crime against you was a pretty long one, with no early release.' Vicky shrugged and sipped her tea once more.

'She had no choice but to work with the man she loved, on a day by day basis,' said Jane finally.

'And of course all of the impossible choices were hers. Bill had his fling with the younger model, and all he had to do was to sign the cheque. Easy really.'

Jane pondered. 'So she had a choice of keeping me as a single mum, an abortion or adoption.'

'I'm not sure which I'd have chosen, but I think she probably made the best decision of the lousy options she had, but I could well understand you thinking differently. I think it's been made more difficult for mum because she's kept it a secret all these years. To put it in a nutshell she just wants to say sorry to you, and you haven't given her the chance. She was a fool. No doubt about it. But I don't think she tried to trap Bill, and my God has she paid a price.'

Jane nodded. 'So when did you find all this out?'

'Only when Jean died. Mum told me everything, and gave me the pen. It shook me to the core I'll admit. I felt betrayed to be honest. Mum and I are so very close. I couldn't believe that she hadn't told me before. So I suppose I get a little of how you feel.'

Jane looked up. 'Betrayed? Yes. That's exactly how I feel.'

*   *   *

Brenda sat alone in her office. The local paper on her desk. Headline news. She turned the paper over, as if to shield her from its bitter words. It was late and even Vicky was out of town. She was very alone.

She spoke aloud to herself, and perhaps to Bill.

'Restore it family ownership…irregularities in share dealings. Bring in professional management. What a pack of lies. What absolute rubbish. Maybe Vicky's right and I should get out of town. You've got to hand it to James and Mandy, they're tying me up in knots.'

James Murgatroyd meanwhile was back in his Docklands flat talking to his boss, the CEO of IPCO.

'Look Bob it'll take a few more days, but the deal is virtually done. We've got enough of the employees to sell, and with my half-sister's nine per cent in the bag I'll have control by the end of next week.'

'From our perspective this ain't too pretty James. The PR is pretty bad, and I gotta letter from the Union demanding a meeting,' Bob's mid western drawl interjected.

James paced the room as he spoke. 'Yes I know I said that I would have control of my mother's shares too, but the minority shareholding won't make any difference to IPCO and Arkwright will sell once she realises the game is up. She's sixty. She'll retire gracefully. Look I know you don't want bad publicity. I'm handling that personally. We'll get her a CBE or something, tea with the Queen, whatever. As for the unions, they're noisy but they don't have much power these days.'

'That's as may be James, but I gotta letter from the council too. They want assurances about the future of the plant. Assurances that you know we can't give. This whole deal looks like hassle we don't need right now.'

'Look I'll handle it here Bob. Just fax it across and I'll

deal with it. The factory here is a joke. We move production to Hatfield to boost margins and leave the R & D and sales function here to keep the locals happy. Frankly you're doing the locals a favour. Globalisation is coming and Murgatroyd's will only survive as part of a volume player with access to third world manufacturing, you and I know that. At least I'm family. Let's keep our nerve. It will be done this week.'

'Okay James. I'll stay with it, but let's get it done huh?' said Bob wearily. He'd had too much of the Murgatroyd feud already.

'Okay Bob, I hear you. I'll get it done. Love to Dolores'

James put the phone down.

'Bloody Yanks. First sign of a problem and they shit themselves.'

Mandy looked up from her magazine and shook her head.

'Well you told them you were getting your late mother's shares old man. Bit of a balls up that. Now the deal looks and smells of hassle. And those radio interviews have backfired spectacularly, what on earth possessed you? Caused big trouble at 'tut' mill old boy. They'll rally around the local girl now, you just see if they don't. Bloody PR disaster.'

James snarled. 'Murgatroyd is mine by birth right, I'm just taking back what's mine.'

Mandy had heard enough. 'You're obsessed James. You're VP of a major US group, a highly successful businessman, but you're obsessed with the past. A tiny little company in a grimy little shit heap of a town amidst the dark satanic mills of the frozen fucking north. Give me strength.'

'But it's my birth right, not Brenda fucking Arkwright's,' James snapped.

Mandy softened. With James in this mood you had to remain calm. She tried, but the words came out all wrong. 'Don't you think that you're being rather pathetic James? You're behaving like a little schoolboy whose mummy took his train set away because he's been naughty. That's pretty much it isn't it? Frankly I've had a bellyful of this in the last 25 years. I've had enough. If you don't mind I don't want to hear about Murgatroyd's anymore. I got fired too remember? The difference is that I've moved on and you haven't.'

19.

2000

There was no easy way to do it. Nowhere seemed right to Vicky. Robert suggested neutral territory. The diaries of two managing directors at a few days' notice were predictably problematic, but Vicky knew that Brenda had to make this meeting.

Vicky also appreciated that the topics of the relationship and the shares must be kept separate, although she personally couldn't see how. But it was one of Jane's conditions.

She decided she had to be devious, and came up with a scheme. She told her mother that she had booked a long weekend for them both in Kent. Then she pondered a suitable venue. She booked a little cottage for them at Ightam Mote.

When they got there, Brenda seemed to have relaxed at last. They had visited Sissinghurst the previous day, and been to Rye too. They bought presents for the girls, and behaved as a normal mother and daughter would for once. They didn't do this often enough, but the combined pressures of Brenda's job and Vicky's young family didn't make it very practical.

They had lunch, and headed back to the cottage. As they got to the gate a grey VW Golf pulled into the car park. Jane got out and smiled at Vicky. They hugged briefly.

'Mother I'd like to introduce Jane Page,' said Vicky.

'Mrs Arkwright, pleased to meet you,' said Jane.

They shook hands. Brenda was truly lost for words. Her mouth was slightly open, as if she meant to speak, but nothing came out. Vicky took command.

'Let's go inside. I'm glad you could make it Jane, mum and I have meant to come here for a while,' said Vicky, keeping the conversation light.

They sat in the sun-filled sitting room, and Vicky made the tea. She kept the conversation sociable, and Jane played along. Brenda did her best, but she still seemed shaken. Vicky had bought double chocolate chip cookies, Jane's favourite, and chocolate shortbread, her mother's. At least they had something in common.

Finally, when they had run out of niceties, it was time to face the music. This was the tough part, because Vicky had no idea how you did this. She spoke, haltingly at first, then with a little more confidence. She had rehearsed the words in her mind repeatedly.

'Mum, Jane, let's get to this, why we're here I mean. Firstly mum I have to say that I was stunned when you told me I had an elder sister I knew nothing about. It was as if an earthquake had shaken the roots of my life, and our very close relationship. But I've just about come to terms with it. Now I need my sister and my mother to at least try to put the past to rights. I went to see Jane, and she agreed to meet. I can see that she has been deeply hurt by the decision you made to have her adopted, and has every right to feel betrayed. I'm sure that anybody would. But it's been a very long time now, and I think it's best for you both to talk things out. I've put you together, now I'm going to leave you to it. Before I do though I've agreed with Jane that this meeting is not about Murgatroyd's, or the shareholding. Jane must make a separate and distinct judgement about her shares, based on her own best interests. Jane are you okay with what I've said?'

'Yes. It's fine Vicky. What about you er... Mrs Arkwright?' said Jane.

'Brenda, please Jane. Well yes it seems Victoria has a plan, so let's talk.'

Vicky hugged them both, and left them alone. She walked around the grounds, her eyes stinging with unshed tears. This was hard, so very hard. Victoria has a plan. Her Mum only called her Victoria when she was vexed.

Back in the sitting room Brenda and Jane were trying to work out what to do next. As far as Jane was concerned she had agreed to meet her mother because Vicky had asked her to, and it seemed the right thing to do. Hear what her mother had to say. For Brenda it was more difficult. She had nothing prepared. But she had thought of what she might say to her long lost daughter many times.

'Well that told me didn't it? Forgive me but I'm not used to my daughter telling me what to do,' she said.

Jane laughed. 'I'm getting used to it. She gate crashed my office.'

Vicky left it an hour, then returned in trepidation. Things seemed calm, they were making small talk once more.

Jane left shortly after. She shook Brenda's hand, and Vicky saw her out. She hugged Jane as she reached her car.

'Thanks Vicky. It was good to talk, 'Jane said, a quiver in her voice.

'I'm so glad we could make it happen,' Vicky replied.

'I've agreed to come up next week to see the factory. I'm going to decide about the shares on a purely financial basis. Being fair to both sides as I see it.'

'That seems very fair Jane. I'll look forward to it. I'll book you a hotel if you'd prefer, but Robert and I would be delighted to have you. Do what you feel most comfortable with.'

Jane smiled. 'That's a nice offer Vicky. I must admit that hotels are pretty soulless. I'll stay with you if I may.'

They hugged once more, then Jane drove off. That's progress, thought Vicky.

She headed back in the house, but her mother had gone out of the back door and was nowhere to be seen.

Brenda wasn't sure how things went, and couldn't face the questions which Vicky would doubtless ask. She walked around the grounds of the house once again. It began to rain, but she couldn't bring herself to go back to the cottage.

On the one hand she was delighted to have had at least one hour of conversation with her eldest daughter. But on the other the absence of any thinking time meant that she had had difficulty framing her explanation. All of the guilt she felt came tumbling out, in an incoherent jumble. Jane had sat expressionless and seemed unmoved.

They had moved on and discussed Jane's career in business. Brenda had of course researched this in some detail previously, and there was a lot more common ground. Jane became animated and articulate. She was so like Bill. Dark haired, same ready smile, same furrowed brow when thinking. Same passion and intensity. Jane knew where her business was going, and how she was going to take it there. In every aspect she was impressive. This was Bill's daughter. It made it more difficult somehow.

They had discussed Bill briefly, but Jane moved off the topic quickly. It seemed clear to Brenda that Jane was reluctant to deal with what she obviously regarded as a closed chapter of her life.

Brenda rationalised and realised that she had wanted far too much. 'I forgive you' was not going to happen after a one hour meeting, and yet she felt so empty. She had explained about the adoption; how and why she, and she alone, had reached the decision.

Jane had clearly made up her mind before the meeting, which she had only agreed to because Vicky had demanded it of her, and there was obviously a bond there which Brenda found touching. They had parted with a handshake. Much as Brenda wanted to hold her daughter it was clear that it would not be appropriate.

The rain was falling steadily now, and Brenda could feel the water dripping from her clothes. She had come out without a coat and was soaking wet. Well at least I'll see her again, she thought. At least Jane had agreed to visit Murgatroyd's to give her mother the chance to convince her that retaining her shares was in her best interests.

She wasn't sure if it was rain or tears that ran down her cheeks, but she made no attempt to wipe them. Vicky appeared with an umbrella, and they went back to the house. She allowed Vicky to run her a bath, and she had a long soak. A large single malt whisky warmed her inside, and she felt better. She nodded off in front of the fire. Much needed sleep which had eluded her recently.

Vicky cooked, and they ate in silence. She said nothing

about the meeting, and neither did Brenda. Finally, when dinner was finished, Brenda was ready. She asked casually if Jane had said anything as she left.

'Not really. Only that she's coming to see the factory. She's staying with Robert and I,' said Vicky casually, as she cleared away the dishes.

'Really? Staying with you?' said Brenda, with an obvious tone of surprise.

'Yes. I offered and she accepted. Frankly the local hotels aren't up to much these days, and it will be nice for the kids to meet their Auntie Jane.'

'Oh I hadn't, well, I suppose I hadn't thought of that,' stammered Brenda.

'She's my sister and their auntie too mum,' explained Vicky, coming back to the table.

'Well I suppose that's something,' said Brenda.

'Rome wasn't built in a day mum,' said Vicky.

'True,' said Brenda, pouring more Scotch. Vicky handed over her glass.

'Look mum you made progress today. You met your daughter and she's agreed to discuss the share question and not just simply sell to James. A good day's work in my book.'

'Yes I know. It's just that, oh I don't know.'

Vicky interrupted. 'She didn't throw herself into your arms and say she forgives you?'

'Well no, I don't mean...'

'That was never going to happen mum. Jane's deeply hurt and confused. She might be bright but she's still trying to come to terms with things. You must give her time. I think that you got all you could from today, and I'll admit that when she agreed to stay with us it was a surprise. Not a bad start considering'.

'I guess,' said Brenda unconvinced.

Vicky laughed. 'When I was younger, you always accused me of impatience, now look in the mirror. The next meeting will be better. You are playing at home and will be talking about the business you built and are rightly proud of.'

'Yes. I know. And we seemed to have more in common when we talked business.'

'There you are then. Look, remember when you described to me the meetings you had with the bank in the early days, when you had to convince them to stay with Murgatroyd's rather than pull the plug?'

'Well it was more Archie really but yes.'

'Well I think that you've just got to treat Jane as an investor. Forget that she's your daughter.'

'Yes,' said Brenda.

There was a pause. The silence punctuated by the grandfather clock.

'She's so like Bill,' said Brenda sadly.

'Yes,' said Vicky. 'I've seen the picture in your office'.

'No, not only does she look like him, she also has the same mannerisms. It makes it tougher somehow.'

20.

2000

Jane travelled up from London by train. She got through a lot of work for the first couple of hours, and then allowed herself to take in the northern scenery. It was beautiful in its way she thought. She was strangely looking forward to returning. Vicky was so very different, but yet great fun. Her direct style matched her own. She quite liked the idea of meeting her little nieces too.

On the other hand, she found Brenda very odd. How this lady could have rebuilt Murgatroyd's was beyond her. She was diffident and uncertain, at times incoherent. But Jane had read the business plan that Brenda had written, and found it imaginative and professional. Keep an open mind Jane, she thought.

She arrived at the station. It could have been awkward, but Vicky hugged her straight away. It was as if they'd been sisters all of their lives, rather than a matter of weeks. In one way Jane found this familiarity difficult, but it was just 'Vicky being Vicky'.

They picked the girls up from school. They didn't in any way find it odd that Auntie Jane had just walked into their lives from nowhere, so Auntie Jane got a hug, whether she wanted one or not.

Jane found the instant love and familiarity disconcerting, but rather sweet. She had always found it difficult to drop her guard, to be herself.

They got back to the house, a three bed semi on a smart modern estate. Then Robert arrived home. Big slobbering kisses from both girls, who clearly loved their daddy.

Jane found herself envying the loud, tumbling fun and disorder of Vicky's life. A life which she could never replicate, and probably wouldn't want to either. The close unconditional love that the family had for each other contrasted with the more reserved adult relationship she had with her own adopted parents.

After a chaotic early evening with dinner and bath time she read a bedtime story to the girls. She realised that she'd never done that in her life before. The Page family was small, and she was an only child used to very adult ways from an early age. A very structured upbringing, but still a loving one none the less.

She found herself admiring Vicky's ability to juggle family life with work. She found her own business life difficult to schedule, but Vicky had to cope with whatever chaos two children could bring. Jane pondered whether she actually had a family life at all really. The business seemed to take every waking hour that she had.

Robert headed out to his local drama group, leaving Vicky and Jane to relax with a bottle of wine.

Vicky was no mug in terms of people management thought Jane. Most people would have tried to pressurise her over the relationship with her mother, and the question of the shares. She was grateful to her younger sister for leaving be. Some might have used the evening to push things in the right direction, but not Vicky.

After a second large glass of red Jane's curiosity got the better of her, and she asked Vicky why she had kept off the subject. Vicky smiled, her sunny open hearted smile.

'I'm not that stupid Jane. You're too bright to fall for that, and you'd see through it in a moment. And I don't think that you're the sort who likes to be handled anyway. I know what I'd like you to do, but it's your decision entirely. I love mum very much, so I got involved because she was hurting. I've given you both the opportunity to talk things out, but now it's up to you both to sort things in whatever way you will. You're both grown adults, and don't think that I've not been hurt by her deception. Far from it. When she told me about you I was gobsmacked. How could she have kept that from me for all those years?'

Jane nodded. She rather wished she hadn't asked. She thought about what to say next, but struggled to frame a response.

Vicky put her at ease. 'All I would say is that whatever decision you make I'd like us to be friends, if you'd like that. It's lovely having a big sister.'

Jane smiled. They left it there, Vicky turned on the TV.

Vicky found her sister equally puzzling. She's great company when the ice maiden melts she thought. Just puts up a good front most of the time. It was so funny when Katie asked if her Auntie Jane could put her to bed. She coped pretty well considering. She does have a nurturing side she thought. She just doesn't show it too often.

The following morning Vicky dropped the girls off at school, then the two women went for a walk above the town for an hour or so, before going to Murgatroyd's.

They entered the boardroom together. Jane's eyes were drawn immediately to the picture of Bill.

'Handsome bastard wasn't he?' ventured Vicky.

'I suppose so,' replied Jane.

'You do look like him you know? Both dark, same hair line, shape of face,' said Vicky studying the picture, then Jane. 'Sorry you probably don't want to hear that.'

'You're dead right, I don't, although I must admit I do look like him. It's uncanny.'

There was an awkward silence, but at that moment Brenda arrived. She hugged Vicky, then shook Jane by the hand.

'Ms Page. Thank you for agreeing to come. I hope that Vicky and Robert are looking after you okay?' said Brenda brightly, if a little formally.

'Yes thank you Mrs Arkwright. I've been made most welcome thank you.' Jane reciprocated with the niceties.

Vicky laughed at the formality of it all. 'Look at you two. It's Jane and Brenda. None of this Ms Page crap.'

Brenda and Jane laughed.

'And mother we've agreed this is a business meeting about Murgatroyd's.' said Vicky,

'Thank you Victoria, I think we do understand that,' said Brenda, more tartly than she intended.

'Okay. I'll leave you to it then. I'm off to work, no peace for the wicked. Goodbye Jane, Robert will pick you up and take you to the station, I've got to pick up the kids okay?'

'Yes that's fine Vicky, and thanks once again,' said Jane, before being hugged again.

'No probs. See you later guys,' said Vicky, then she was gone.

Brenda laughed. 'Well that told me again didn't it? Okay, to business Jane. You've had the business plan, and you'll doubtless have some questions, but I thought we should start with a tour of the factory.'

Jane nodded. 'That's fine Brenda.'

Brenda continued smoothly. 'Then I've arranged lunch with my senior team. I'm keen to develop the next generation of management as you will see. The business plan is a collective work, not just my vision. You'll note we each signed it. A bit old fashioned I guess, but when we sign up we deliver.'

Jane pondered. 'Fair enough. Why not?'

Brenda got up.

'Let's drop you down to Paul Higginbottom first. He's my operations director. Much of what you see comes from the learning he got in a three month secondment to Nissan. Lean manufacturing, Kaizan, that sort of stuff.'

Jane nodded. 'Yes. I've read the books. Simple concepts but impressive results.'

They headed to a cubicle on a mezzanine above the shop floor. From this spot you could see virtually the whole production facility, much of it automated.

'Jane I'm going to leave you with Paul, who will show you around. Then you will have time with each of the Directors. We'll all have lunch together in the boardroom, and then you can quiz me as you wish. None of them are yes people. There are some warts which we won't hide from you. We make mistakes, but we try to learn from them.'

Jane nodded. Quietly impressed. This was a different

Brenda, on her home turf. An obvious leader so different from the emotional wreck she'd met in Kent.

Brenda concluded. 'I believe that to come to a rational decision you must not only have confidence in the business plan, but crucially in the ability of each member of the team to deliver it, myself included.'

The tour took an hour, then she talked to the marketing and technical directors, and finally the finance director. Each had an MBA she noted. Average age probably just under forty, although the technical director was probably older. The marketing director and finance director were female. The rest were male. Over lunch the team debated the plan and seemed to be energised. Brenda sat back, taking it all in. She spoke only occasionally, to correct or encourage. Jane concluded that they couldn't have been coached. This was the true Murgatroyd's she was seeing.

After lunch they all shook hands warmly, leaving Jane and Brenda alone over coffee.

Warm sunlight flooded into the boardroom, lighting the picture of Bill like a ghost. Jane puzzled why Brenda kept it in position, but realised that next to it was an older print of Bill's father, and one which she took to be Jean. Perhaps a break from the past was more difficult in a multi-generational family business she thought.

'So. To business. Did you enjoy the factory tour? I hope

Paul Higginbottom didn't bore you. He's fantastic, but a bit obsessive about his factory,' said Brenda crisply.

'I like factories Mrs… Brenda. I run one remember? Not as big as this but, well the principles are the same,' said Jane.

Brenda nodded. 'And your assessment? You can be blunt as you like. In this office people speak honestly.'

Jane considered for a moment. 'Too small for high volume production. You've done the best you can, and the lean systems are great, but at these volumes you can't get economies of scale. As simple as that really.'

'True. Fair comment I think.'

Jane looked at her notes. 'In my view IPCO could, as they say in their business plan, cut costs by ten percent at least just by moving it to Hatfield, and with their distribution channels they could generate the volumes that you lack. They buy in volume already, so they could consolidate components and buy them from their Indian factories. Just keep a bit of final assembly in UK to protect the brand.'

Brenda countered. 'We already source from India, and I've great hopes for the joint venture out there as we discussed over lunch.'

'Yes I agree it's impressive what you've done Brenda, I'm just not sure where you can go next. You must admit that IPCO could do a pretty good job of taking it to the next level?'

Brenda realised that Jane was not only highly intelligent, but also articulate and streetwise. Whoever had been her mentor had taught her wisely. At thirty she had the gravitas of someone much older.

'Yes. I'd have to concede that. But we can do the low volume high margin stuff well. I had this made up in the development shop. Take a look.'

Brenda handed over a boxed pen. It was an exquisite design, simple and classic. Jane held it and realised something.

'I've seen that pen somewhere before haven't I,' she said.

Brenda looked at her directly. 'Yes Jane. Well at least one rather similar. We've restyled it slightly. It's slightly slimmer, and with simpler lines.'

Jane returned her gaze. 'It's beautiful Brenda. Just like the other one.'

Brenda paused. She could have talked about the origin of the design. But this was not the time or the place. Stick to the facts she thought.

'We made one very similar recently for the Queen, hence the royal warrant. They retail for five thousand pounds. The gross margin is seventy five percent. We offer them through only a few selected outlets, mainly in London or major capital cities. The latest is in Dubai. Hand made to order.'

Jane took out the original from her handbag and compared them.

'Impressive,' she said simply.

'May I?' said Brenda.

Jane handed over the original pen, which Brenda had not seen since 1969. The monogram WM was still as clear as the day it had been made. He had shown her it in Florence, and promised to have one made for her. It never happened. Only later did Jean show the one Bill had given to her. Seeing it again didn't help her mood, especially with the picture of Bill on the wall staring down at her. She handed it back without comment.

Jane took the pen and replaced it in the box. Brenda took the new one, and rolled it between her fingers as she spoke.

'Look everything you've said thus far is absolutely true. Is there any future for UK manufacturing? Blair says we're a service economy now. I think that we've got to do all we can to keep it, but that means that we must produce low volume lines with high added value to the luxury market. We can't put all of our people in call centres can we?'

Jane understood the strategy well. 'Yes, I saw the Queen's Award for export outside. We hope to win one this year. We've got some strong intellectual property, so we are hoping that we can float next year. Did you never think of floating?'

Brenda became hesitant as it was an obvious question, although there was an equally obvious answer.

'Well no. As you might understand communication

between the shareholders has been somewhat limited. We let sleeping dogs lie to be honest. Not necessarily the best thing for the business but you see how it is.'

'I'm sorry Brenda that was a stupid question,'

'No it wasn't Jane, it is a very logical question. One I've asked myself and was tempted to raise with Jean on many occasions. The reality is that we could have grown Murgatroyd to become a volume player, but it would have needed a new factory, probably overseas and substantial investment in the brand. We are a classically under-invested UK business. To have floated would have invited a takeover bid from James, and neither James nor Jean would talk the ownership issues out after the bust up. I was just a hired gun with a minority stake.'

'I think you undersell yourself. You're running a fine business Brenda. It does you and your workforce credit.'

'Thank you Jane. My congratulations on your success too. It puts mine in the shade somewhat.'

Jane smiled. 'Different times Brenda. Information Technology is a fast moving animal and you can make a lot of money very quickly. I just developed the right thing at the right time. The only trouble is if you don't keep moving and back the right technology you can fall from grace just as quickly. The internet is going to change everything in the next ten years. Retailing will be transformed. It's going to mess up distribution channels, differential pricing between markets, the whole world is going to change.'

Brenda nodded.

'I know what you mean Jane. I'm trying to keep up to date. I'm pretty good with word processing and spreadsheets. But I do agree with you about the internet. We're already making plans. Ah – I think Robert's just arrived. Gosh the time has moved on. Was there anything we haven't covered?'

Jane looked at her notes. 'No I don't think so.. Oh well yes there was one more thing. Forgive me but I must ask about your own aspirations? You've got a decent team for young managers, but no obvious successor.'

'A good question. I'm working on Paul, but I don't plan to retire for a few years yet by which time I think he will be ready. I love this Company and this town. In my view, and in Jean's, we have a corporate social responsibility. I completely agree that IPCO's offer represents an excellent deal for shareholders, and better than me or my management team can achieve with the resources we have. But don't expect me to sell. Jean left me the shares because she knew I wouldn't sell the town out to anyone, and I won't break that confidence. But your position is very different and you must obviously make up your own mind. In your position I wouldn't blame you if you chose to sell.'

Jane was taken aback at the unabashed honesty of this

lady. 'Thanks Brenda. It's been a pleasure. Thank your team for their time, it's given me much to consider. Please give my love to Vicky.'

Brenda extended her hand, and Jane shook it. Brenda added her other hand to clasp hers. For once in the meeting Brenda showed signs of emotion.

'Well thank you for at least giving me a chance to put my side of the argument. It's much appreciated. I'll come down with you.'

They said their goodbyes in the car park, and Brenda went back to the boardroom. She looked at the picture.

'I gave it my best shot Bill, but if she's as financially savvy as I think she is she'll sell. Nothing more I can do now.'

21.

2000

The following day Jane was in her office reflecting on the events of the last few weeks. Whilst her initial research twelve months previously had given her the bare bones of her family history, in the last few weeks it had become suddenly real and very personal.

She had come to realise that her upbringing had been loving but highly intensive and adult focussed. She never really fitted in. She was too bright to be bothered by some of the gibberish her classmates talked about. More comfortable with her head in some book, computing mainly.

University had broadened her horizons, and her presentational and social skills had improved. In business situations, talking about her subject, she was fine. In fact she was more than fine.

But she was never comfortable in domestic social situations. She got bored easily, and didn't watch TV or go to concerts, so she had no real conversation beyond business. Fortunately her adopted father didn't have much to say either, so such social events were rare. Her mother had tried to get her to go to the school leaver's do, but she stubbornly resisted.

Looking back she was probably bullied at school, over her boyishness, her intelligence and her figure. She was different and, in school, different is definitely not cool. But actually Jane didn't notice very much, and cared even less.

But she didn't know how to fail either. So she developed her business with passion and intensity, working ridiculous hours along with a couple of likeminded colleagues. Her father coached her and gave her the initial money to set up.

When it came to negotiating with the bank her father put her in touch with a personal friend who coached her in how you dealt with financial institutions. Her presentation was well rehearsed, and very professional. The bank said yes, as they had throughout the years of double digit growth in the business.

So she didn't do or need the personal stuff which Murgatroyd's entailed. Vicky was fun because she was totally different. Chalk and cheese. Her refreshing honesty made a change in a world full of business bullshit.

And talking business with Brenda was fine too. They had a common interest and Jane admired what her birth mother had achieved. But at the cost of giving away her first child? Too big a price to pay. No way would she have done that.

So she was still minded to sell the shares be done with it. She could pop up to Vicky's from time to time and play Auntie Jane to Bethany and Katie, for whom she had developed an instant affection. Brenda would make a fortune when she sold her shares, so if she wanted to save her home town she would have plenty of money to do so.

Then why did she not just ring James and sell? Something was troubling her. Something was wrong in the wiring. But she couldn't figure that bit out. It was emotional not logical. And her mind worked on logic mostly, well actually all of the time.

She remembered little Katie putting her hands up to her as she left, and the sticky slobbering kiss which followed. The smell of Vicky's perfume as she bear hugged her before leaving. The song Robert sang as he drove her to the station.

She was still thinking when the phone rang.

'Good morning, Jane Page,' she said.

'Hello Jane, James Murgatroyd here.'

'Good afternoon James. Are you in the UK?'

'No I'm in New York. My body clock's all over the place as usual. I just wondered how your trip around the factory went?'

Jane pondered what to say. James was keen to talk. Too keen. 'Very well James. Brenda runs an impressive operation,' she said positively.

James agreed, although grudgingly. 'Yes, she's not done a bad job considering. Have you read the consultant's report we commissioned on the IPCO offer?'

'Yes I have. It was pretty conclusive. Open and shut case really.'

'I agree with it entirely. I've thought for a long time that bringing IPCO and Murgatroyd's together was an obvious way to generate shareholder value and turn Murgatroyd's into a proper global brand. Neither Brenda or my mother would hear of it I'm afraid. Look I was born and bred in the town, and I'm as fond of Murgatroyd's as Brenda is, if not more so being family and all that, but you've just got to move with the times as far as I'm concerned.' James spoke with a slight American twang which kept slipping into his fading northern accent.

'Yes. I can see the business logic.'

'Good well I can update you on IPCO's position as of last night. They don't want a protracted wrangle over the shares, so they've offered both of us an extra fifty pence a share conditional on signing over the shares within forty eight hours. I've accepted of course.'

James was in aggressive selling mode. Jane didn't like pushy salesman. James seemed too desperate to get the deal done.

As if reading her mind he continued.

'To be honest Jane the yanks don't like the adverse PR coming out of the UK. It's a small acquisition from their perspective, but as European VP I see it as a key brand for the future. I'm taking over development of emerging markets shortly, although it's not been announced yet, and the Murgatroyd brand, added to IPCO's global promotional capability has massive potential.'

'Yes I can see that James, and of course the improved offer is quite attractive from my perspective. You will understand that I have a business of my own to run, so I'd welcome closure on this matter as soon as possible.'

James was cheered by her response. Nearly there he thought.

'That's fine then. I assume that you'll dial in to the shareholder's meeting the day after tomorrow as I will? We can get the deal done and dusted soon after that?'

'I'll speak to you then James,' said Jane, and put the phone down.

Decision made she thought, although the nagging guilt remained. But why should she feel guilty? This had nothing to do with her. It was a complete intrusion on her life and she just didn't need this hassle over a lousy nine percent, and the cash could be ploughed into her businesses. She didn't need or even want the money. Bill Murgatroyd's conscience money.

At Murgatroyd's those few days went by slowly. Brenda

tried to focus, but found it quite impossible to do. The absence of any contact from Jane meant the worst. She would sell her shares and hand control back to James and then to IPCO.

Brenda couldn't fault the logic of her doing so, in spite of the business plan which was entirely credible and deliverable. If IPCO did it right then they would pick up a global brand, ripe for development, at a sensible price. She had received an email from IPCO advising her of the increased offer, which seemed the last nail in the coffin.

She was waiting for the axe to fall as she knew it must. The clock was ticking down to two pm on Friday and the shareholder's meeting. She had twenty four hours left as Managing Director.

James had phoned her previously to offer an olive branch. A seat on the Murgatroyd's Board, and a ceremonial role as patron of the new Murgatroyd's foundation created by IPCO to fund educational and arts projects in the town. He had requested that she stay for three months and then retire on a substantial severance package. He had said that her management team would be looked after with IPCO stock options. She thanked him politely but said she still wouldn't sell.

She had contemplated ringing Jane, but thought it looked desperate and in any event to do so was more than likely pointless.

She began to think about the future. Perhaps she should take James' offer? She had fought a good fight, and if the factory closed as she was sure that it would then who could really blame her? She had urged employees not to sell their shares but they had done so in spite of her plea.

The fact was that she feared being lonely and suddenly felt old for the first time. Murgatroyd's was her life, as sad as that might be. She didn't really have material needs, and her Murgatroyd pension was more than enough to keep her comfortable. The bungalow she had bought was hers and all paid for. The bottom line was that she would be rich if she sold, but what good would it do her?

She hadn't planned to retire and couldn't really contemplate how she would spend her time if she did. She had some charitable roles which she enjoyed, but it didn't have the same buzz as being the managing director of Murgatroyd's. She had travelled all over the world. She had a real purpose for living. What purpose would she have in retirement?

'Better face it Brenda your sell by date is pretty much up. Better work out your future old girl,' she murmured to herself.

The following day at 2pm she sat in the boardroom with Martin Braceby awaiting the dial in to the teleconference. Almost on cue both James and Jane dialled in.

The pleasantries duly exchanged Martin brought the meeting to order, in his capacity as Company secretary.

'I have circulated the consultant's report into Murgatroyd's, and I am aware that Ms Page has also had a copy of the Murgatroyd business plan. Have you all had adequate time to consider the findings and recommendations?'

There were murmurs of assent.

'Then perhaps I'll invite comments?'

James was inevitably first to speak. 'Well for my part I'm delighted with the findings. Obviously I have a potential conflict of interest as an employee of IPCO, so I'm glad that a fully independent report endorses the IPCO proposal as offering the best value to shareholders and the best future for the business. I think you'll agree Brenda that even Archie couldn't vote against this offer.'

The reference to Archie was a bitter twist of the knife, but Brenda let it pass.

'I will not sell irrespective of the consultant's report. I've made my position plain. The town depends on Murgatroyd's and its closure will have enormous social consequences which I cannot contemplate,' she replied.

James changed the subject. 'Mr Braceby can I ask that you update us on the shareholding position please?'

Martin checked his notes. 'As at close of business yesterday IPCO has acquired 2.1% of the Company from the employees, and with Mr Murgatroyd's shares pledged to them it would take their shareholding up to 42.1%. Mrs Arkwright has 46% and Ms Page 9%. Self-evidently Ms Page, you have the balance of the shares and if you sell to them IPCO will have effective control. Would you care to add your comments?'

Jane's voice came on the line. It was business-like and formal. 'Well obviously I have listened to both sides of the argument in the last few days, and I have to say that the IPCO offer is a very generous one. I am of the view, and I've shared it with Mrs Arkwright, that Murgatroyd's is not well placed to meet the challenges of global competition. Bluntly I think that given the trends in manufacturing costs it is unlikely that it will be possible to sustain the current Murgatroyd manufacturing plant irrespective of which side gets control. I believe that Mrs Arkwright and her team have done an excellent job thus far, but that is my considered opinion and that of my financial advisor. Subject to appropriate legal documentation I am prepared to sell my shares to IPCO on the revised terms.'

Brenda heard a barely audible gasp of yes from James, and that was it. Martin Braceby brought the meeting to an end, and the lines from James and Jane were dropped, ending the conference call. He looked up at Brenda. He could see that she was close to tears.

22.

2000

Mandy sat in the docklands flat she shared with James. They led quite separate lives in many ways. James was in the US a good deal of the time, but also increasingly the Far East. His latest promotion made him a main board director of IPCO.

So in many ways the acquisition of Murgatroyd's was a side show, almost a vanity project in some respects. James phoned her after the meeting. Jane was selling he said excitedly, and Murgatroyd's was his.

She had put him right. Actually he had just flogged the family business to a Yankee predator. Sometimes Mandy liked to prick the pompous balloon that James' inflated ego created.

Then she softened. She did of course realise how much restoring the family business meant to James. She couldn't forget that awful day when she got fired. The difference was that he wanted vengeance. She couldn't hate Jean, or Archie, or Brenda for that matter. It was all so long ago, and she could see that what they did was entirely right. James was young and headstrong, and she got caught up in the excitement of the business, and was in the heady months of really being in love, probably for the first time. The decisions they made had put the business at risk, and Archie was right to take James' job away. And hers.

On a good day James would in his heart of hearts agree with that assessment, but it still burned within him that he had been humiliated.

He had told Mandy that he would close that factory within six months, and not a trace of Murgatroyd's would be left. Manufacturing would be moved to Hatfield, and he had created a project team to make it happen. Sales and marketing would be conducted out of the small Murgatroyd offices near Bond Street.

She was troubled. This was a vindictive James wreaking revenge and enjoying the slaughter. She wanted no part of this.

And there was something else.

James was flying in tonight to celebrate. They were booked into La Gavroche for the following day for lunch, a fortunate last minute cancellation. But she had no real appetite. There was something else they needed to discuss, but that would need to wait. The meal was excellent and James was of course in a jubilant mood. She tried to share his joy, and put on a brave face.

She waited until they were back at the flat. James had opened another bottle of champagne, although she didn't feel like it. Time to get this over with.

She stood, and waited for James to pause.

'James, who's Tracey Lewis?'

James looked startled. She recognised the look. The schoolboy caught with his hand in the sweet jar. 'What?'

Mandy had rehearsed this many times. She felt scared, but exhilarated.

'Simple question. Who's Tracey Lewis,' she said.

'Why?'

'A simply question. Who is she?'

James shrugged. 'She's a PR rep in Hatfield.'

Mandy nodded, then she looked at him more directly. 'And Stephanie Stevens?'

'What?'

Now James was worried. Plough on Mandy.

'Who's Stephanie Stevens, simple question.'

The rabbit was in the headlights.

'Why?'

'And Freya Westcott, who's she?'

James stood. He was now in full understanding of where this was going.

'Mandy I don't see....,' he pleaded.

'What don't you see? It's pretty obvious isn't it?' said Mandy.

James shrugged. He had nothing to say.

'And finally, when is Lisa Jarrold's baby due James?' she looked at him darkly.

She threw her glass of champagne and it shattered against the double glazed window.

James knew the game was up. How did she know all this?

'Next month,' he said quietly.

'Next month. So let's count back. Ah yes that was Rome was it. The European pen convention that I couldn't go to,' she said with icy calm.

'Yes.'

'Makes a change from Florence I suppose. I've heard this before haven't I James? Or rather your poor mother did? But I'm not a lesbian Bill, and I haven't loved anyone but you for twenty five years. Twenty five fucking years. I forgave you the first one, that slut in New York. But the others, so many others.'

James made to hold her, but she shrugged him off.

'Look I've already told her I won't leave you. It's you I love Mandy.'

'Sorry James. Change the bloody record. I've heard it played too many times.'

James was angry now, but only because he was reacting defensively to being caught cold. How did Mandy know? She still had the odd friend in IPCO, but surely nobody that knew of his affairs?

'Well I'm sure you've been shagging that business partner of yours. All those parties while I've been in the states. I've seen how he paws you and flatters you. A bit of a slimy frog but maybe you like that sort of thing.'

She stared at him coldly.

'How dare you.'

James laughed. 'So you're going to try to deny it?'

'Yes. I absolutely do deny it. For your information Jean Jacques is gay James. I'm sure Claude his partner of twenty odd years would confirm it, if you wish to speak with him that is.'

There was silence. James stood and stared out of the window.

Mandy collected her thoughts. How dare he accuse her? She had been faithful to him throughout. Not for the want of offers either. The bloody cheek of the man. Now he stood there with nothing to say, waiting for her next move.

The irony of the situation had not occurred to James, but Mandy had of course been pondering the situation for some time. She had determined that history was not going to repeat itself.

She sat. Choked back the tears.

'I had lunch with Jane the other day. She let me see the letters from your father and from Brenda. Jane's life has been haunted by not knowing who her parents were. Brenda's has been riddled with the guilt of a mother who gave her daughter away.'

She paused for a moment.

'So?' was all James had to offer.

Mandy continued. 'You're not going to be let off as easily as your father got off. You will stand by Lisa and her baby publicly and live with the consequences. No adoption. You will look after the child you've brought into the world, not buy out your obligations with a big fat cheque as your father did. We will divorce so that you can honour your obligations to her and the baby. Marry her or don't marry her I don't care. Now I'm going away for a few days so you can think things through and follow your Murgatroyd obsession through to the bitter end. I've had enough of Murgatroyd's and the misery your obsession has caused amongst the rest of the carnage you've caused.'

With that she went to the bedroom and took out a case she had packed earlier. She phoned for a cab and headed for the door. James sat in silence staring ahead. He heard the door close as Mandy left.

James now realised that history was indeed repeating itself, and put his head in his hands.

23.

2000

Brenda sat in her office waiting for the call. It was Friday, and it was pouring with rain. The factory was producing and the canteen had that Friday aroma. It was always fish on Friday. Brenda remembered the day in 1976 when they shut the executive dining room and Jean, Archie and herself had marched into the canteen and queued with Derek Dawson for their fish and chips.

It had been an emotional day, because it was a symbol of them and us. To the workforce, seeing the management on site and queuing for their lunch with everyone else was a clear sign that things at Murgatroyd's had changed.

For many months in the early days Brenda had shared an office with Archie as they operated as a war room. Every purchase requisition was signed by Archie and they spent nothing that wasn't absolutely essential.

They had a weekly manager's meeting, and toured the shop floor regularly. Some might have called it micro management, but to Archie it was common sense. The sales force got used to a regime of filing weekly reports on sales activity, and that failing to achieve sales targets resulted in departures. It was tough, some might say ruthless management. But it had to be done. As soon as their company cars arrived back in the car park Archie sold them.

They had been long, long days. Brenda had often left at midnight. She was young and driven, with boundless energy and enthusiasm. She thought nothing of heading for the packing line to get an urgent order out of the door. It was what Brenda did, leading from the front. And they respected her for it.

But it cost her marriage too, and she wasn't convinced that Vicky had always had the support she deserved.

Her thoughts were interrupted by the telephone buzzer. She picked it up. Martin Braceby. This is it she thought.

'Brenda I've just had a very strange phone call from Jane's solicitors. He tells me that she has pulled out of the sale. I gather she's had a change of heart, but what her plans are now I don't know.'

And thus it was that the share sale collapsed. For James Murgatroyd, reading the fax from Jane's solicitors was a terrible end to an awful week.

'Following a re-evaluation of her future intentions we have been instructed by Ms Page that she no longer intends to sell her shareholding in Murgatroyd's at this time. She thanks

IPCO for their generous offer but intends to work with the current management team to develop the Murgatroyd business, in conjunction with other shareholders.'

James was horrified and completely perplexed. They had only spoken forty eight hours ago.

The states woke up in three hours he knew. He had to fix this by then. There was still one thing which Mandy didn't know. The fact that James needed the money from selling the shares he had inherited. James had invested in high risk dot com stocks which were now crashing around his ears. He had property in Florida, New York and London with big mortgages. He had the life of a US corporate executive, with spending to match.

Mandy on the other hand had handled her own business frugally but very effectively. Her works were in demand, and some had become retail works selling at higher volume. The bespoke work was increasingly collectable, so she had amassed quite a substantial personal worth, in stark contrast to her husband.

He tried Jane repeatedly, but it just went to voicemail. He spoke to the solicitor, but he simply said that his client had contacted him to say that she had had a change of heart.

He rang Mandy too, in desperation. They had not spoken since she had left him earlier that week. Her phone was off and her PA at the gallery said she was in Paris.

In the end James had to ring the states. He reasoned that it was important to be seen as being in command rather than have them ring him to extract the bad news. Having spent considerable sums on due diligence they were predictably very dismayed. James was humiliated.

Brenda briefed her senior team on a confidential basis, but could tell them very little. She tried to contact Jane, but to no avail.

Jane was actually on her way north. She wanted to speak with Brenda face to face and discuss the way forward. She intended to speak with James later. She arrived just after lunch to Brenda's surprise. She declined to discuss her reasons, simply saying that they were personal. Brenda had no desire to cause a further reconsideration by trying to find out more.

Jane suggested that her non-executive chair, Paul Reynolds, became a director of the Company to look after her interests. Paul lived within fifty miles of the factory and was very experienced. Brenda was only too happy to agree.

Jane planned to return south that evening, but Vicky managed to get her to agree to stay with her until the following day. She intended to get to the bottom of things.

Later on that evening Jane was at Vicky's. They were on the second bottle of red and the children were asleep.

'Look Jane if you don't want to tell me why you changed

your mind I'll respect your privacy. But everything you discussed with Mum suggested that you found the IPCO offer so compelling that you would sell. You almost convinced her that the Murgatroyd factory had no future in any event and she should sell too, if only to look after my legacy and that of the kids.'

Jane smiled. The question was inevitable.

'It doesn't have a future Vicky. I'm afraid it probably has five years, ten at the outside.'

'Then why not sell?'

'Well it's a pretty stupid and completely irrational reason really,' said Vicky.

'Yes? Come on Jane I promise I won't tell mum.'

'Well I had arranged to go into the solicitors to sign, but then Mandy Brice Cooper showed up at the office.'

'What? That's James' wife isn't it?' said Vicky, very puzzled.

'We met for an hour over lunch. She told me some things.'

'What things?' said Vicky.

'Sorry Vicky, but even between sisters some things must be kept private.'

Vicky decided not to press things. 'Okay but I want to know why you changed you mind. You were going to sell weren't you? That's what your business head told you to do.'

Jane thought for a moment and sipped her wine. 'Well let's say that Mandy painted a picture of a not very nice man. She showed me the press releases, played me some of the news footage. I saw how he portrayed himself and your mother.'

'Our mother,' said Vicky quietly.

'Whatever. He tried to portray your mother as having somehow embezzled the shares and run the Company poorly. That was thoroughly untrue, and disreputable behaviour.'

'So that, and these stories you don't want to share, that's why you didn't sell?' said Vicky.

'That and one more thing I will tell you about,' said Jane.

'Go on.'

'I understand that at an office party in London last month James got drunk and caught two female employees kissing in the corridor. He sacked them on the spot. I understand he told them he considered it conduct likely to bring the Company into disrepute. He also said, and I quote, 'I don't want any of those lezzie sluts in my company'. The girls had been in a steady relationship for three years. It was fairly common knowledge I gather.'

Vicky was stunned. Now it all made sense. 'Oh that's awful. He must be so very bitter and unhappy.'

Jane shrugged. 'Yes. I think he is. Anyway I have strong views on equality. I won't tolerate any form of discrimination in my workplace.'

Vicky nodded. 'Okay Jane, but that's not quite all is it?'

Jane seemed puzzled. She looked at Vicky questioningly.

Vicky smiled. 'You're a lesbian aren't you Jane? I saw her picture, Alex isn't it? But you don't let on do you?'

Jane relaxed and looked sad all of a sudden.

'No. Alex and I have been together for a few years now. My parents know and are fine with it, but some of my customers haven't yet made the journey. I'm floating the Company this year. Dot Coms are going berserk in the US, and my advisors say that I'd be mad to miss out. I don't want to take any chances. I don't know why I care really, and I'm sure it wouldn't make any difference. I just don't like my private life being broadcast. But I don't have to do business with dinosaurs like James Murgatroyd. End of story.'

24.

2014

The old lady pulled her coat together and adjusted her scarf to protect her from the biting cold wind. Eventually she came to the site, although the new housing confused her and she took a wrong turn before realising her mistake. The old mill in front of her was being converted into flats, and the factory had just about been levelled. Piles of bricks and concrete were all that were left. She gazed at the old gatehouse with its windows smashed and willow herb growing out of the door.

She looked sadly at the wreckage, and her heart felt as heavy as the dark grey clouds.

She was right then our Jane, thought Brenda. Eight years it lasted, but we had to close the old girl in the end. They still had a sales unit on the industrial estate outside the town, and a workshop making those expensive models they sold to Harrods. Everything else was imported now though. At its peak it employed 800. Now it was just 70, no longer the town's biggest employer.

She had last visited the site just after the closure. She asked to walk the old site one more time alone.

She went first to her old office and the boardroom. It was eerily quiet. The picture hooks were still in the wall and the faded paint framed the areas where the paintings had been. She had debated retaining the one of Bill for herself, but then decided that it would be disrespectful to Jean, and it still brought back too much pain alongside the nostalgia. It was shipped off with all the memorabilia to the Murgatroyd Pen Museum, a recent addition to the town's tourism offer, limited though it was.

Then down to the factory, and the packing line where it all began, so many years ago. Empty now, everything shipped out to Poland or India, she couldn't remember which.

She went into the old foreman's office, and remembered his hand touching her. She shivered. Then to the old union office, Derek Dawson's personal fiefdom. An old union notice was left where it had fallen after the old filing cabinets were removed. Dusty and covered in cobwebs it was signed by Derek. She put it in her handbag to give to his son as a reminder of his father now long gone.

Then into the canteen. The canteen that had once been two until the barriers had been torn down by the bare hands of Jean and Derek as a gesture to the new Murgatroyd's. If you looked hard enough you could still make out where the executive dining room had been, with its lovely view over the mill pond at the back. She looked out for a final time, allowing the emotion to wash over her.

It was empty now of course, yet it was as if it was in suspended animation, waiting for the customers to return. Except that the factory was closed for good, and the hundreds of human beings who had lost their jobs had moved on and would never return.

The camaraderie of the shared lunchtime community was lost. The servery stood as it had been left. Those that had left it had pride she noticed, and although some dust had accumulated from disuse it had clearly been left spotless. The floor still showed the signs of human traffic. The till had gone, but the old price list taped to the counter still offered the final day fare. Fish and chips was today's special. Well if it's the last supper why not?

As she walked through there was a ghostly echo, and suddenly a movement activated sensor caused a fan vent to spring into life, as if hope was springing eternal that the people might return. This was a factory, a livelihood, but more than that it was a community, and the canteen was its community centre.

It was where they had the Christmas tree, the Christmas party, the long service lunch and the retired employees welfare gathering. It was also where an ashen faced chairman of

Murgatroyd International PLC had announced the closure of the plant.

A solitary balloon, long since deflated, hung disconsolately from a light fitting, too high to be removed. A reminder of the closing day party, where the no alcohol rule was abandoned for the day.

The notice board still had the notice of closure on it, as if the workers wanted to mark their betrayal forever. A single word 'Why?' was scrawled in ballpoint pen on the bottom right and corner. The site was still profitable but overseas was still cheaper. I'd like to see their staff canteen she thought. If they're given time off to eat of course.

That's enough Brenda she thought. Enough nostalgia. Move on. She turned for one last look then left the site. She had said her goodbyes.

Now, months later she stood and wondered what would happen to the rest of the vast site which had mainly been cleared. Just the perimeter fence had been kept and the old mill headquarters building, ready for its new role as desirable flats looking out over the mill pond and the hills beyond it. The old Murgatroyd arch still stood defiantly against the march of time, protected by a preservation order.

Brenda had retired. Murgatroyd's was eventually floated by the management team she had built, using the experience and skills of Paul Reynolds as executive chairman. She sold most of her shares after the float. She'd earned that. She bought a lovely place on the coast near Scarborough with a sea view, and spent much of the summer there. She spent the winter in Lanzarote, out of the cold, but winter was early this year.

She still missed Murgatroyd's. Most of her friends still lived locally, but a number had died. James too had passed away, just last year. He had become a less bitter man in later life, and had made some peace with his past. He and Mandy never divorced.

Brenda walked a little further, to where the cricket field still remained. She was glad that she had at least managed to keep that in trust for the town. As she looked on, Vicky arrived. No spring chicken yourself young Vicky, thought Brenda. They looked ever more alike as she got older, though Vicky wouldn't have thanked her for saying so.

'Hi mum. Isn't it a bit cold up here? Come on I'll walk you back,' said Vicky, taking her arm.

'Oh no don't be silly. Must keep my exercise up. I'm not ready for the Zimmer frame yet you know.'

Vicky knew better than to argue. They walked back around the front once again. Brenda noticed that the 'for sale' board now had a sold sign on it.

'I see someone's bought the site then? The developers and our Mister Reynolds will be pleased.'

As they reached the gate a new open topped sports car pulled out and stopped opposite them. The driver's side door opened, and Jane got out.

'Look what the cat's dragged in,' said Vicky as she hugged her sister warmly.

'Hello Jane, I didn't expect you until next week,' said Brenda as she hugged them both.

'Hi mum, how have you been?' said Jane.

'About as bloody-minded and awkward as ever Jane,' said Vicky interjecting.

'I'm well Jane. Ignore her. Is Alex with you?'

'No. Not this time Mum, I'm here on a business trip,' said Jane.

'Business trip? Not much business up here these days,' said Brenda.

'Mum's just noticed that the site has been sold Jane?' said Vicky, a twinkle in her eye.

'More bloody retail I suppose. No real jobs,' said Brenda, enjoying one of her hobby horses.

Vicky laughed knowingly, and Jane smiled.

'Actually that's why I'm here. We completed the purchase last week,' she said.

Brenda was confused. 'Sorry I'm not with you? You did what?'

Jane shrugged with frustration. 'Oh it took an age for the

EU grant to come through. We should start building our new distribution centre shortly. It will only employ fifty at first, but hey it's a start.'

Brenda finally understood and hugged Jane tightly. The wheels of progress had completed another rotation, and the town would begin to reinvent itself once again. Brenda was not sure what Josiah Murgatroyd would have made of it, but to her it felt right.

They got into Jane's car, with Brenda eventually installed in the front passenger seat, still smiling to herself, and Vicky moaning about the lack of legroom in the back.

The new distribution centre opened later that year, bringing life to the site once more. Jane bought an apartment in the old mill where Brenda's office had been, overlooking the mill pond. Jane was a fantastic businesswoman, her employees respected her, the town came to know and love her. But it was Brenda Arkwright who cut the ribbon at the opening ceremony.

16719702R00207

Printed in Great Britain
by Amazon